Mojave Dese

Gary J. George

ISBN-13:978-1532798412
ISBN-10: 1532798415

The characters and events in this book are fictitious. Any similarity to real persons, living or dead, is coincidental and not intended by the author.

For Ginny

You're the one

CONTENTS

Chapter 1

Las Vegas, Nevada

March 23, 1961

On a Friday afternoon, Kiko Yoshida was in the middle of her shift at the Serengeti Hotel in Las Vegas when one of the other Keno girls tapped her on the shoulder.

"Kiko, supervisor wants to see you. He sent me to cover your section until you get back."

"He say what he wanted?"

"Nope. Just told me to get you."

Puzzled, Kiko made her way across the casino floor.

"Phil, you wanted to see me?"

"Yeah. Mr. Mazzetti and Mr. Meyer want to talk to you. Take the restricted elevator up to the offices."

As she walked to the executive elevator, she thought about those two names. Everybody who worked at the casino knew that Mr. Mazzetti was Eduardo Mazzetti, casino manager and one-time associate of Al Capone. General Manager Melvin Meyer also had a history of problems with the law. She could think of no reason such powerful men even knew she existed. She was just one of hundreds of faceless, casino-floor employees, not even as far up the pecking order as the cocktail waitresses who threaded their way in skimpy costumes through the sea of gamblers, enduring crude remarks and casual groping in exchange for the occasional big tip.

When she stepped out of the elevator, the receptionist took in her Keno-girl outfit and gave her a dismissive look.

"Yes?"

"Kiko Yoshida. I'm supposed to see Mr. Mazzetti and Mr. Meyer."

"Regarding?"

"No idea. My supervisor sent me up."

"And you're a Keno girl?"

"That's right."

The receptionist picked up the phone.

"Alicia? There's a Keno girl out here, Kiki something or other. Says she's supposed to see Mr. Mazzetti and Mr. Meyer. Do you know anything about this?"

Whatever the person on the other end of the phone said, the receptionist suddenly sat up straight.

"Yes. Yes, certainly. I'll send her right back."

She hung up the phone and favored Kiko with a bright smile.

"Mr. Mazzetti and Mr. Meyer are expecting you, Miss Yoshida."

She rose very quickly and opened one of the frosted-glass double doors to the right of her desk.

"Go right on back. Alicia will show you into Mr. Mazzetti's office."

Kiko found it interesting that she was suddenly "Miss Yoshida."

Beyond the double doors was another receptionist, this one even blonder and taller than the first one. She gave Kiko a dazzling smile as she rose from her desk.

"Right this way, Miss Yoshida."

She led Kiko to a door and opened it for her.

"Mr. Mazzetti, Miss Yoshida to see you."

Kiko saw a man sitting behind a huge desk. His white sport coat and white tie contrasted sharply with his black shirt and the red carnation in his buttonhole. His carefully combed hair glistened with oil. He rose and extended his hand.

"Hello, Miss Yoshida. I'm Eddie Mazzetti."

When she took his hand, he covered it with his other hand in a grip favored by politicians.

"Yes sir. I know who you are. Everybody at the Serengeti does."

"I'd like you to meet Melvin Meyer. He's our general manager."

Kiko realized she hadn't seen the man standing off to the side in the conservative gray suit when she walked in because she had been focused on the notorious person in front of her.

Melvin Meyer extended his hand as well.

"Pleased to make your acquaintance, Miss Yoshida."

She heard the door open behind her, and Eddie Mazzetti spoke again.

"And this is Herman Silverstein, our credit manager."

Kiko turned from Mr. Meyer to face Herman Silverstein. Silverstein was not physically imposing, but he had the chilling look of a snake eyeing a robin's egg. When Kiko shook his hand, she had to resist the urge to wipe her palm on her uniform.

"Sit down, Miss Yoshida. My associates and I want to talk to you about somethin' important."

Kiko took the plush chair directly in front of the desk. Silverstein and Meyer took similar chairs on either side of her.

"Miss Yoshida, is it okay if I call you Kiko?"

"Certainly, Mr. Mazzetti."

"And call me Eddie, okay?"

"All right."

Mazzetti opened the file in front of him.

"I see you've been with us since the first of the year."

"Yes sir, that's right."

"Eddie, Kiko. I'm Eddie to my friends."

"Yes, Eddie."

"I see nothin' but good stuff here. Smart, catch on quick, show up on time, don't call in sick. Other employees and the gamblers like you."

And I see here you been to college. Berkeley, right?"

"Yes."

Kiko had no idea where this was heading, but she began to relax a little. This wasn't about something she'd unknowingly done wrong.

"You done good for the Serengeti. We appreciate it."

"I'm glad to hear that, si..-uh Eddie."

"But now my friends and I want you to do somethin' else for us, somethin' big. How's that sound?"

Kiko hesitated.

"Well, I guess that depends on what it is. If it's something reasonable, I'd be willing to do it."

Eddie Mazzetti smiled and spread his arms wide as he addressed Meyer and Silverstein.

"What I tell ya, huh? This is one smart cookie. Wants to know if it's reasonable. No wonder the supervisors say she catches on quick!"

Meyer and Silverstein both smiled.

"Kiko, I'll get right to it.

You have caught the eye of Mr. Pescatore, a very important man in the Serengeti organization."

Alarm bells went off in her head.

"When you say 'caught the eye' ...."

"I mean Mr. Pescatore seen you on the casino floor, thinks you're really a looker. You know, a real doll."

"That's very flattering, Eddie."

"So see, here's the thing. Mr. Pescatore's from the head office in Chicago. He's here to represent the Serengeti at a meetin' of very important people – owners, politicians and so forth. You know, all big shots."

"Yes?"

"He wants you to go with him to this big meetin'. As his date. This is real important to him, so it's important to us we do this for him, you know, set this up for him."

Kiko stood up.

"Whoops! Oh, no. No. No way. You've got the wrong girl, Mr. Mazzetti. I don't do that kind of thing."

"Please, sit down. And remember, it's Eddie.

8

Look, Kiko, you're gettin' this all wrong. All we want you to do, go to this fancy dinner with this man and the other big shots. Listen to some people make speeches. Mr. Pescatore wants to impress everybody there.

Soon as he seen you, he come to me, had me pull your file. He was very impressed with your college background. I swear, these were his exact words, 'I show up with this girl on my arm, they're gonna drop dead jealous. And when they talk to her, they're gonna know she's smart. Not some empty head. She's gonna make me look good'."

"No, Eddie. I don't think I'm your girl. I'm sure you can find someone else. There are lots of girls working here who are prettier than I am and would love to do this."

"Look, Kiko, gonna buy you the most beautiful evening dress in Vegas. Yours to keep after the dinner. Gonna give you diamonds and pearls to wear – course, you'll have to give those back after."

"That's very generous, Eddie– and Mr. Meyer and Mr. Silverstein, but this is still not something I want to do."

"Okay, one more thing before you say 'no' for sure, Kiko. I seen in your file you come to Vegas to be a dancer. How's that workin' out?"

Kiko was still nervous, but Eddie had her attention.

"Not well. I thought maybe I could catch on in a lounge show somewhere. But no luck. No call for a little Japanese girl. I can't even get an audition."

"We might have somethin' for you."

"In the Moulin Rouge Revue? An Asian girl in with all those tall blondes? That woman from Paris who directs the show would have a heart attack!"

Eddie knew he had found his hook.

"Kiko, I'm lettin' you in on a little secret here. The Flower Drum Song is comin' to the Thunderbird in December."

Kiko was stunned.

"The Broadway production?"

"Some of the people, not all of them. They're gonna hire some locals. Now, Melvin and Herman and me, we got contacts over the 'Bird. We put in the word, you're in the show. You interested?"

Eddie's smile lit up the room.

"Certainly."

9

"Okay, you do this one favor; we get you in that show. And believe me, all you gotta do is be a arm piece. We get you the dress, the jewels. Beauty parlor here at the hotel does your hair and nails. People from the Rouge Revue do your makeup. I'm tellin' ya, you'll be the knockout of the dinner. Once the thing is over, back in the limo, straight back to the Serengeti, done for the night. And guaranteed a singin' and dancin' part in a big, Las Vegas show."

"It sounds interesting, Eddie, but ..."

Melvin Meyer spoke.

"Miss Yoshida, we understand you are leery of big promises. Given your level of intellectual sophistication, that's not surprising. We didn't expect you to be naïve. So, we'll sign a contract with you. If Mr. Mazzetti, Mr. Silverstein and I don't get you into that show, the Serengeti will pay you two thousand dollars."

"One more sweetener," added Eddie.

"You get back tonight, move into the showgirl wing here at the Serengeti. Those are big, fancy rooms. Stay there, rent free, long as you work here."

The dress, the jewels, a room in the showgirl's wing: none of those things would have persuaded her. But the Flower Drum Song! Kiko was almost twenty eight years old. If she was ever going to do anything as a singer and dancer, it had to be soon. She had come to Las Vegas hoping to land a spot in a lounge show as a stepping stone to something better. But the Flower Drum Song? A real Broadway show with some of the original cast? That would be a dream come true. She would never get another chance like this. She couldn't turn it down.

"All right, Eddie. I'll do it."

"That's our girl, Kiko! Check in with Alicia out front. She'll take care a alla details. Time you get done at the beauty parlor, Mr. Meyer will have the contract we talked about."

Kiko got up and shook hands with everyone before leaving the room.

When she was gone, Eddie let out a sigh.

"Man, that's one nervy little slant-eye. I was runnin' outta stuff to offer. I was thinkin' gold-plated chop sticks, maybe. You'd think her people won the war. Now we have to get her into that show or pay her two large?

Jesus, why can't Frankie Pescatore just get a regular hooker like everyone else Chicago sends out here?"

"He has an eye for them gooks," said Herman Silverstein, "and Frankie is from The Outfit. Frankie "The Whale" gets whatever he wants while he's here.

It's a good thing they don't send him very often. Regular guy should be back on the route next month."

"Little smart ass makes you almost wish Frankie'd knock her around a little," said Eddie.

"Well, once she voluntarily steps across the threshold of that room, I don't care what he does with her, or to her, as long as he goes home happy," said Meyer.

"Are you really going to draw up a contract? I mean, I know that was the clincher, but she gets the dress and the jewels, might be enough."

"I certainly am going to draw it up," said Meyer. "And we're all going to sign it. This girl is no dummy. Believe me, you don't want to hear from Frankie if she doesn't show.

That reminds me, Herman. I'm going to call Chicago and tell them to head for the safe phone. Get to an outside phone and call them at two o'clock. That'll be four o'clock their time.

Remind them Frankie's leaving tonight with the skim."

"Yeah," said Herman Silverstein, "this is the part I don't like. Our end should be done when their guy walks out of the countin' room with the skim. But they say it's on us until Frankie puts the case in Sam Genovese's hand.

Usually, I don't get too nervous, but I sweat every time they send Frankie. I don't think he's the most reliable guy. He likes to play the big shot. Claims nobody would dare to bother him. Takes the case to his room with him the night before his flight! That's not only stupid, it leaves us hangin' out."

"I don't like it either," said Eddie. "But you'd better never let "The Whale" hear you talk like that. He's a made man, for Christ's sake. Top of that, he's related to Sammy Genovese's wife, Delores, somehow. So whadya gonna do? The Outfit's money, The Outfit's rules."

"It *is* their rules," said Melvin Meyer, "and if it doesn't get to Sam, they're going to accuse us of going off the record. If they do, we'd have no choice but to make it up from our end. We'd have to skim the money twice and keep it quiet. Unless we want Tommy Bones coming after us. Sammy Genovese may be the front man, but the guy who really runs the show is Thomaso."

"Jesus! Don't even say that. I knew Capone, and he was a wild man, but Thomaso Cortese is scarier."

Mojave Desert Sanctuary

CHAPTER 2

Las Vegas, Nevada

March 23, 1961

At 6:45, on a very cold and windy evening in Las Vegas, a driver in a black, Chrysler 300 picked up Kiko Yoshida outside her apartment and drove her to the Serengeti Hotel and Casino. At seven o'clock, she was standing outside the door to a suite in the high-roller, Serengeti-showgirl wing of the hotel. She was very nervous.

She was wearing an elegant, strapless, black evening dress. She had on an exquisite diamond bracelet and diamond earrings. The tastefully expensive string of pearls around her neck contrasted beautifully with her dress. She had a small, gold lame purse over her shoulder. The dress, the jewelry and the purse had been provided to her by the management of the casino. Her hair had been styled in the hotel beauty salon, and her makeup had been done by the people who prepared the showgirls for their performances of the Moulin Rouge Revue.

Kiko took several deep breaths to calm herself while she decided whether she was really willing to do what she had agreed to do. She was feeling uneasy. Common sense told her the evening could go badly in any number of ways. But then she thought about the signed contract back in her room, the one that promised her a role in the Flower Drum Song in December. Lord, she wanted a spot in that show! It could be the spark she had been hoping for.

What was the worst thing that could happen? Some executive trying to grope her in the back seat of a limousine? She could handle that.

She screwed up her courage and knocked on the door.

There was no answer.

She knocked again, louder.

"Who is it?"

"Kiko Yoshida. Mr. Mazzetti sent me."

She heard the rattle of the chain coming off the door, then two separate clicks.

The door opened.

She saw an enormous man in a bathrobe.

The "hi" was already on her lips, and it popped out before she could stop it as a huge hand took her by the elbow and yanked her into the room.

Before she could protest, the man slammed the door, locked both locks and slid the security chain back in place.

"You don't have to be so …."

"Shut-up!"

The enormous man stood with his ear pressed against the door.

"Sure you come alone?"

"I think so."

"Didn't see nobody followin' you?"

"I wasn't looking."

"Did you tell anyone else you was comin' here?"

"No, not exactly."

"Whadya mean, 'not exactly," honey. You did or you didn't."

"I told my roommates I had a date. I didn't tell them where I was going."

"Anyone else know you're here?"

"Mr. Mazzetti, Mr. Meyer and Mr. Silverstein all know."

The big man seemed to relax.

"That's okay. They're on the up."

"Excuse me, but shouldn't you be dressed? Aren't we going to be late?"

"Honey, don't have to get dressed to do what we're gonna do. In fact, you got way too much clothes on."

14

Kiko's brain went into high gear. This was what she had been afraid of. She decided to play dumb to buy some time.

"But Mr. Mazzetti told me I was going to be your date for a fancy, executive dinner party."

Frankie laughed. It was not a pleasant sound. "Boy, that Eddie! Got a gift for the gab, don't he? Fancy dinner, huh?"

"That's what he said."

"There's no dinner, doll. Just a appetizer, and you're it."

She realized she had made a serious mistake by coming. She knew the mob ran Vegas, but it had never hit her head-on before. This immense man with his dead eyes was a gangster! And she had come into his room! She knew about the mob's lock on the Las Vegas Police and Sheriff's departments. No matter what happened, she could forget pressing charges for rape if the guy wouldn't let her leave.

"By the way, Eddie paid you, didn't he?"

Dumb hadn't worked, so she decided to try outraged.

"Paid me?"

"Yeah. I don't know what you charge, but he should have paid up front. The Outfit don't pay for nothin' in this town."

"What I charge? Listen, I'm not some cheap trick."

"Sure, sure you're not. But you're here, ain't you? Means you got a price. Eddie shoulda paid it. Not to say I won't leave a good tip, you was to do good."

"Look, I don't know what Eddie Mazzetti told you …."

The smile left the big man's face. His voice went very cold.

"I'm Frankie Pescatore. They call me Frankie "The Whale" behind my back. The ones who called me that to my face are all dead. I'm not some chump. I'm from The Outfit. Eddie Mazzetti don't tell me. I tell him."

"Eddie Mazzetti runs the Serengeti. Everybody knows that."

"That's for the citizens, dummy. Eddie Mazzetti is just the local bozo."

Kiko looked doubtful.

Frankie's face got red. He wasn't used to being questioned.

"Don't believe me?

See that case over there on the table?"

"The metal one?"

"Jesus, see one ain't metal?

Yeah. Metal one, combination locks.

Know what's in there? More money you ever seen in your life. Over a half a million dollars, off-the-books money. Money don't get reported. And Frankie Pescatore is the man The Outfit trusts, carry it to Chicago. Know nobody's gonna mess with Frankie!

Eddie Mazzetti?" The big man laughed. "Compared to me, Eddie Mazzetti's a putz."

"If you're such an important man, why am I here? I'm just a Keno girl."

"You stupid or somethin'? You can't figure it out?

Look, was walkin' through the casino and seen you. Pretty sharp little fortune cookie. Got a thing, you oriental types. Look like little dolls."

"Fortune cookies are Chinese. I'm Japanese."

"Chinese, Japanese, whatever."

"So, you never had Eddie pull my file?"

"Pull your file? Think this some job interview? I'm Frankie Pescatore, for Chrissake. Don't interview whores, high priced or low priced.

Now, quit yankin' my chain, get them clothes off. Let's get the party started. I gotta catch the redeye at two in the morning, and I wanna get some sleep before I go."

Frankie stood up and dropped his robe to the floor.

Kiko stood there horrified and speechless. She was looking at an obscenely obese man wearing nothing but tiny underpants that had almost disappeared into disgusting rolls of fat and the thatch of coarse, black hair covering his stomach and groin. A man who weighed at least three hundred and fifty pounds. A man who clearly expected her to have sex with him in the next few minutes.

I wonder how he walks with those fat thighs rubbing together, she thought, and was immediately alarmed. How could she be thinking such a stupid thing when she should be devising an escape plan?

She was clearly in trouble. The fat man might not be very swift, but there was no way she could get to the door, get the security chain off and unlock both locks before he reached her. And if she tried such a move and failed, she would not have another chance to get away.

Options flashed through her brain.

She shifted gears. Dumb hadn't worked, and outrage had failed, so she decided to try charm. He apparently thought she was a high-priced call girl trying to get a big tip, so she decided to act like one.

She ran her eyes up and down his body and licked her lips. "My goodness, you're a big man. What's the hurry? Let's enjoy this and have some fun."

Her eyes flicked to the wet bar in the corner of the big room.

"How about I fix us a little drink?"

Frankie kicked the tent-sized robe away from his feet and sat down on the leather couch. It groaned as it accommodated his bulk.

"That's more like it, doll baby.

Scotch rocks for me. Whatever you want for yourself. Make it quick."

Kiko moved to the bar.

As a dancer, she was very aware of her body and also aware of the effect it had on many men. She put everything she had into the movement as she walked away from him.

A whistle escaped his lips.

"Hey, baby, I like the way you move. Hurry with them drinks. I can't wait to get you on my lap."

As she put ice cubes into a glass and covered them with scotch from a heavy, crystal decanter, she thought about the man sitting on the couch.

The fact that he was sitting down was good, but the real element in her favor was that he was barefoot. She wasn't.

She walked back toward him with his drink and the decanter.

"Hey, you ain't got no drink."

"Don't need one, Frankie. Not with a big man like you."

He groaned with the effort as he rose to his feet, looking at her suspiciously. Maybe she had overplayed the charm thing. Now that he was standing up, part of her advantage was gone.

"Go the bedroom, you'n me. Big, round bed in there you're really gonna like. Mirrors on the ceiling."

Kiko deliberately flicked her eyes to the door.

Frankie picked up on the movement.

17

"Hey, don't get no ideas. You ain't gettin' out of here 'till I'm done with you. After that, can jump out the window, all I care."

Kiko hoped she now had him thinking she might make a dash for the door. From three feet away, she threw the glass full of scotch at his face. When he put his hands up to deflect it, she raised the crystal decanter with both hands and smashed it to the white marble floor.

As the crystal shattered and the air filled with the sharp smell of whiskey, she took two steps toward the door.

He moved to his right to cut off her escape.

Kiko quickly changed course and went the other way.

His face contorted in fury, Frankie tried to change directions too, but overcoming the inertia of over three hundred and fifty moving pounds and pivoting in a different direction is not easy. Especially not on a wet, marble floor.

Frankie went down. Hard.

Kiko had already rounded the couch and was headed for the door from the other side when she realized Frankie was not only down, he was making strange noises and didn't seem to be able to get to his feet.

Afraid it was some kind of trick to gain him time, she went quickly to the door, unhooked the security chain, and turned both locks before she looked at him more carefully.

Frankie "The Whale's" eyes were open wide and darting frantically from side to side. His mouth was moving like a fish out of water. A pool of blood was rapidly spreading out from beneath his head.

She realized what had happened.

As Frankie twisted, lost his balance and fell, he had landed on a substantial, upright shard from the base of the shattered decanter. The sharp edge of the big fragment had jammed into his neck and hit an artery. Blood was spurting straight down onto the marble floor beneath him.

Frankie had landed on his left side, and his left arm was trapped beneath his bulk. With his right hand, he was clawing at the shard, but the heavy fall had dazed him, and the effort was feeble. Even if he had been able to pull it out, he would not be able to stop the heavy flow of blood pumping out of his body. Kiko made no move to help him. She didn't want to go anywhere near him.

Even as she watched, his hand fell away from his neck. His fingers began to twitch, and his eyes went out of focus. A long, shuddering sigh escaped his lips. A moment later he voided his bladder, and the yellow stain spread onto the floor below his groin. It mingled with the pool of blood. Then his sphincter let go.

Keeping her eyes on the now-motionless man, Kiko put her ear against the door and listened. It did not escape her that she was mimicking an action she had seen the giant mobster make not long before. As she listened, she was aware of the sharp odor of raw whiskey mixed with the iron scent of blood, the pungent smell of Frankie's urine and the reek of his bowel movement.

There was no sound from the hallway.

She put the security chain back on the door and turned both locks.

Her legs were suddenly weak. She moved to one of the chairs and sat down with her head between her knees. She concentrated on taking deep breaths to bring her racing pulse and spinning thoughts under control. This was no time to panic and do something foolish. She had made one mistake when she knocked on the door. She couldn't afford to make another if she hoped to stay alive.

As her breathing evened out, she went to a special place in her mind. It was a pond. The surface of the pond was calm and smooth under the light of a full moon. She hovered above the pond. In the bottom of the pond was a smooth, round stone. She entered the pond and then the stone and remained there, perfectly still, for a time. When she was completely calm, she left the stone and the pond behind and returned to the hotel room in Las Vegas.

She considered her options. They were not good.

She obviously couldn't call Serengeti Management for help. The mobster who lay dead on the marble floor of the luxurious suite had made it quite clear he outranked the locals in a criminal organization. No matter the circumstances surrounding the man's death, someone was going to pay a heavy price. She didn't want to be that someone.

She knew calling the police would be the same as calling Eddie Mazzetti.

She looked in her tiny purse. Nothing in there but a California driver's license, a five dollar bill, and sixty five cents in change.

She looked across the room at the case Frankie Pescatore had bragged about while he was trying to impress her. She got up and walked over to look at it. The metal had a flat finish. There were combination locks beneath each of the latches. On the off chance that Frankie had not set the locks, she tried both latches.

No luck.

She hoisted the case. It was heavy. Frankie's words echoed in her head. "Know what's in there? More money you ever seen in your life." If Frankie hadn't been exaggerating, there was more than half a million dollars inside. She had five. She didn't dare go by her apartment to get more.

She got up and walked over to Frankie's corpse. An incredible amount of blood had pumped out of the man's body. The huge pool, some of it now spreading toward the door, had engulfed most of the pieces of scattered glass. Then there was the deadly shard stuck in his throat. She had smashed the decanter that had produced that shard, but she felt no guilt about what she had done. She thought again about Frankie losing his balance as he tried to pivot and cut off her escape.

She returned to the chair and sat down again to think logically about her next moves.

She thought of movies she had seen about people trying to get away with murder, not that she thought she had murdered Frankie. They were always concerned about fingerprints. She thought about everything she had touched in the room and realized her prints were on some of the broken glass scattered on the floor. She didn't think that mattered because Eddie would already know she had been in the room. After all, he had sent a driver to take her to the "date" with the dead man.

She also didn't think Eddie was going to call in the police in any official capacity. She knew he would have to make arrangements for the body. That would take cooperation from some of the cops he owned, but Kiko was positive Eddie wouldn't tell the police about the woman who had been in the room and the missing money. The money Frankie had called "off the books money."

Unbidden, a phrase popped into her head. A line her English Literature professor at Cal had quoted from a D. H. Laurence novel: "But she might as well be hung for a sheep as for a lamb."

In that moment, she made her decision. She wasn't going to be an easily slaughtered lamb. She was going to run, and she was going to take the money with her. But she wasn't going to run in a panic. She was going to think things through.

That's when the finality of it all really struck her. The moment Frankie had and fallen, her life had changed forever. She started to cry. But she was not crying tears of hysteria. She was crying for her lost life. She let the tears flow freely. She had time.

Somebody would come for Frankie. There was no way he was going to the airport alone with all that money. Not the man who was so afraid someone might have followed her that he almost yanked her arm off pulling her into the room so he could slam the door. But the mobster had told her he was going to catch a flight at two o'clock in the morning. He said he wanted to get some sleep first. That meant his driver or escort or whatever he was wouldn't knock on Frankie's door for a while.

She sobbed until she had cried herself out.

"There," she thought. "No more tears. Down to business."

She began to think about what she had to do to survive.

First, she had to disappear. Her immediate need, of course, was to get out of Vegas, but beyond that, Kiko Yoshida had to cease to exist. That meant she couldn't contact anyone she considered a friend for help. She was sure Eddie's people would go to her apartment. They would look through all her things, or simply pack them up and take them. They were going to have her address book, so they would be watching her friends and family. She just hoped they wouldn't do anything worse than watch them.

Second, the money in the case was the key to her survival. In fact, she realized she would probably have to make it last for the rest of her life. But she couldn't take the case with her when she ran. She was going to be on public transportation, or even worse, out on the highway hitchhiking. What if someone got the case away from her? She would be a dead woman.

She had to secure the money somewhere, get out of Las Vegas for at least a few months, and then come back for it. As much as it frightened her just to think about ever returning, she couldn't imagine trusting someone else enough to have them pick it up for her.

Her thoughts turned to the man who would be looking for her.

If Eddie Mazzetti really was a "putz" compared to Frankie Pescatore, he was in as much trouble as she was. When he found out Frankie was dead and the case was gone, his first concern would be the missing money. He would pull out all the stops looking for her and the case.

But he couldn't let very many people know the money was missing. He would be desperate to find it before "The Outfit" even knew Frankie "The Whale" was dead. Eddie would confer with Silverstein and Meyer and then send men he could trust to search for her. Men well up in the criminal organization.

There couldn't be that many high-ranking gangsters available on such short notice. And even the ones Eddie thought he could trust he'd have to send in teams of two so they could keep an eye on each other. After all, since they were high up in the organization they would know about what Frankie had called "off the books money." Once Eddie told the men to look for her and the case both, they'd know the case was full of money, even if they didn't know how much.

The critical question was: how many teams would he have? Maybe two, maybe three, maybe four? Surely no more than that. She had to believe his resources were limited. If they weren't, she'd be dead before the sun came up.

Okay. Okay. Push those kinds of thought away.

First car to the airport, since that was the fastest way to get the farthest away from Las Vegas.

Probably wouldn't check the Union Pacific Depot because the two daily passenger trains had already come and gone. Eddie would know the schedule from sending cars to pick up very important guests.

Second car to the bus station. That left two.

Third car to her apartment.

And the fourth car? That one would slowly cruise the city. She shivered when she thought of it rolling silently through the streets with the windows down, driver and passenger scanning the faces for a Japanese woman.

Since there was a good chance they would not discover Frankie was dead until after midnight or one o'clock, she might have a chance.

But she had to move, and move quickly.

All she had in her purse was five dollars and change, but she had jewelry worth a good deal more. If she could somehow get to L.A., she could turn it into enough money to hide out until things cooled off and she could come back for the case.

She took off the diamond bracelet, the pearls and the diamond earrings and put them in the little purse.

She walked over to the case. She realized the metal finish and the combination locks made it unusual and memorable. She didn't want it to draw attention to her when she was on the street. She went into the bedroom and took a pillow case off one of the huge pillows. She walked out and shoved the courier case inside it.

She moved to the door, circling well away from Frankie's corpse. She stood listening at the door again. When she was satisfied she could hear no sounds, she gathered her courage. She knew this was a dangerous moment. The blood was almost to the door. If someone were passing by, they would not only see her but might also see the blood. She removed the security chain and unsnapped both locks. When she peered into the hallway, she saw no one. She stood for a moment, listening for voices or footsteps. She heard none. She pulled the door wider and eased into the hallway. She switched off the lights. No reason to have someone wonder why light was showing under the door of the suite later that night.

She pulled the heavy door closed and headed off down the hall, hoping she would meet no one before she reached the stairwell.

The ground floor exit door took her into the parking lot behind the casino. She walked across the lot and forced her way through the oleanders separating the Serengeti parking lot from the Silver Slipper. She crossed the Silver Slipper lot and one more before exiting onto the Las Vegas Strip. She crossed to the south side and turned east toward Fremont Street and downtown Las Vegas.

It was very cold. She was freezing in her strapless, elegant and completely useless evening dress. The garishly lighted, early evening Strip was jammed with cars. The streets were packed with people. She moved along quickly, the heavy container in the pillow case under her arm. She tried to avoid eye contact as she moved thorough the sea of people. She needn't have worried. They were all rushing past her to get to the next place to throw away their money.

There was no way she could afford a cab. And even if she had been able to, she could just see some cab driver saying, "Japanese girl? In an evening dress? Yeah, I picked her up and took her to the Union Pacific train depot."

She walked as fast as she could in her high heels. When she got to Fremont Street, she headed to the Union Pacific depot. Inside, she moved quickly to the luggage lockers. She opened the door to one and put the box inside. She put in a quarter and turned the lock. She put the key in her purse and hurried out into the street. She had been inside less than two minutes.

Even so, she was sure someone in there had noticed her. But because she hadn't walked over to look at the arrival/departure board or asked about ticket prices, she hoped she had only been seen by tourists and not Union Pacific employees.

From the depot, Kiko headed west toward the bus station, thinking hard as she walked. She was Japanese and elegantly dressed. Either one of those elements could get her remembered, but there was nothing for it. With only five dollars in her purse, she had no other way to get out of town.

She pushed through the doors into the station and walked to the ticket window.

"How much for a ticket to Los Angeles?"

"Fifteen dollars."

23

"How about Barstow?"

"Seven fifty."

"Is there anywhere I can go for less than five dollars?"

"Three fifty will get you to Baker."

"When does the next bus leave?"

"Ten minutes."

She put her five dollar bill on the counter.

Fifteen minutes later she was looking out the window into the dark night as the bus rolled past the "Leaving Las Vegas" sign. Her reflection, frightened and uncertain, stared back at her in the smeared glass.

Chapter 3

Las Vegas, Nevada

March 24, 1961

At one fifteen in the morning, Eddie Mazzetti was just drifting off to sleep when his phone rang. He answered with an irritated, "Yeah."

"Boss, it's Clemente. We got a problem."

Eddie was instantly wide awake.

"Are you at the airport?"

"That's the problem. I'm still at the hotel."

Eddie kicked off the satin sheets and sat on the edge of the bed.

"Why?"

"Cause, Frankie ain't answerin' his door."

"Well, knock louder."

"I did, boss. I pounded on the thing. I been knockin' since one. Nothin'."

"Did you have the desk call his room?"

"Thought it'd be best if I didn't. If there's a problem, I don't think we want everyone in the hotel knowin' about it."

"Yeah, yeah. Good, Clemente."

There was a momentary silence.

25

"Go get Melvin Meyer. Don't call him. Go to his house.

I'll meet the two of you in the casino near the craps tables."

"Gotcha."

A half hour later, Eddie Mazzetti, Melvin Meyer and Clemente were gathered outside the door of the suite.

"Knock once more, Clemente. Give it a couple good whacks."

Clemente hit the door three times with the flat of his big hand.

There was no response.

Eddie produced the key to the suite and unlocked the door. The odor hit the men immediately. He started to step inside. Clemente put his hand across Eddie's chest.

"Hold it, boss. That's blood."

"Shit. Hold the door a minute."

Eddie stayed in the hallway, reached inside, and turned on the lights.

The source of the tremendous amount of blood was immediately obvious.

"Okay, we all need to get inside without steppin' in that."

Clemente pushed the door all the way open and managed to skirt the blood. He held it open while Eddie Mazzetti and Melvin Meyer followed the same path. When they were clear, he pushed the door closed.

The three men stood in the luxurious suite looking down at Frankie's enormous body, naked save for his tiny undershorts.

"Do you think he's dead?"

"Jesus, Melvin, do you really think a man can lose that much blood and still be alive?

And he's been here a while. I mean, he's stuck to the floor for Chrissake."

"What killed him?"

"That's not the first thing we need to know. We need to know where the skim is."

Melvin Meyer, who had been very calm about the dead body in front of him, turned pale. He turned to Clemente.

"You know what we're looking for?"

26

"Sure. I been takin' guys to the airport carrying that case for a long time."

"Okay, let's search the place."

Fifteen minutes later, they had scoured the suite with no success.

The three men gathered beside the body again.

"Dumb bastard," said Meyer. "Had to be the big shot, just like Herman said."

"So, now what?"

"Now we get the hell out of here and away from this stink.

Clemente, round up Guido Battagliano, Lino DeLuca, Vincenzo Zamparo and Fiore Abbatini. I'll get Herman Silverstein. My office, half an hour."

At two-thirty in the morning, the eight men were all in Eddie's office. Eddie, Melvin Meyer and Herman Silverstein were seated behind Eddie's desk. The other men were standing in front of it.

"You are here because of your loyalty to the family.

The worst possible thing has happened. Frankie Pescatore is dead. Frankie's body is in his suite.

Melvin and I are going to meet with a detective from the Las Vegas Police Department. This is a good cop. We bought him and he will stay bought. We also have a deputy coroner in our pocket, plus we have a local doctor with a big gamblin' problem gonna sign the death certificate.

This will be an 'unattended death.' Seems Frankie had a sudden and massive heart attack. Poor guy never had a chance. There will be no autopsy. Frankie will be taken to the funeral parlor where he'll be embalmed and dressed. Casket be on the train to Chicago later today.

Which brings us back to right now.

Frankie died because he fell on a piece of crystal from a whisky decanter that was smashed on the floor. A piece of the crystal stabbed him in the throat and hit his car ... cart... Melvin, what's the word I'm lookin' for here?"

"Carotid artery, Eddie"

"Right. That artery thing that Melvin said. He bled to death in a few minutes."

27

Clemente interrupted. "Yeah, man, you shoulda seen him. He was completely white. He looked like a big gob of Crisco covered with black hair, and he was wearing …"

"Clemente. That's enough."

"It just creeped me out. And the smell …"

"Clemente."

"Okay, okay. Sorry, boss."

"So, here's our problem.

Frankie had the skim with him, his room.

It's gone.

We sent a girl up to his room. Uppity little nip bitch. She's in the wind, money's gone. We gotta find her quick. There's pictures of her for everybody on the desk.

Guido, you and Fiore take the transportation. Hit the airport first. All the airlines and even charters. That's the quickest way out of town. If she hasn't been there, do the bus station.

"What about the train depot?"

"Trains have already come and gone.

Clemente, you do the cab companies. I want to know if anybody picked this girl up last night or early today.

I know we had her picked up at her place for her date with Frankie, so she didn't have wheels here.

Lino and Vincenzo, go to the girl's apartment. Here's the address. If she has roommates, find out the last time they saw her. Find out if she had a car. If she didn't, find out if she borrowed one of theirs. Find out if they knew where she was goin' last night. If nobody comes to the door, break in.

And hey! Find out where they work. Lean on them. Lean on them hard.

Now, before you go, the money is in a metal case about so big. It has a combination lock underneath both latches. If you find it, call me. Then bring it straight here.

There's a lot of scratch in that case, but don't get no funny ideas. Just remember, it belongs to The Outfit. Even more important, it belongs to Tommy Bones. So, watch each other. Cause if one a you takes the money and runs, his partner's gonna take his weight.

Got it?"

28

There were murmurs of assent.

"Then get outta here. Find that broad. And bring her and the money to me."

After the two teams left, Eddie addressed Clemente.

"If you find a cabbie that picked her up, bring him here. If not, I want you to shadow the team at her apartment. Make sure they turn over every rock."

Clemente hurried out of the room.

Eddie, Melvin and Herman were silent for a moment.

Eddie spoke first.

"Melvin, how long you think we have before we have to call Chicago?"

"Frankie's plane is due at O'Hare at seven twenty. That's five twenty our time. Somebody will be there to meet him.

If the plane's on time, by five forty five they'll know for sure he wasn't on it. They'll call here as soon as they know.

So we've really got no time at all."

"Then we better call Sam at home, soon as we get done with the cops and the coroner.

We have him get to a safe phone and call us. We tell him what we're doin'.

Then we hang up and wait about ten minutes. When the phone rings again, it'll be Thomaso Cortese. He'll scream at us."

"If we're lucky he'll scream. But if he's really pissed, that crazy bastard will whisper in that 'Tommy Bones' voice, and you'll have to strain to catch every word," said Herman.

"I hope he screams," said Eddie.

"Jesus, I hope he doesn't come out here."

Melvin shuddered. "Me too.

You know, on second thought, maybe we better call Sam right now. You know, get out in front of this? Tell him what we're doing to try to control the whole thing."

"Nope. We get the clean-up started. The dead whale in that room makes me nervous. Then tell Sam what we done."

At four fifteen in the morning, Eddie made the call, waking up a very unhappy Sam Genovese. He kept it short, simply saying that something very important had happened, and Sam should get to the safe phone.

Fifteen minutes later, passersby on Fremont Street were treated to the sight of two of the most powerful men in Las Vegas squeezed into a phone booth next to a black Chrysler parked on a hydrant. While the pedestrians were unaware of the identities of the two men, an officer behind the wheel of a Las Vegas Police Department prowl car recognized them immediately. He had slowed to ticket the car for parking in the red, but when he realized who the men in the phone booth were, he accelerated and drove on past.

It was crowded in the booth. It was also awkward because the two men were trying to position themselves so both of them could hear the conversation.

Eddie dialed the number for the safe phone.

It was answered immediately.

"This better be good, Eddie."

"Frankie Pescatore's dead. We found him lyin' in his own blood in one of our suites."

There was a long silence.

"Where's the skim?"

"Jeez, Sam, don't you even want to know what happened to him?"

"No as much as I want to know where the money is."

"It's gone."

There was another silence.

"You know what Tommy Bones gonna say, don't you? He's gonna say this is on you 'cause the money never got to us."

Melvin leaned over and shouted into the phone.

"Sam, this is Melvin Meyer.

I really don't think that's fair."

"Tommy don't give a damn what you think, Melvin. That's our money, and you'd better get it back. We know the count to the penny. Frankie called when he had the total. Almost seven hundred thousand dollars, and that's how much you owe us, plus the vigorish."

"What's the vig?"

"The usual. Ten percent a week."

30

Eddie broke in.

"Come on, Sam, we're all friends here."

"Hey, Tommy Bones don't have no friends when it comes to The Outfit's money. That money could be loaned out to patsies, be at work for us all month. You lost it, you gotta make it good. By the time the courier gets out there, you'll have that money, plus the vig, plus next month's skim. Otherwise, Tommy Bones may think he has to come out there personally."

"Okay, okay, we'll have it, but don't bury us! It's going to be hard to make up that much, so how about a break on the vig?"

"I'll ask Tommy.

Now, let's leave Thomaso Cortese out of this for a minute. What the hell happened to my wife's cousin?"

"He slipped and fell on a shard from a crystal decanter. It cut the artery in his neck. He musta bled out in minutes."

"He did this all by himself?"

"No.

Eyeballed this girl he liked, we sent her to his room. Japanese girl, worked the Keno floor.

She wasn't no pro, but we sweetened the pot with somethin' she really wanted and talked her into goin'."

"Ah, Jesus. Always with them oriental broads, that Frankie."

"Anyways, we really don't know exactly how it happened. Some kind of struggle, maybe."

"Struggle? How big was this broad?"

"A hundred pounds, tops."

"A hundred pound girl put Frankie on the ground? C'mon!"

"I don't know. Maybe she was one a them judo champs or somethin'."

"Very funny.

So, what are you doing to clean up the mess?"

"We already met with a cop and a deputy coroner we own, plus a local doctor with a bad gambling jones who signed off on an unattended death. This was officially a heart attack. Easy to believe, guy Frankie's size."

We have the right kind of ties to a local funeral home. The body is there right now. Frankie's casket will be on the train to Chicago before the day is over.

We have cleaners, a bunch of our soldiers, in the room. Place will be spotless before the sun comes up."

"How's the body look?"

"Other than no blood, pretty good. When he's embalmed, made up and dressed, he'll look like he's goin' to a weddin'."

"Good. We'll have a big funeral for him here. Open casket. Let all the goombahs have a look at him. Local press, too."

"Right. Be a short piece in the Review Journal out here about the heart attack. Frankie'll be described as a 'visitor'."

"Okay, Eddie.

Thomaso will expect you to be in Chicago for the funeral."

"Wouldn't miss it. Besides, I'd rather come there and talk to Thomaso than have him out here."

"Agreed. I don't want you guys distracted. You find that money, find that little whore."

"Like I said, Sam, she wasn't a pro."

"Yeah, yeah. Just find the bitch and take care of her."

"You got it."

"And Eddie, give me the number you're callin' from and stand by."

Eight minutes later the phone rang again.

Eddie could barely hear Thomaso "Tommy Bones" Cortese.

"Sam told me what happened.

I don't like it."

"We don't like it either, Thomaso, but whadya gonna do?"

"What you're gonna do is get us our money. Plus the vig.

Sam asked me for a favor for you, so I'm gonna give you a big break. The vigorish? Ten percent the month, not each week. Best deal I ever give anybody, ever!"

"Thanks, Thomaso, we really appreciate it."

"And you're gonna get that little chink."

"Japanese, Thomaso. She's Japanese."

"Yeah, yeah.

Sam told me about you guys takin' care the mess, makin' the arrangements. Done good on that.

Now, how much head start this girl have?"

"Pretty good one. The doc said Frankie probably died between seven and nine. But we had guys out trying to pick up her trail right after we found the body at twenty till two."

Thomaso raised his voice slightly.

"Not regular soldiers!"

"No, no. Family guys. Got them in pairs, watch each other."

"Just remember, we want the money, but the girl, too. Really want her! Nobody kills a made man from The Outfit and gets away with it."

"We'll find her, Thomaso."

"One more thing. When you come for the funeral, bring the card you fingerprinted the girl when you hired her."

"What do you need that for?"

"I'm puttin' a contract on this girl. Ten large for the goombah gets her. But he has to bring me her fingers, prove he killed her.

Somebody will call your office and tell you when the funeral will be."

Eddie started to speak again, but Tommy Bones had already hung up.

A few minutes later, Eddie Mazzetti and Melvin got back in the car. They were having an earnest discussion when the LVPD prowler went by again. Just as before, the driver pretended not to notice their car

At five in the morning, Eddie Mazzetti, Melvin Meyer and a very nervous Herman Silverstein were in the executive office when Clemente Malaleta walked in.

"Boss, no one at the cab companies picked her up.

Guido and Fiore picked up her trail at the bus station. Guy there remembered her real good. Said she only had enough money to buy a ticket to Baker, so that's where she went. They're on their way there now."

"Did she have the case with her?"

"He didn't know."

33

"What time did she buy the ticket?"

"She went west on the 8:50 bus."

"Shit! She's way ahead of us.

We talked to Chicago. They want their money and they want this Kiko broad to disappear. Forever.

Tommy Bones has put a ten thousand dollar price on her head!"

When Guido and Fiore pulled into the east end of Baker, the town was almost completely dark. Their headlights picked up nondescript buildings on both sides of the highway.

"Jesus! What a dump. Can't believe people live here."

"Yeah, well, I guess everybody gotta live somewhere, Fiore."

"Spare me the philosophy. Start lookin' the bus station."

They drove slowly through town.

"There, on the left."

"Closed."

"Better check the motels, then."

"Guido, if the chick didn't have enough money for a bus ticket to anyplace other than here, how's she gonna pay for a motel room?"

"You may be right, but you wanna tell Eddie we didn't check the motels?"

Fiore made a U-turn, and they started checking motels

The last one they stopped at was on the very north edge of Baker. It was so run down they hadn't even realized it was a motel when they had first driven into town. It looked more like a collection of abandoned shacks.

"Hey, if she had fifty cents she coulda got a room in this dump!"

When they pulled in, the office was dark. The "motel" sign was hand-painted. The place didn't even have a name.

They parked in front of the closest cabin and walked to the office door.

It was locked.

There was a piece of cardboard taped to the door that read "Press button for after-hours service."

Guido pressed the button.

34

They could hear no sound from inside.

Fiore hammered the door with the flat of his hand.

Nothing.

They waited a few minutes, and Fiore hammered again.

Still nothing.

Fiore stepped back and began to kick the glass door. It rattled in its cheap, aluminum frame.

There was no response from inside. No lights came on.

"Get me the tire iron out of the trunk."

When Fiore returned, Guido wedged the flat tip of the iron between the frame and the door and heaved his considerable bulk against it.

The door popped open.

The two men walked into the office and went behind the counter.

Guido tried the knob on the door there. It didn't turn.

"Want me to knock?"

"We're done knockin'."

Fiore lifted his foot and smashed it into the door next to the knob. The door flew open and banged against the wall in the next room.

There was a disheveled young man coming awake on a couch. Empty beer cans were scattered around the room. There was a girlie magazine splayed open on the man's chest.

"Hey, bozo, get up!"

"Huh?"

"Get your lazy ass off that couch."

The young man was suddenly wide awake. He looked at the splintered door jamb.

"How'd you get in here?"

"Through the door, stupid."

"You can't come busting in here like that!"

"We just did.

Now get up."

"Look, I don't know who …"

Which was as far as he got.

Fiore reached down, grabbed the lapels of a ratty bathrobe and yanked the kid off the couch and onto his feet.

"Stop talkin', unless we ask you a question."

The young man started to say something, and then thought better of it.

Guido held the picture of Kiko in front of him.

"You seen this woman?"

"No."

"You sure?"

"Yeah. There's only two people staying here, and she isn't one of them."

Fiore pushed the man hard, and he fell awkwardly onto the couch.

"Have another beer."

The two men stomped out of the room. The young man heard a car start, but by the time he got off the couch, pulled on his pants and shirt and got into the office, it was gone.

When he saw the ruined glass door, he picked up the phone and dialed the Smoke Tree Sheriff's substation.

The last stop Guido and Fiore made was at the Bun Boy restaurant. False dawn was brightening the sky above the distant Kelso Mountains when they walked in.

"Two for breakfast?" asked the waitress.

"Nah.

You seen this woman?"

Guido showed her Kiko's picture.

"No."

"What time did you come on?"

"Midnight."

"Who was here before that?"

The woman hesitated.

"I'm not sure if ..."

Fiore interrupted her. "Look ... Debbie," he said, gripping her arm as he read her name tag, "We gotta find this woman.

36

Now, who was on last night before midnight?"

"Hey," she said, trying to pull free, "you're hurting my arm!"

Fiore squeezed harder.

The door to the kitchen swung open and a boxy man wearing slacks and a short-sleeved white shirt with a clip-on tie walked toward them.

"Mike, these men …."

"Shut it, lady."

"Do we have a problem here, gentlemen?"

"Not yet, but might.

You the manager?"

"That's right."

"Let's go talk in your office."

Mike saw the fear in Debbie's eyes and nodded to the men.

"Follow me."

The "office" was a small desk in a storeroom full of paper products, cleaning supplies, canned food and stacks of hamburger buns. The room smelled like insecticide. There were dead roaches on the floor.

Guido and Fiore squeezed inside and closed the door.

Mike found himself crowded against his own desk.

"We're lookin' for a woman made some big trouble in Vegas.

We need to talk to someone was workin' the swing shift last night."

"Well, I don't know …"

Guido held out his hands, palms down.

There was a fifty dollar bill sticking up between the fingers of his left hand.

"Look, Mike. We don't want no trouble, but my partner here, he gets a little rough at times. I have to hold him back. We don't let him out in polite company a lot.

Now, you tell us where to find the waitress who was on last night so we can show her a picture of this woman, the Benjamin is yours.

You don't, I can't be responsible for what this guy might do."

Mike swallowed.

"That would be Maureen."

"There you go! We just want to show her this picture, see this woman was in your place last night. Won't take two minutes.

Where can we find this Maureen?"

"Down the street. Take the highway toward Death Valley. Half mile you'll see a mobile home on the left. Got a bunch of those wooden airplanes with propellers that spin in the wind all over the place."

Guido handed Mike the fifty, and he and Fiore turned to go.

Guido stopped in the doorway and turned back.

"And Mike?"

"Yes?"

"If we learn you called her after we leave, I'm gonna come and get my fifty dollars back, and my friend here? Re-arrange your place.

Now, you sit right here until you're sure we're gone."

The two men walked out into the restaurant.

Debbie was sitting in a booth having a cup of coffee and a cigarette. Her hand shook as she raised it to her mouth.

Guido stopped at her booth.

"Debbie, sorry if my pal hurt your arm. He gets real excited sometimes. Don't know his own strength."

He reached in his pocket and pulled out a roll of bills. He sorted through them until he found a twenty.

He put it in front of her on the table.

"Now, Debbie, I want you to sit here until we're gone."

He wagged his finger.

"No fair peekin' out the window at our license plate.

Okay?"

Debbie looked away.

"Sure, mister, sure."

Guido drove past the mobile home, made a U-turn and parked the car far enough down the road that it would be almost impossible to read the license plate.

They walked back to the mobile home and roused Maureen from her sleep. She opened the door only as far as the security chain permitted. When they showed her Kiko's picture and encouraged Maureen's memory with a twenty, she opened the door and invited them in.

The three of them sat in the tiny living room.

"You know my name, but I don't know yours."

"Uh," stammered Guido. "I'm Sammy and this is Frank."

Maureen smiled.

"Oh yeah. I think I caught your act on the strip."

Guido and Fiore stared at her.

"That's a joke. I know you're not going to tell me your names. But the girl in the photograph was in the Bun Boy last night around eleven o'clock. She stood out, you know?"

"Not sure I do. Tell me."

"Well first, the place was dead. When it's quiet like that, I usually notice when a car pulls into the lot, but I didn't see one. The door just opened and she walked in.

Second, as you can tell, she's some kind of an oriental. I don't know which kind. I can't really tell them apart.

And she was wearing a black, strapless evening dress and high heeled shoes. Don't see that a lot at the Bun Boy.

But what was really odd was she didn't have a jacket. She must have been freezing 'cause it was really cold last night."

"Did she have any luggage with her? Case of some kind?"

Maureen thought for a minute.

"I'm not sure."

"How long did she stay?"

"Not long.

She ordered a burger and went after it like she was starving.

But then, a bunch of young guys came in."

"How young?"

"College guys would be my guess. Looked like they had been drinking. When they saw the woman they made a beeline for her.

I didn't hear everything they said, but it sounded like they wanted her to go to Vegas with them."

"What'd she say?"

"She was polite at first. Said she wanted to go to L.A. But those boys wouldn't take 'no' for an answer. They got pretty insistent.

I went over and told them to leave her alone. While I was arguing with them, she went out the door.

I tried to slow them down, but they went out after her."

"Then what?"

"In a few minutes, I saw the boys tear out of the parking lot. The woman wasn't with them."

""The girl come back in after they left?"

"Nope. Never saw her again.

And I didn't see another car pull out after those boys left, so I don't think she was driving a car of her own."

"So, you have no idea where she went?"

"Don't know where she came from. Don't know where she went.

Mystery woman."

"Thanks for your time, Maureen. Sorry to wake you up."

"Twenty bucks for answering a few questions? You can wake me up anytime, boys.

Tell you something for free, though."

"What's that?"

"Girl that pretty, dressed like that? She walks out on the highway and sticks out her thumb? She's gone in two minutes."

At nine o'clock that morning, Eddie Mazzetti, Melvin Meyer, Herman Silverstein, Clemente Malaleta, Guido Battagliano, Lino DeLuca, Vincenzo Zamparo and Fiore Abbatini were gathered in Eddie's office far above the casino floor. Only Eddie, Melvin and Herman were seated. The other men were arrayed in front of Eddie's desk.

"All right, things are worse than before. Chicago's pissed. Believe me, we don't want to be remembered as the clowns let some little slant eye kill a made man from The Outfit, steal the skim, just walk away."

There were nods and murmurs of assent from the five standing men.

"Just so everybody knows what everybody else knows, Guido and Fiore, tell us about the bus station."

"Guy there remembered her real good. We asked him if she had luggage with her. He didn't remember, but he told us she only had enough money for a ticket to Baker.

We drove down there.

I gotta tell you, that's one sorry ass town. I mean, whadya gotta do wrong to have to live in a dump like that? Checked all the motels. No luck.

Then we started at the restaurants. She was seen at a place called the Bun Boy at about eleven o'clock.

We greased the manager, and he told us where the night manager lived. We drove out there, give her twenty bucks. She fell all over herself talkin' to us.

Said the girl was there."

"Did you ask about the case?"

"Said she wasn't sure."

"Go on."

"Said the girl come in, ordered a burger, didn't get to eat it. Some college boys came in, started botherin' her. Wanted her to come to Vegas with them. She wasn't interested, but they wouldn't leave her alone, so she left.

This woman said the boys went out the door after her, but she saw them drive off a while later. Said the girl wasn't with them."

"Did the woman see the girl again?"

"No, but she said somethin' made sense. Said a broad that good lookin', dressed like that? Goes out on the highway, sticks out her thumb, gone in two minutes."

"Vincenzo, Lino, tell us what you found when you went to the broad's apartment."

"Her roommates was there. Squeezed them pretty good.

And by the way, they ain't gonna complain. Turns out they both work for the Serengeti.

Anyway, they hadn't seen her since yesterday mornin'. Hadn't heard from her, either. They both work the swing shift and they were gone before she woulda come home."

"Did this Kiko have a car?"

41

"No."

"She didn't take one of theirs?"

"Nope.

They only got one car between the three of them. It was in the parkin' lot."

"So, they're due at work this afternoon?"

"Yeah. One's a cocktail waitress. I coulda guessed that by the bazoombas on the broad. Probably gets a five dollar tip every time she bends over."

"And the other one?"

"Plain Jane. Works one of our restaurants."

"Okay. Get them out of town.

Melvin, give Vincenzo six thousand.

Vincenzo, give each a them three thousand. Tell them to pack up their stuff and get out of Dodge. Right now. Tell them the 'Welcome to Las Vegas' sign don't apply to them no more. Ever. Make sure they understand what will happen if we see ever see them back. We don't want nobody talkin' it around about this Kiko person missin'."

"What if they put up a fuss?"

"About what? Christ, for three thousand they can buy a new Thunderbird!

Stay there until they've loaded up and gone. Then get all the Kiko broad's stuff, bring it with you.

This girl's got a family somewhere.

I want to know where they live.

She must have friends somewhere. Bound to. Was in college.

We're lookin' for address book, letters, phone numbers. Anything can help us figure out where she's goin' to go to ground.

He turned to Silverstein.

"Herman, we still got that house on the dead-end street in Henderson?"

"Yeah, Eddie."

"Okay, that's gonna be the headquarters for this search.

42

We'll meet there seven o'clock tonight, hand out the assignments.

Now, get movin'."

By the time they met that evening, they knew a few things. They knew Kiko's parents lived in Salinas, up by Monterey. They had an address for a friend in New York and one in Seattle. Eddie assigned Vincenzo and Lino to check on the family. He assigned Guido and Fiore to check on New York. Clemente was to take a quick trip to Seattle.

"Clemente, soon as you're done Seattle, get back here. Gonna run the search from this house. I don't want you other goombahs comin' and goin' through the casino or hotel to my office. Scares the citizens.

You other guys, remember, Clemente's only one who comes here.

Okay, this broad's in more trouble than we are. She don't have much she can use. Got a case with a ton of money in it. Maybe she's got it with her, maybe she don't. If she does, got no easy way to get into it while she's on the run. She's wearin' the only clothes she has. She's got some expensive jewelry she can pawn, but we already put out the word and her description to all the shops in L.A. She tries to turn the stuff into cash, we'll know about it.

Now, I gotta go to Chicago as soon as they call me. Frankie's funeral. Melvin will be in charge until I get back.

One more thing. Just so you know how serious this is.

Tommy Bones has put a price on this Kiko woman's head. Ten large, the guy finds her. But you have to make her disappear. And I mean forever!

I'm takin' the employment card with her fingerprints on it to Chicago with me."

"What for?"

"Tommy wants it. If you get the girl, he wants proof. He'll pay the ten thousand when he gets the fingers that match the prints."

Fiore laughed.

"Hell, for another yard, I'll throw in her feet."

43

Chapter 4

Las Vegas, Nevada, Smoke Tree, California

Oatman, Kingman, and Parker, Arizona

Twentynine Palms, California

And the mountains of the Eastern Mojave Desert

Thursday, May 11, 1961

When Clemente walked into Eddie Mazzetti's office, he was worried about the meeting. He knew Tommy Bones had been all over Eddie. That meant Eddie was going to be all over him.

Eddie was behind his desk. Melvin Meyer was sitting on one side of the desk facing Eddie and Herman Silverstein on the other. There was a vacant chair in the middle.

"Siddown, Clemente."

He sat down. All three men stared at him.

"So, Clemente. Been runnin' the search for that little Jap bitch since March with no luck.

Take us through everything again."

"Like you say boss, haven't had much luck.

Seattle was a dead end. Girl up there hadn't heard from this Kiko broad in years."

"You sure?" asked Meyer.

"Yeah." Way I asked, I guarantee she woulda told me if she'd heard."

"Okay," said Eddie. "And New York?"

"Guido and Fiore tracked down the New York connection, squeezed her. Hard."

Silverstein broke in.

"Aren't we afraid she'll go to the cops?"

Eddie laughed.

"Come on, Herman. Half of the NYPD is on a pad to the Family. The other half's coverin' for them.

Clemente, tell these guys what the girl told Guido."

"This girl was her roommate in college. The both a them studied dance and theater stuff along with all that other college crap. They decided they would go to New York after they graduated, try show biz.

Month before graduation? Kiko broad gets herself knocked up. Tells her mom. Mom tells Kiko's pop. He hits the roof. Tells her she has disgraced the family, whole Jap nation. Says he don't have no daughter no more."

"Why? Japanese women don't get pregnant?"

"Not unless they're gonna get married they don't. And not by some white guy. That's even more important than the not married part."

"So who's the daddy?"

Some mutt from a rich family. He's about done with law school, don't want no half and half bambino. Tells her get rid of it.

She tells him she ain't dyin' from no back-alley butcher job. Wants enough money to get the job done someone knows what they're doin'.

Mutt comes through with the money. Her and the roommate goes off to New York."

Meyer interrupted.

"This other girl, she Japanese too?"

"Nah. Regular white broad.

The two a them audition for some stuff, don't get nowhere."

"What are they doin' for money? She woulda run through the abortion bucks before too long. Family decide to help her after all?"

"Nope. This other girl? The roommate? Parents back in California are bucks up. They're slippin' the white girl enough dough she can take care a the both a them.

Kiko gets too far along to audition, works as a waitress, put some money in the kitty. Does that until she can't work no more, checks into one a them unwed mothers places. Has the baby. Gives it away.

Turns out she never intended get no abortion. Was just tryin' to get enough dough to go to New York. "

"Then what?"

"They're both doin' the temporary job thing, still tryin' to catch a break.

The roommate? She's a real looker, and stacked! Guido told me he woulda porked her in a minute!

Anyway, she starts to get some work. Little stuff, ya know?

But this Kiko broad? Nothin'. Not a lot of jobs for slant-eyed girls, I guess.

She keeps tryin' a while, sees New York ain't her ticket, goes back to California."

"And does what?"

"Back to school.

See, this little Jap is super smart. Degree in some kinda science stuff. Song and dance shit was extra.

Anyway, she's in some kinda after-regular-college school, gets another degree a some kind while she works doin' some science things, a lab at the college."

"What kind of science stuff?"

"Jeez, boss. I dunno. The roommate tried to explain it, Guido and Fiore, they couldn't make heads or tails. Somethin' to do with some kinda bugs."

"You mean spiders and roaches and shit?"

"Nah. Little tiny bugs. Gotta look through one a them microscopes to see 'em."

Herman interrupted.

47

"She's so damn smart, all these degrees, how'd she end up workin' as a Keno girl?"

"This roommate? The stacked broad? She says this Kiko still had a jones for the song and dance. Leaves the science gig and comes to Vegas, see if she can break in here."

"Okay, how about Vincenzo and Lino in this Salinas place."

"Told me it was a real dump. Nothin' but wetbacks and vegetables and dirt.

They knock on the door, *papa san* don't ask them in. They're out on the porch talkin' to him, but when Vincenzo mentions the Kiko broad's name, says don't have no daughter that name. Slams the door in their face.

They're standin' on the porch decidin' whether to kick down the door when *mama san* sneaks out, talks to them. Tiny woman. Apologizes, her husband. Starts to cry. Whole time she's talkin', keeps drippin'.

Says, 'Please, tell me where Kiko is. I'm worried about my daughter.'

They say, 'We don't know where she is. Why we're here.'

Says, 'My husband thinks Kiko disgraced the family. He never wants to see her again. But she's my daughter. I worry about her.'

Vincenzo says the woman probably woulda said more, but *papa san* opens the door, says somethin' in Japanese. Woman gives a little bow, goes in the house. *Papa san* slams the door again. Harder this time.

Vincenzo and Lino go for coffee and talk it over. Decide the parents haven't heard from Kiko. But don't wanna let it go at that.

They drive to San Francisco, North Beach, talk with the Family Underboss about a way to keep a loose net over these Japs. Turns out there's a crumb works at the post office in Salinas has a bad habit thinkin' he can pick the ponies. Into a Family-connected bookie and shylock for over three large.

Vincenzo and Lino go back to Salinas, brace the guy. At first he almost craps his pants, thinks they're gonna bust him up bein' late with the vig. When Vincenzo tells him he wants a favor that will erase half what he owes, he falls over himself askin' what he can do. Vincenzo gives him the name, address of the Yoshida family. Tells him his job is to watch for a letter from the daughter.

When they get back to Vegas, Vincenzo mails the guy a page from the girl's diary so he can see the handwritin' 'cause Vincenzo don't think she's dumb enough to put a return address on a letter."

"Why don't the guy just steal the letter?"

"Scared of the shylock, not scared enough to lose his job."

"Guido and Fiore back now?"

"Yeah. The New York Family keepin' a eye on the roommate. Not hard to track. Got a little part in a show on Broadway, won't be leavin' town."

"Anything else?"

"The other Families, New Orleans, Kansas City, Milwaukee, Cleveland, Pittsburgh, Boston? Give pictures the broad to their crews. Shows up anywhere, she's dead. The Commission approved the contract, so even open cities like Miami? Whoever nails her, gets them fingers, picks up the ten large."

"Clemente, you think we're gonna find her?"

Clemente was silent for a few moments. It was clear he was not comfortable with answering.

"Don't look good, boss. She's for sure got the money out of the case.

I don't know how much was in there, it's not my business to know, but I gotta think it's enough to blow the country.

I think she's maybe in Mexico somewhere. Can go there without no passport. Same with Canada."

"Okay. You wanna step outta the office a minute? Me and Melvin and Herman gotta talk about somethin'."

Clemente was glad to get out of the room.

Eddie settled back in his chair.

"Okay, so we made up the skim, right Melvin?"

"Yes, we made it up by the April pickup, but I think Chicago screwed us."

"What makes you think that?"

"Sam told us there was almost seven hundred thousand in the case. I think that was bullshit. You know they never tell us what the skim count was. They just send the guy out at the end of the month. He spends a few days havin' a good time. Then he picks up the money their guy in the count room has been stuffing in that metal box all month. Their inside guy gives the money to the courier, and the guy locks it in the special briefcase and heads back to Chicago.

But we never know how much he takes. I mean, we can guess, because we know how much used to come in before this started. But the action on the casino floor has picked up a lot. Maybe doubled, maybe tripled. But we have no way of knowing with that parasite in the count room because we never get a month without a skim. And sometimes, especially with Frankie, these guys even go to the casher's cage and skim the cream there.

And by the way, that creates a real problem for us, because we have to go back afterward and falsify the fill slips for the chips going back out to the floor so the gambling commission doesn't sniff out the scheme. And that isn't easy. It takes four signatures on each of those slips. Thank God Herman here is a forger as well as a slick accountant.

Anyway, I think they lied to us about the count, but we had to make it up on top of what the courier picked up from the regular skim.

It was very difficult! The official books for the month make it look like we were closed!"

"That's not our worst problem, Melvin. Tommy Bones is breathin' down our necks. He wants this girl dead. Says The Outfit's losin' respect from the other Families in the Commission – their courier, and a made man to boot, took down by a little girl."

"At least we're square on the money."

"But we gotta find this girl, or at least find out where she went if she's out of the country. I'm tellin' you, don't want Tommy Bones out here. He draws the Feds like flies, and I don't want them lookin' at us with new eyes. No way."

"That brings up another thing," said Herman. "And Sam understands this, even if Tommy Bones don't.

As far as we can tell from our sources inside, the Feds haven't tumbled to this skim business. That's a lot of dough leakin' out of here. And not just here but from the other casinos. It's all pre-tax money that's bein' siphoned off to the Families.

If the IRS ever gets even a whiff of this, we're screwed. 'Cause remember, it was the IRS accountants put Capone away. Not the boys with the guns."

"Good point."

Eddie picked up the phone.

"Send Clemente back in."

When Clemente was sitting in front of them again, Eddie started with a question.

"You've been talkin' to the boys, the other Families. How sure are you this woman isn't in Seattle, Salinas or New York?"

"Boss, I'm not sure of nothin' here."

"Okay, forget 'sure.' What's your best guess?"

"I think she ain't in none a them places. I don't think the people we squeezed are givin' us the run around – they really ain't seen her, heard from her.

I think she's gone. In another country, livin' large."

"You think she got out, even with the Families watchin' the airports?"

"That's just it. The *big* airports. There's a hunnerd other ways outta this country. No way we can watch 'em all. And once she's out, she's gonna be hard to find."

Eddie turned to Meyer and Silverstein.

"You guys agree with Clemente on this?"

"Makes sense to me."

"Me too."

"Well, I disagree. Course, I got no way of knowin', but I think she's still around somewhere."

"Not in Vegas?"

"No, she could never hide here."

"Then where?"

"You ever drive across this desert?"

"Christ, not if I can help it."

"Me either. Borin', ugly place. Not a blade of grass or a drop of water. And huge. Miles and miles of nothin'.

What better place to hide until she thinks we've given up?"

Clemente spoke again.

"Man, Eddie, if I had the kinda dough that broad has, I'd be somewhere I could enjoy it."

"I know you would. Clemente. I know you would.

And that's just it. You're not her!

We know she's smart, and I think she went to ground around here somewhere because she knew the more she moved around the better chance we'd find her.

51

But, just in case, send Lino and Vincenzo to New York to watch the roommate.

I know the New York Family's watchin' her, but she's not as important to them as she is to us. The roommate's the person Kiko's tightest with. If she's still on the fly, that's the place she might show up."

"Okay, boss."

"And here? Back here, I want you to send Guido and Fiore to all them Podunk towns down on the desert."

Eddie pulled a map out of his desk drawer and unfolded it.

"Smoke Tree, Kingman, Parker, places like that."

He tossed the map to Clemente.

"Have them show her picture round. They can do it nice or do it hard, whatever way they think works, each place they go.

I think she's around here close somewhere. Little bitch is laughin' her ass off, knowin' we're lookin' everywhere else in the country for her."

He retrieved two badges from the drawer and put them on the desk.

"Here's a couple Vegas Police Department badges. They're real. I picked them up from some retired guys who owe us a favor or two. Tell Guido and Fiore they can flash these if they think it'll help with certain people. But have them be careful about that.

The rest of the time they can use these."

He reached in the drawer and got out two more badges.

"These are private investigator tins. They can say they're lookin' for this woman because the family hasn't heard from her, or she's come into some money. Whatever they think will work.

And hey? Tell them to dress good. Blazers and ties. And keep the blazers buttoned so the guns don't show, unless they need to show them."

"Jeez, boss, they're gonna cry the blues about that. It's hot enough out on that stinkin' desert without wearin' no jackets and ties."

Eddie didn't reply. He just sat staring at Clemente.

Then he exploded.

"Goddamnit, Clemente, you think I give a shit if those goombahs sweat a little bit?

Let me explain somethin' to you.

Tommy Bones comes out here with a crew, there's a chance you and me could end up countin' fish at the bottom of Lake Mead."

Clemente held up his hands.

"Sorry, sorry boss. You're a hunnerd percent right.

I'll get right on it."

He hurried out of the room.

At noon the following day, Guido and Fiore were headed south on Highway 95. Fiore was at the wheel as they entered Searchlight, Nevada.

"Pull over. Stop at the Casino."

"That dump? Jesus, a woman with that kind of money's not gonna hang around a place like that."

"Get somethin' through your head, you stupid Guinea. She's not 'hangin' around.' She's hidin' out. Maybe somebody here seen her."

"Okay, okay."

They pulled off the highway in front of the casino and coffee shop and went inside.

The three blackjack tables were covered. There were some old guys sticking nickels and quarters in a couple of slot machines. The place smelled of cigarette smoke, spilled beer, and desperation.

A chubby man wearing a plaid sports coat, a shirt with horizontal stripes and a bolo tie, spotted them when they came in. He walked over, evaluating their clothes as he came.

"You gentleman looking for some action? I can get a dealer behind one of those tables right away."

Reaching in his pocket, Guido said, "Nah, we're lookin' for this woman."

He pulled out Kiko's picture and held it in front of the man.

The man stepped back.

"Jesus! You guys carrying?"

"What if we are?"

"Come on, not in the casino."

Fiore stared at him. It was not a friendly stare.

"Hey, pal, in your crappy casino or anywhere else we want. Got it?"

Guido moved closer to the man, still holding the picture.

"Answer the question. You seen this broad?"

The man held up his hands, palms out.

"Okay, okay. Give me a second to look, all right?"

He studied the picture for a moment.

"Uh uh.

And who wants to know?"

Guido looked around to see if anyone was listening.

"Tommy Bones, you dumb sonofabitch."

The man looked like someone had jabbed him with a cattle prod.

"Holy shit! Why didn't you say so?

No, I haven't seen her or anyone who even looks like her. Okay? And sorry for the hard time. I didn't know who you was askin' the question for."

Guido put the picture back in his pocket. The two men headed for the door.

"Hey, you guys come back anytime. Anytime at all, okay?"

"Yeah, sure," said Fiore as they went out the door. "Count on it."

They pulled onto the highway. As they left the desert hills where the remnants of Searchlight crouched abandoned and decaying under the indigo dome of a cloudless sky, they could see the New York, Ivanpah and Clark Mountains stretching away to the west. Of course, neither man knew the names of those ranges, nor of the Newberry or Black Mountains turning on the eastern horizon, nor of the Dead Mountains far to the south.

For these men were at home on city streets and in alleys of asphalt. Comfortable on concrete. Completely uninterested in the natural or undeveloped world. To them, the Mojave was a place best avoided: preferably flown over. And if they were forced by circumstances to drive across it, they hugged the highway. They lacked any desire to put their feet on anything that had not been put in place by the hand of man.

Guido Battagliano didn't like the desert. He was indifferent to it.

But for Fiore Abbatini it was different. The hostile, implacable landscape troubled him in ways he could not define. He was offended by the vast emptiness. It made him feel small and unimportant. And beyond feeling offended, he felt an unnerving unease. As if something ominous were concealed

54

behind a distant ridgeline or crouched in some desiccated, stone-filled dry wash, waiting for an unwary traveler to leave the road.

As he drove, Fiore could see three dust devils spinning across the empty plain below the descending highway. They were all that moved in all the inverted, south-sloping bowl below them. There was not another vehicle anywhere.

After a long drive, a railroad crossing came into sight ahead of them. The crossing gates were down, and a long freight was going by. Beside the highway, just before the crossing, there was an old service station.

Fiore's voice, when he spoke, seemed unnaturally loud to his ears, but he could stand the silence no longer.

"Jesus. Look at that place. Damn near fallin' down."

"No wonder. Been there forever. Check out the old gas pumps. Those are the old hand crank kind with the glass measures on top."

"Yeah. Haven't seen those since I was a kid back in Jersey."

"Pull in."

"What for? You think that Kiko woman is hidin' in them junked out cars in the back?"

"No. But I want to be able to tell Eddie and Clemente we checked every place we saw.

You got a better idea?"

Fiore guided the big Chrysler under the overhang.

"Man, I can't get over them pumps. Still got the flyin' red horse on them."

They sat in the car for a moment, reluctant to get out of the air conditioning.

"Ah, nobody's comin' out. Let's go inside."

The instant they got out of the car, they started to sweat. They walked to the steps and climbed to the screened-in porch.

As they did, the caboose cleared the crossing and the crossing gates went up.

Fiore pushed open the screen and they went inside.

A very thin old man, wearing green canvas pants, a green T-shirt and a green, long-billed cap, stepped out of a door behind the counter to meet them.

"Sorry, gents. I didn't hear your car pull up. Them freight trains makes a lot a noise.

Hep you with anything?"

"We just want to ask you a question," said Guido as he reached in his jacket and pulled out his private investigator badge and the picture of Kiko.

"We're private investigators from Las Vegas. We're lookin' for this woman."

"Why?"

Fiore interrupted. "What's it matter 'why'. We're lookin' for her. Have you seen her?"

Guido gave him a hard look and put his hand on Fiore's arm before he turned back to the old man.

"Sir, she's gone missing. She came to Las Vegas a while back and never returned home."

The man peered at the photo.

"She's right purty, but shouldn't you be lookin' for her in Las Vegas?"

"Believe me, sir, we have. We've been to every hotel and motel. She stayed at the Flamingo, but she checked out and never got home.

So now we're searching the outlying areas to find out if anyone has seen her."

"Let me ask you men a question. My curiosity has just plumb got the best of me."

"Go ahead, sir."

"I never met no private eyes before, but I notice you men is heeled. I thought only private eyes in picture shows carried guns."

Guido put on a false smile, trying not to be impatient.

"Well sir, you never know what you're going to run into in this business."

"That must be it.

Can I ask one more question?"

Guido sighed.

"Ask away."

"What kind of money you boys make for a job like this?"

"Hey, old man, we're in a hurry. Just tell us if you seen this bitch."

The old man dropped his hands off the counter. Something changed in his eyes. They looked like black marbles.

"Don't think I like your mouth, mister."

He paused.

"Don't think I like it at all.

If you was workin' for this girl's family, you never would use such a ugly word for her. No, I don't think you're workin' for her family. So even if I'd seen this here girl, I surely wouldn't tell you."

Fiore lost it.

"That's enough from you, pops. You need to learn some manners."

He started to reach across the counter.

The old man took a step back. As he did, he pulled a short, double-barred shotgun out from beneath the counter. The gun was so old it had exterior hammers.

"This here's a coach gun, sonny. Ten gauge. It's old, but it works real good. Both barrels is filled with double aught buckshot. You take one more step toward me or reach for that gun, I'll splatter your grits all over that screen behind you."

Fiore laughed. "With that old piece of junk? How do you know it even works."

The old man cocked both hammers.

"You willin' to bet your life it don't?"

"Old timer, I don't think you've got the nerve for it. You might get one of us, but you won't get us both"

The man smiled over the shotgun.

"Fought in World War One in Belgium and France. Was shelled, shot at, gassed and bored almost to death. Takes more than a low rent gangster such as yourself to scare me.

Now git!"

He motioned with the shotgun.

Fiore started to speak, but Guido held up his hand.

"We're wastin' time here. Let's go."

He turned and pulled the screen door open and walked outside.

Fiore reluctantly turned and went with him.

The old man followed them to the door. He paused, then pulled it open, keeping the shotgun pointed at them.

"One more thing, boys."

Guido and Fiore stopped and looked back.

"Next time you lads comb your hair of a mornin'? Leave a little Brylcream in the tube for the next day."

Guido touched his hand to his head in a limp salute.

"So long, old timer."

When they were back on the road, Fiore vented his frustration.

"Goddamnit, Guido. We should go back and ice that old fart."

"What for? It wouldn't help us find the girl. Forget about it!"

"Well, I don't like it."

"No?

Listen, Fiore, if you think about it, it's pretty funny. An old man with a piece a junk shotgun gettin' the drop on two button men from Chicago."

Fiore slammed his fist against the dashboard.

"I don't think it's right, and I ain't forgettin' about it."

"Well, if you wanna come back, do it on your on time."

Guido's voice got hard.

"And from now on, you let me take the lead. Stand around a look tough or somethin', but don't talk!

Every time you open your mouth, you say somethin' stupid and queer the deal."

By the time they reached Smoke Tree, Fiore's mood had worsened. Guido knew he was going to have to keep him on a short leash for the rest of the trip.

Goddamn *Sicilianos*! Couldn't reason with them.

The first place they checked in Smoke Tree was the 66 Truck Stop Cafe. Guido had Fiore pull around behind the cafe and back the black Chrysler 300 into the deepest corner of the parking lot.

When they got out, Guido said, "Pop the trunk."

"What for?"

"We're gonna put our guns in there. In case you hadn't noticed, guns make people nervous."

"So what? We want em nervous."

"Nervous people sometimes call the heat. I don't want that.

And another thing. We're gonna go with the P.I. thing in this town. We're just tryin' to help a worried family find their daughter.

No rough stuff!

In fact, just watch. You might learn somethin'."

Fiore was defensive. "From you?"

"Listen, chump, was doin' my first hit when you was still droolin' your mama's titty. I been at this a long time. Sometimes, you need muscle, and sometimes, you need somethin' else.

This is a 'somethin' else' time.

Now, open that trunk. Put your gun in there, and let's get to it."

They worked Smoke Tree from one end to the other. The motels, the gas stations, the grocery store, both drug stores, restaurants, the works.

And came up with nothing.

At the south end of town, they came to the place where Highway 95 split off and headed southwest. Fiore pulled to the side of the road while Guido checked the map.

"That road goes to Parker. We'll hit it later.

We want to stay on 66 and check out Kingman."

When Fiore pulled back onto 66, they could see the narrow green strip that paralleled both banks of the Colorado River as it flowed east of the highway. The green swath looked out of place against the sere, desert backdrop.

Fifteen miles later, they crossed the bridge over the river and came to a bump in the road called Topock.

They stopped at the tiny diner just beyond the bridge for a late lunch.

Their waitress was a pretty young girl. She looked Italian. Guido gave her the spiel and showed her Kiko's picture. The girl hadn't seen Kiko.

Fiore tried to flirt with her. She was obviously repulsed.

After the girl took their order, Guido pointed across the highway and asked, "Where's that road go?"

"Down to Shorty's Camp and then on to Catfisherman's Paradise."

When they were finished with lunch, Fiore paid the bill and put a ten dollar tip on the counter. The girl left it there and walked away. Fiore picked up the money before he went outside.

They got in the car, waited for a break in traffic, and drove across the highway and down the hill.

Shorty's Camp was little more than a dock with a couple of boats to rent and a marine gas pump jutting out into a backwater of the river. There was a snack bar next to the dock.

No one there had seen Kiko.

They got back in the car, and Fiore started to drive back up the hill toward the highway.

"Where you goin'?"

"Kingman."

"The girl at the diner said there's another place down the road."

"Come on, Guido, they ain't seen the Kiko broad here. She ain't gonna pop up down the road in the bushes next to this swamp."

"Lemme ask you again: you wanna tell Eddie we skipped a place?"

Fiore grumbled, but he turned the car back down the hill.

Catfisherman's Paradise turned out to be some picnic tables and a combination bait shop and grocery store inside a stand of massive, ancient aethel trees.

A bell on the screen door tinkled when they went inside

It was very damp and dark. The room was heavy with moist air pumped out by an ancient swamp cooler. There were cats everywhere. The warped wooden floors smelled of cat pee, wood rot and something Guido couldn't identify. Flies and mosquitoes hovered in the damp breeze. He slapped at one on his neck. His hand came away bloody.

There were two parallel rows of shelves. They walked down the aisle between them. The top shelves were the only ones with any goods. The one on their right held jars of mayonnaise and mustard and bottles of catsup. Because of the moisture put out by the swamp cooler, most of the labels were sagging off the containers. Haphazardly jumbled next to the jars were piles of various kinds of sardines and potted meat that looked like they had been there for years. Some of the tins were rusty.

60

The top shelf on their left held a few loaves of white bread. One of the loaves had a transparent cover, and Guido saw a thick coating of mold inside.

On a stool behind the counter at the back of the store sat an immense woman wearing a dirty T-shirt too small to cover her belly. Rolls of fat spread out from under the shirt and overtopped a grimy pair of faded, red pedal pushers that threatened to burst their side seams.

Guido took two bottles of Coke from an ancient, red refrigerator with the Coca Cola label painted in white on the door. He carried them to the counter. It was covered with Styrofoam containers sealed with clear plastic lids. Through the lids he could see various kinds of worms.

Next to the counter was a large tank made of galvanized metal. There were dead minnows floating belly up on top of the water. Guido's nose told him they had been dead for some time.

He peered into the tank to see if there were any live ones. Crawling around on the bottom of the tank were strange creatures that looked like miniature dragons.

"What the hell are those things walkin' around down there?"

"Them's water dogs. Guarandamnteed to catch you a bass. Better'n them minnows, even.

You and your friend gonna do some fishin'?"

"Not today. Just the Cokes will be fine."

The woman rang up the sale, took his money and gave him his change.

Guido got out the private investigator badge and the photograph of Kiko. He put the photo on the counter.

"My partner and I are private investigators from Las Vegas."

"The hell you say!

Jeez, I wish't my Vern was here. He run into Smoke Tree on a errand. He reads them True Detective magazines and them Mike Hammer books all the time. He's gonna be real disappointed when he finds out he missed you boys."

"Well, I'm sorry he's not here. But, can you tell me if you've seen this woman?"

The woman picked up the photo. She held it with her immense arms extended, arms so fat she seemed to lack both elbows and wrists. She squinted at it for a moment. Then she reached under the counter and pulled out a pair of glasses. They had greasy, finger-marked lenses.

She turned the picture this way and that, trying to get a better look at it in the dim light. There was black grime under her stubby fingernails.

"Looks like some kinda chink."

"Yes ma'am. She's Japanese."

The woman wiped the picture on her T-shirt before handing it back.

"Mighta smudged it a mite there. Allus fergit to hold them photographs by the edges."

"Have you seen her?"

"Not hide nor hair."

"Well, thanks for your time.

Can you tell me what's farther down this road?"

Guido pointed off to the east.

"Well sir, this here's the old Gold Road. Was Highway 66 in the olden days. Man, cars come up and down this road back then! Just a steady stream of 'em.

Then they brung the highway down from Kingman t'other way, over there to Yucca. And built a new bridge at Topock.

The traffic through here stopped overnight. One day it was a comin' through here; the next it warn't. Killed the bidness here. Just killed it!

Anyways, on up that road is Oatman."

"What's Oatman?"

"Ghost town. Used to mine gold there, way, way long time ago. But it run out, and so did the people. Now it's just old, deserted shacks up in them hills and burros all over the place."

She leaned toward him and lowered her voice.

"And there's some strange types squattin' in some a them shacks."

She leaned back.

"But the hotel is still open, and the saloon downstairs."

"There's a hotel in a ghost town?"

"You never heard of the Oatman Hotel? Why, that place was famous. Clark Gable and Carole Lombard stayed there on their honeymoon. Yessir. That's God's truth."

"Thanks for the information."

"Y'all gonna drive up there?"

"Yes ma'am."

"Be careful. Road's not in good shape. Gum'mint don't take care of it no more."

The sun was setting over Topock Slough by the time Guido and Fiore headed up the hill. Stillness had settled over the water. Bats chased bugs above the cattails and the snags of dead trees beside the road. Fish flopped, making concentric rings in the still, dark water. The setting sun cast longer and longer shadows as it dropped. It could have been a scene from prehistoric times. It reminded Guido of the movie, "The Creature from the Black Lagoon."

He resisted the urge to drive faster because the road really was in terrible shape. There were sections where they had to slow to a crawl to keep from damaging the car. It was well after dark when they entered what remained of the main street of Oatman.

They had no trouble finding the hotel, but they had to drive well past it to find a place to park because there were cars and pickup trucks all around the building. As they drove by, country and western music blared into the street.

Before they got out, Guido turned to Fiore.

"We may need the guns here."

They got out, opened the trunk, took off their blazers and slipped on their shoulder holsters. They put the blazers back on and buttoned them to cover the guns.

They stepped up onto the ancient, raised sidewalk and headed for the hotel. There were hitching posts embedded in the walkway, and some of the sections were made of wood instead of cement. The hillside behind the stores on the opposite side of the street was mostly dark, but here and there weak, yellow light shone through windows.

As they approached the hotel, the music was louder.

"Goddamn shit-kicker, hillbilly ass music. Hate that crap!"

"Hold that thought, Fiore. We need to walk in pissed off to deal with this crowd."

"I was born pissed off."

They went inside.

Directly in front of them was a staircase. To the right was a deserted lobby. To the left were swinging doors that led into a bar.

They pushed through the doors.

The band inside was blasting through a rendition of "Alabam."

A tall, statuesque woman came down the bar to take their order. She was wearing tight, black Levi's cinched to her waist by a wide, leather belt fastened with a silver buckle the size of a dinner plate. A white, western shirt with mother-of-pearl snap buttons and embroidered flowers was tucked into the pants, and the pants were tucked into tooled leather, high heeled cowboy boots. Around her neck was an ornate, squash-blossom necklace.

She had heavy, purple eye liner around her brown eyes. The thick mascara on her eyelashes was the same color.

This broad puts on her makeup with a shovel, thought Guido.

He couldn't help wondering how many cans of hairspray the woman used to hold her towering beehive hairdo so rigidly in place.

"Get you boys something?"

Guido pulled his Las Vegas Police Department badge holder out of his blazer and flipped it open.

"I'm Detective Kinston. This is detective Blake."

The woman cupped her ear and leaned toward him.

"Gonna have to speak up, officer. Can't hear you."

Guido shouted the message.

"Yeah, so?"

He put the picture of Kiko Yoshida on the bar.

"We're looking for this woman. Have you seen her?"

The woman glanced at the picture and shook her head.

"Do you mind if we ask your customers?"

The woman surveyed the lively crowd and smiled.

"No, I don't mind.

Tell you what. I'll even get you a microphone."

She came out from behind the bar and walked toward the riser where the band was finishing their song with a final flourish.

Guido watched her put her hand over the lead singer's microphone and talk to him. She turned and motioned Guido forward.

"Come with me," he said to Fiore.

The two men crossed the floor and stepped up onto the riser. They stood side by side, facing the crowd.

Guido banged on the microphone a few times.

"Hey, listen up."

The noise level dropped. People turned to look.

He held up his badge.

"Good evening. I'm Detective Kinston and this is my partner, Detective Blake. We're from the Las Vegas Police Department."

The room fell silent. The only sound was the squeak of two ancient, black ceiling fans trying to stir the thick cloud of smoke and overheated air in the room.

Guido noticed several of the men and a couple of the women were beginning to edge toward the door.

He held up the picture of Kiko.

"We're looking for this woman. My partner and I are going to come around with her picture. If you've seen her, we want to know about it."

A voice came from the crowd.

"Piss off."

Another voice chimed in.

"Yeah. Little out of your jurisdiction, ain't ya?"

"We're working in cooperation with local law enforcement."

"That's a good one, bozo. Local law enforcement don't come here.

Any of you seen any 'local law enforcement' lately?"

That got a laugh.

The second voice came again.

"We don't like cops here. Get your sorry asses out of town!"

The crowd surged forward.

Fiore reached inside his jacket.

A deep voice called from the back of the room.

"Hold it. Hold up, Goddamnit."

The crowd came to a halt.

"These guys ain't cops."

"What are they then?"

A large, thick, muscular man shouldered his way to the front of the crowd. There was a huge spider tattooed on the side of his face.

"I don't know the guy with his hand in his jacket, but the guy at the mic is Guido Battagliano. He's a made man with the Chicago Outfit. And before you decide to push him, you should know he'd just as soon kill you as look at you."

The crowd moved back.

The first man who had yelled spoke again.

"How you know that, Spider?"

"He did a nickel jolt a Leavenworth when I was there. Stand up con. Nobody messed with him. Not even the screws."

He turned back toward Guido and Fiore.

"Member me, Mr. Battagliano?"

"Yeah, sure, Spider. See you're still clankin' that iron.

What's the haps?"

"No haps, Mr. Battagliano.

If you hand me that picture, I'll have everyone take a look for you. That okay?"

Fiore took his hand out of his blazer.

"Sure, Spider. Come ahead."

The man came forward. Guido handed him the picture.

Guido and Fiore watched as Spider circulated the room with the photograph. They noticed that everyone looked at it very carefully.

The man brought the picture back to Guido.

"Don't look like anyone's seen her, Mr. Battagliano."

Guido took the picture and turned around and showed it to the band. Nobody recognized her.

He turned back to the silent room and spoke into the microphone.

"Thanks for your help. Get back to your dance."

Behind him, the drummer did a rim shot on the snare and hit the cymbal.

The crowd laughed. The tension went out of the room.

66

Guido stepped down and walked over to Spider.

"Glad you spoke up. Partner's a little crazy. Probably woulda shot a couple people."

"You don't mind me askin', who is he?"

"That's Fiore Abbatini."

The man paled.

"Jesus!"

"How do we get to Kingman from here?"

"Just keep going up the hill, Mr. Battagliano."

"Any motels there?"

"Lots. Kingman's on 66."

"Thanks."

Guido turned to leave, then turned back.

"And hey?"

"Yessir?"

"That woman ever shows up here, call me."

"Sure. How do I reach you?"

"Just call the Serengeti in Vegas. Have them put you through to Eddie Mazzetti. Tell him I told you to call. There'll be somethin' in it for you, the lead pans out."

"You've got it, Mr. Battagliano. Glad to help."

As Guido and Fiore walked out, the band launched into "Fallen Angel."

Guido and Fiore drove the narrow, winding road from Oatman to Kingman where they got dinner and a motel room. After breakfast the next morning, they worked their way through town, once again leaving their guns in the trunk and using the private investigator story. No one had seen Kiko Yoshida.

By midmorning, they were headed west on Highway 66. They crossed the Colorado at Topock again. Noon found them at the 66 / 95 split on the south side of Smoke Tree. They turned onto Highway 95 and headed for Parker, Arizona.

Two hours after crossing the Colorado into Arizona, they had worked their way through the little town with no success.

They were back in California when they arrived at the agricultural inspection station at Vidal Junction. After they confirmed they were not carrying any fruits or vegetables from Arizona or points east, they parked the car and showed Kiko's photograph to the inspectors. None of them had seen her.

Leaving the junction, they took Highway 62 to Twentynine Palms. By late afternoon, they were entering the town.

After checking into a motel, they went out for a look at the place.

"Man," said Fiore, "There ain't nothin' out here but dirt and jarheads. Never seen so many guys with white sidewalls."

"Was you ever in the military, Fiore?"

"Nah. The service is strictly for suckers."

The next morning after consulting the map, they headed east on Amboy Road. After passing miles of abandoned shacks, the road turned north over Sheephole Pass. As they drove down the hill on the other side, the desert stretched out endlessly brown and unbroken below them as far as they could see in every direction.

"Man, I seen enough desert, last me forever. Can't wait to get back to Vegas, get a good meal, good broad."

"Yeah, me too."

At the bottom of the pass, the road cut across Bristol Dry Lake, a place as barren of vegetation as the surface of the moon. After they passed the salt works settling ponds, Amboy Crater rose up on the west as they approached Highway 66.

They got out of the air conditioned car at Roy's Cafe in Amboy. Even though it was early May, the temperature was already over a hundred degrees.

They showed Kiko's picture in the cafe with no success.

"What's the shortest way back to Vegas from here?" Guido asked the man at the counter.

"Go on down the road toward Smoke Tree. You'll come to a turn-off that says Kelbaker Road.

Take it. Stay on it. You'll come to a place called Kelso. The road splits just past the train depot there. Go to Baker. You'll find the L.A. to Vegas Highway."

They took the road that rose up past the Old Dad Mountains. As they approached the Granite Mountains, the road abruptly turned to dirt.

Fiore stopped the car.

"We get stuck out here, nobody find us but the buzzards."

""Yeah, well, we're not goin' the long way around. If that guy at the diner thought we couldn't get through, he'd a said somethin'."

"He's probably back there laughin' his ass off. Probably sends ten tourists a day up this road to get stuck in the dirt."

"If we get stuck, I'll go back, make sure he never laughs again."

When they drove across the asphalt onto the broad, dirt road, a huge cloud of dust scrolled out behind them. After they went over the pass east of the Granites, the road turned to pavement again.

As they drove down the hill, the desert rolled away on all sides. After two turns, they could see a green swath far below.

After they crossed the Union Pacific tracks at Kelso, they stopped at the depot.

"Hey," said Guido. "Look at this place! Must have been somethin' a long time ago."

"Yeah? Well it's a dump now."

They went inside. There was a lunch counter with no customers. They showed Kiko's picture to the waitress. She hadn't seen Kiko.

Guido gestured toward the north.

"Where's that road go?"

"Cima."

They left the depot and got in the car.

"We already checked Baker. Go this other place."

They drove east on a narrow road with countless dips. The Kelso Mountains hung on the southern horizon. A freight train at least a mile long passed them on its way down the grade.

After a few miles, they came to Cima. There was nothing there but a combination store and tiny post office.

The woman there didn't recognize Kiko.

"What's off that way?" Guido asked the woman.

"Nipton."

Twenty minutes later, they were in Nipton, another almost-deserted place. They showed Kiko's picture at the little store with the usual result.

"Where's that road go?" asked Guido, pointing east.

"Searchlight."

"How about the other road?"

"Hooks up with the Vegas Highway."

They trudged out to the car and drove to where the road intersected with the highway to Las Vegas. They joined the stream of traffic heading that way and stopped at Stateline to check at the casino and gas station. No luck there either. Once they got back on the road, Fiore put his foot in it and took the big Chrysler up to a hundred miles an hour, recklessly passing anything slower on the two lane highway.

After a few miles at that speed, the temperature gauge began to move toward the red.

"Hey, dumbass, we're gonna boil over. You either have to slow down or turn off the air conditioner. And if you turn off the A/C, I'll kill ya."

Fiore sighed.

"What a huge waste of time."

"Hey, we work for Eddie. We do whatever he tells us to do, so quit your bitchin'."

Fiore settled back into disgusted silence.

As they got closer to Las Vegas, they saw a sign for Goodsprings.

Fiore looked over at Guido.

"Do we hafta? She wouldn't try to hide out this close to Vegas."

"How do we know what that broad would do?

Take the turnoff."

Goodsprings was a bust.

It was twilight before they reached the Las Vegas Strip.

Chapter 5

Smoke Tree, California

San Bernardino, California

And Highway 66 between those two towns

Friday, May 12, 1961

Horse

On Friday, Lieutenant Carlos Caballo, commander of the San Bernardino County Sheriff's Department Smoke Tree Substation, known throughout the Lower Colorado River Basin simply as "Horse," was in San Bernardino. Once a month the lieutenant had to drive there to meet with Sheriff Frank Bland, his staff, and the other substation commanders. It was a trip he didn't like to make.

It wasn't the two hundred mile drive that bothered him. Anyone who lives on the Mojave is used to long drives. Besides, Horse loved the desert and never grew tired of its beauty. Nor was the meeting with his boss, a man he respected and admired, something he objected to.

What bothered him was leaving the desert behind at the top of Cajon Pass and descending into the sprawl that began at the bottom of the hill and extended all the way to Los Angeles.

San Bernardino County was twenty two thousand square miles, bigger than seventy of the countries in the world. San Bernardino County could, for example, contain the entire country of Switzerland inside its borders and still have room left over. But ninety percent of the population was concentrated inside the four hundred and eighty square miles on the down slope side of Cajon pass. The other ten percent of the people were scattered over the deserts and mountains of the remaining nineteen thousand square miles of the county like a handful of sand flung into a high wind. The result was a population density of far less than one person per square mile.

And that was the problem. As far as Horse, a typical desert rat, was concerned, less than one person per square mile was just about right. There were just too many people packed into the section against the foothills of the San Bernardino and San Gabriel Mountains. Too many cars. Too much noise. Too much eye-burning, lung-choking smog. And way too much concrete and asphalt smothering the earth.

After the meeting in San Bernardino was over, Horse treated himself to an early dinner at Bing's before he headed home. The sun was setting when he crossed the Mojave River at Victorville with its beautiful stand of green cottonwoods stretching along the trickle of water.

By the time he drove from Victorville to Barstow, the last of the light was leaking out of the sky. The Calico Mountains to the north of the town were only a vague outline.

When he reached Ludlow, night had fallen. The tiny community marked the westernmost border of his area of responsibility. At over twelve thousand square miles, the twenty seven million acres he and his deputies policed was a huge area with very few people. But what it lacked in permanent residents, it made up for in transient population. Except for the traffic that split off at Barstow to head for Sin City, the bulk of the cars and trucks heading east from the coast stayed on 66 until they crossed the Colorado River into Arizona just south of Smoke Tree. That meant thousands and thousands of people moving through Horse's area every day of the year.

Most of the travelers were ordinary, decent people going about their lives or business. That's not to say some of them didn't get in trouble. Sometimes, they got off the highway onto some desert road and then broke down on a day when the temperature was over a hundred and twenty degrees. When that happened, Horse's deputies had to go search for them. Many times the travelers were dead before they could be found. But some of the transients were bad guys. And these were the people who accounted for most of the crime in his part of the Mojave and Colorado deserts.

Driving down the hill from Ludlow, he passed through the driest part of an arid region. The tiny outpost of Bagdad had once gone over two years without a single drop of rain falling. And yet, when the rain finally came, the creosote bushes, which had lost all their leaves and looked for all the world like they had died months before, put out new leaves and turned green again. You had to love a plant that tough! The Cafe Bagdad and the old gas station were still open for evening travelers.

An hour later, Horse crested South Pass and started the descent into the Mohave Valley of the Colorado River. It was not long before the lights of Smoke Tree appeared to the southeast. All the rest of the valley was inky black. As the lights came into view, Horse felt the tension from the long drive leave his neck and shoulders. It was good to be coming home.

Smoke Tree was an isolated little town without charm. Many of the desperate people fleeing the dust bowl in the 1930s thought they'd made a horrible mistake coming to California when it was the first town they came to after crossing the Colorado River on the Mother Road.

Smoke Tree was a railroad town. The Santa Fe was its heartbeat. The railroad provided a living to almost everyone in Smoke Tree, either directly or by the railroad workers supporting local businesses. The Santa Fe depot and rail yards were the most important part of town. The rest of Smoke Tree had sprawled haphazardly along the highway over the years, like many of the towns along Route 66. Most of those who didn't work for the Santa Fe had jobs that depended on the traffic that came though the center of town on 66.

Smoke Tree wasn't much to look at. A cracked, shabby and shopworn gemstone embedded in a beautiful setting on the banks of the Colorado River. The housing stock was mostly old and worn out. Many of the streets were in bad shape. There were very few rich people, and except for the impoverished Native Americans struggling to survive in the Mojave Indian village on the north edge of town, very few really poor ones. It was the most blue collar of blue collar towns, almost entirely middle and lower-middle class.

The few stores in town carried only basic goods. Clothing for men was limited to Levi's, flannel shirts, khaki work clothes and white T-shirts. For women, the choices were cheap, print dresses, one color blouses, and pants and "sensible" shoes. Anyone who wanted more drove one hundred miles north to Las Vegas.

Horse had grown up in Smoke Tree and lived there all his life except for the years he was in the service during the Korean War. When Horse had been at Smoke Tree High School, a lot of his classmates talked about getting away from "this hick town." Not Horse. It was the only place he wanted to live. He was a small town person to his core. Smoke Tree may have been run down, provincial, cloyingly insular, dilapidated and drab, but it was his home. He loved the place and intended to liver there for the rest of his life.

Even though they had only been apart since early morning, Horse was looking forward to seeing Esperanza, the wife he loved so much it sometimes made his heart ache. They had been sweethearts since junior high. They married as soon as he got home from Korea.

But first, he went by the office. When he walked into the substation, all was quiet. The relief dispatcher was at his desk doing the Los Angeles Times crossword puzzle.

"Evening, Myles."

"Evening, Lieutenant. Good trip?"

"Good as could be expected. Glad to be home."

He walked into his office and turned on the lights.

His desk was covered with call-back slips.

He shuffled through them and put them in the order in which the calls had come in.

He walked out the door and called to the dispatcher.

"Myles, any idea what all these calls were about?"

"Fred told me everyone who called said it wasn't an emergency, but they all wanted to talk to you, not him."

Horse walked back into his office and looked through the slips again. He soon realized there was a pattern to them. The first call was from the far north end of town, and last one was from the southern city limit. The other part of the pattern was that they were all from business stretched out along the highway.

He examined the slips again to see if he could find any business owners who might still be at work.

He picked up the slip for William Milner, owner of the largest market in town. Horse knew Billy often worked late on Friday evenings, calling his managers in the other markets and convenience stores he owned in Parker and Blythe.

He dialed the number. It rang for a long time, and Horse was just about to give up when a gruff voice said, "The market is closed."

"Hello, Mr. Milner. Horse here. Thought I might find you in the office."

"Evening, Horse. When I called earlier today your dispatcher said you were in San Bernardino. Thanks for calling me back."

"What can I do for you?"

"Just wanted to report something strange that happened at the store today.

A couple guys came in. They were well dressed: slacks, shirts and ties, blazers. They approached all the cashiers. They showed each of them a picture of a pretty, young oriental woman and asked if they had seen her. None of them had.

But they didn't stop there. They started walking through the store and showing the picture to customers.

Dave Sodermeyer was up here in the office. He looked out over the floor and noticed what was going on. He went downstairs and talked to the guys. They gave him some song and dance about being private investigators helping a family find a missing daughter.

The older of the two showed Dave the picture and asked him if he'd seen the woman. Dave glanced at it and said he hadn't.

The younger guy leaned over, took the picture, shoved it in Dave's face and said, "You didn't look at it good. Look again."

Dave told them to quit bothering customers and leave the store.

The younger guy looked like he wanted to make a fuss, but the older one said, "Don't mind my partner. He's a little eager," and they left.

Dave told me there was something about the two that made him not believe their story. And he described the last look the younger guy gave him as pretty hostile.

It seemed like an odd thing. I thought you should know about it."

"Thanks, Mr. Milner. I'll look into it."

When Horse hung up, he picked up the slips and studied them again.

One was for the '76 station. Horse knew Jim Garret often worked the Friday evening shift at his station.

Garret answered on the first ring.

"Smoke Tree '76, Jim speaking."

"Hi, Mr. Garret. Horse here."

"Oh, hey, thanks for calling back.

Had a couple of guys in here today. Something about them just didn't seem right."

"Two guys, well-dressed, with a picture of a woman?"

"Yeah. How'd you know?"

"Just got off the phone with William Milner. They were in his store.

How'd they act at your place?"

"Well, it was like you said, they had a picture. They showed it to me. Young, oriental woman. Real pretty. Looked like some kind of professionally done shot.

Anyway, the passenger showed it to me and asked if I had seen the woman. When I said I hadn't, the driver told me to take another look. And he didn't say it in a friendly way.

I wrote down the license number.

The car was a black, Chrysler 300. Nevada license WLP 1537."

"Good thinking, Mr. Garret. We'll run the plate."

"Say, the dispatcher said you were in San Berdoo."

"Yes. Just got in."

"Well, thanks for taking the time to return my call."

"Anytime. 'Night, sir."

Horse turned off the lights in his office. As he walked by the dispatcher, Horse gave him the license plate information.

"Myles, run this plate for me. Put the information on my desk."

"Will do, Lieutenant."

"Hope we have a quiet night."

"I'm sure we will, until the bars close."

The next morning, rested from a good night's sleep and full of Esperanza's *huevos rancheros* and black coffee, Horse was back in his office. The information about the Nevada license plate was on his desk. The Chrysler was registered to the Serengeti Corporation.

Horse began working his way through call-back slips. Because of his good relationship with the community, he did not intend to leave any of those calls unreturned even though he already the information he needed.

76

Local residents often called his department instead of the Smoke Tree Police because they knew Horse ran a much tighter ship. The Smoke Tree Police Department was a famously incompetent bunch, run by a chief who had come in from out of town. Horse was a local boy many of them had known for years. Also, the STPD had a collection of officers who were mostly rejects from other departments, so it was easy to understand why the locals preferred the sheriff's department.

As he worked his way through the slips, he became more and more intrigued. The two men had worked the town from north to south, hitting service stations, restaurants and motels. Horse wondered where they had gone once they were finished. Their choices were east to Kingman, south to Parker, or back to wherever they had come from.

Horse picked up the phone and called the little diner just across the Arizona border in Topock. The men had been there. The waitress who had served them was the owner's daughter, and she said they had showed her the picture. She also told him the younger of the two men had been crudely flirtatious, and something about him made her very nervous. She had been glad to see them leave.

When Horse asked if she'd noticed where they were headed when they left, she told him they had driven across the highway and down the road toward Shorty's Camp. A call to Shorty's revealed the men had driven east from there on the old Gold Road. If they'd stayed on that road, they'd have wound up in Oatman.

Horse dialed the Oatman Hotel. There was no answer. That was not surprising since the place was a hotel in name only. It was really a big building full of empty rooms except for the saloon on the ground floor.

Horse spent the rest of the morning catching up on some other things that had come up during his absence.

After he got back from lunch, he dialed the hotel again.

Maggie McKellep answered. When he described the two men who had been in Smoke Tree and asked her if they had been in her place, she told him an interesting story.

When she finished recounting the events of Friday night, Horse asked her if there was any chance she remembered the names the two men had used at the saloon.

"Yes, I do. Because the band was so noisy, I made them show me the badges. The names were Kinston and Blake."

"And it said 'detective' on the shields?"

77

"That's right. Gold shields."

"One more question, Maggie. You said this Spider guy recognized one of the men and called him by name. Do you remember that name?"

"Yes. It was the older man, the man at the microphone. Spider called him Guido Battagliano."

After he thanked Maggie for the helpful information, he leaned back in his chair and put his feet up on the desk for a long think. Then he picked up the phone and called the Mohave County Sheriff's Department and asked for his favorite contact, Captain Taylor. The captain wasn't in, but when Horse asked, the dispatcher said there had been calls that morning about two men who claimed to be Las Vegas Police Detectives showing a picture around town.

Horse had just put the phone down when his dispatcher buzzed on the intercom.

"Call for you Horse. Mr. Milner."

Horse picked up.

"Morning, Mr. Milner."

"Morning, Horse.

Say, those guys who were in the store on Friday?"

"Yes?"

"They were in my store in Parker a while ago. Showed the picture to the cashiers. This time they claimed to be police detectives from Las Vegas."

"Thank you, sir. These guys left quite a trail. Be interesting to see where they turn up next."

Horse ended the call and dialed the Las Vegas Police Department.

The LVPD had a reputation for corruption unmatched by any other department in the United States except for the Clark County Sheriff's Department. Horse knew the mob ran Las Vegas. That was no secret. But he also knew they had compromised the LVPD and the Sheriff's Department to the point that they were practically extensions of the criminal organizations themselves. The two agencies shared jurisdiction, with the LVPD taking half of the town and the Sheriff's Department controlling the rest, plus the rest of Clark County.

When he reached the department, he was told the two detectives he wanted to talk to were both retired.

By the time Horse left the office that evening, he had decided he was going to pay the Serengeti a visit. He knew it was customary to contact local law enforcement when entering their territory. He also knew if he did that he might as well tell the Serengeti he was coming.

Chapter 6

Las Vegas, Nevada

Monday, May 15, 1961

Horse

On Monday morning at eleven o'clock, Horse parked his cruiser in the parking lot at the Serengeti Hotel and Casino. He locked his handgun and holster in the trunk, along with his shotgun.

He had heard eleven o'clock was the worst time of day for a business meeting because people were getting hungry and irritable and thinking more about lunch than the meeting. That suited Horse just fine. He didn't want this to be a pleasant visit.

By eleven fifteen, he was waiting outside the executive offices. He had been announced. He was not kept waiting long. A woman emerged from the double doors behind the receptionist.

"Lieutenant, Mr. Mazzetti will see you now."

As he was ushered into an impressively large office, a smiling, darkly handsome man with capped, white teeth stood up behind his desk and extended his hand.

"Good morning, Lieutenant. I'm Eddie Mazzetti. What brings the San Bernardino County Sheriff's Department to the Serengeti today?"

Horse shook the extended hand. He did not return the smile.

"Business."

"Please, Lieutenant, have a seat."

"That won't be necessary. This won't take long.

You let a couple of your boys off the leash. They ended up in my backyard."

"Really? My boys? I'm not sure I follow you."

"A black Chrysler, Nevada license plate WLP 1537, was in Smoke Tree, California, on Friday afternoon. The two guys driving it worked the town, passing themselves off as private investigators. Ring any bells?"

The man pretended to think it over.

"I don't think so, but that might be one of our cars. I'll have to check to see if one has been stolen."

"Come on, Mr. Mazzetti, you and I both know it wasn't stolen. And these two guys had private investigator licenses. Looked like the real thing, according to my sources."

"And your sources were ...?"

"The owner of a number of markets, for one."

"Some guy peddlin' pork roasts and produce? I'm supposed to be impressed?"

Horse did not respond.

"'But let's say, Lieutenant, that we do own such a car and it wasn't stolen. So what?"

"That's where it gets interesting. The two wiseguys in the car turned up that evening at the saloon in the Oatman Hotel where they introduced themselves as LVPD detectives Kinston and Blake."

"Lieutenant, as you may or may not know, we work closely with the Las Vegas PD to suppress crime in Las Vegas, but I don't think I recognize those names."

"Maybe that's because they're retired.

And somehow, Mr. Mazzetti, your two men got hold of their badges and were flashing them around. But someone in the saloon recognized one of your guys, a Guido Battagliano, and called him by name. I still don't know the name of Mr. Battagliano's associate, but I'm sure you do."

"These are serious allegations, Lieutenant."

"Yes, they are. Impersonating a sworn officer of the law is a felony."

"And you say this incident took place in Oatman?"

"That's right."

"Isn't that in Arizona?"

"I see you studied a map before you sent these boys on their little errand."

"And that makes it a matter for the Arizona authorities, doesn't it?"

"Yes, it does. I've passed the information on to the Mohave County Sheriff's Department."

"Funny. I haven't heard from them.

You don't seem to be sayin' this Mr. Battagliano and his associate impersonated sworn officers of the law in your jurisdiction, so since I'm a very busy man, maybe you could explain your business here so I can get back to work."

"I'll get right to it.

Your boys were circulating a picture of a young woman they were trying to find, apparently on your behalf. If this woman has committed some kind of a crime, why didn't you have the LVPD contact my office and ask for my help? Could it be that you don't want whatever happened on the record? Not even with a department everyone knows you have in your pocket?

And while we're talking about this, I think the same two guys were in Baker early one morning back in March. They broke down the door of a motel and shoved the picture of a woman in the face of the young kid who was working there. Demanded to know if he'd seen her. Scared the hell out of him."

"Come on. Lieutenant, why would the Serengeti be tryin' to find some Japanese broad?"

Horse smiled for the first time.

"I didn't say the woman was Japanese."

Eddie was silent for a few moments. Then he pressed his intercom.

"Alicia? The lieutenant's leavin' now.

Please come in, show him out."

"Before I go, here's the most important thing.

The reason the guy in Oatman recognized this Battagliano is because Battagliano did a stretch with him at Leavenworth Federal Penitentiary. Not a place they send small-time offenders.

So here's the message: keep your greaseballs out of my county."

Eddie's eyes went cold.

"Greaseballs? A crude word, lieutenant. And pretty close to "greaser," wouldn't you say?"

"Just not as honorable."

"And I have a final thought for *you*, Lieutenant. I'm sure the Serengeti has some friends in San Bernardino County government."

Horse laughed.

"I'd like to see that!"

Alicia entered the room.

Eddie held up his hand.

"You'd like to see what, Lieutenant?"

"You sleazy bastards trying to get Sheriff Bland in your pocket."

"Wasn't talkin' about the sheriff. Talkin' about his bosses. The Board of Supervisors. I'm sure we've comped one or two of them, time to time."

"Sheriff Bland is an elected official. He only answers to the voters."

Eddie smiled.

"And just like in Clark County, the Board of Supervisors controls his budget."

"But not one of them would like to get in a political pissing contest with a very popular sheriff who has a flawless reputation."

Horse was angry, but he did not raise his voice.

"Do what you want up here in Clark County, Mr. Mazzetti. But don't let it ooze over the border into *my* county. If these guys, or any of your other thugs, show up in my part of San Bernardino County again, they won't like what will happen. And neither will you."

He turned past an open-mounted Alicia and left the room.

Chapter 7

Smoke Tree, California

And the mountains

Of the Eastern Mojave Desert

June 8, 1961

Aeden Snow

It was already one hundred degrees at ten a.m. on June eighth in Smoke Tree, California. I was sweating heavily as I finished loading cement blocks, two by fours, sheets of plywood and drywall, bags of cement, and rolls of tarpaper and roofing material onto an International flat bed at Smoke Tree Hardware and Building Supply. A string of shiny, black, yellow-eyed starlings watched me from the telephone line next to the yard. I lashed everything down and then re-checked to make sure the load was secure. The big springs were compressed so far that the bed was nearly touching the back wheels.

In the low humidity of a summer day in the middle of the Mojave Desert, sweat doesn't last long. By the time I crunched across the gravel of the lumber storage area and crossed the yard to the office, my shirt was nearly dry.

Inside, the swamp cooler was blasting. Betsy Halverson had the piles of papers on her desk weighted down with river rocks.

"Mrs. Halverson, do you have the invoice for the Stonebridge delivery?"

She rifled through some papers under a large, round stone.

"Here you go, Ade. Two copies. It was paid in advance, so just get his signature on our copy.

And before you go, Keith wants to talk to you. He's out in the store."

Keith and Betsy Halverson were good people to work for. They treated me kindly and paid me double the one dollar minimum wage. At my age, I was lucky to have such a well-paying job. I worked hard to be worth my wages.

Out in the store, an even bigger swamp cooler was blowing. The sliding glass door to the parking lot was open so the roof-mounted unit could move enough air through the building to keep it cool. The signs tacked to the walls for Black and Decker power tools, Briggs and Stratton Engines, Scott's Fertilizer, and McCulloch chainsaws were curling at the edges. They rattled in the artificial breeze. The odors of coiled garden hoses, machine oil and pesticides mixed with the familiar, summer smell of wet cooler pads

I found Mr. Halverson sorting bolts, nuts, washers and screws in metal bins. He looked up at me over his bifocals as I reached him.

"Seems like I spend most of my days sorting this stuff. Customers mix them all up when they're looking through them."

"Yessir, I've noticed that.

Mr. Halverson, the truck's all loaded. I'm ready to go. Mrs. Halverson said you wanted to see me before I left."

"That's right. You've got a big load on the truck. Tied her down tight?"

"Yessir."

"Stop and check everything now and then, okay? I know I should probably have you take this load in two trips, but with the cost of gas and all, I thought we'd better get it there in one. And you'll be taking another overload up tomorrow. We're really carrying four loads in two trips.

I'm counting on you to get this stuff there safely. Those roads up where you're going are pretty rough, so take it slow. It'd be real easy to bounce some of that stuff off in a wash or slide it off on a curve."

"Yessir. I'll be careful."

"And you're sure you know where the Stonebridge place is?"

"I've been there a few times with my dad. Dad and Mr. Stonebridge are good friends."

"Got lots of water with you?"

"I've got the two gallon desert bag hanging on the front of the truck."

"Good.

You've got plenty of fuel. The gas tank is three quarters full, and the propane tank was just topped off. She climbs better on gasoline, but when you're on level ground, switch her over to propane. It's cheaper.

Put your car in the back of the yard. If you get back after we've closed, just take the truck home with you tonight.

Have a safe trip."

I drove my car to the back corner of the storage yard.

When I got out, Will Bailey was ripping three-quarter-inch plywood into custom-sized pieces. The saw shrieked when it first bit into a sheet. Then the shriek turned to a low growl as the saw got deeper into the cut. The sweet scent of pinewood, blended with the sharp tang of the chemicals in the glue that held the laminated wood together, drifted across the yard on the hot wind.

I climbed into the cab and started the engine, grateful I'd left the windows rolled down. I eased the truck out of the yard. I drove through the residential streets on the east side of town before joining Route 66 where the motels and gas stations began to line the road.

Once I left the city limits, I caught glimpses of the Colorado River a quarter mile to the east through the mesquite thickets. Discarded beer cans and pieces of broken glass winked in the sun along the shoulder of the highway.

At the place where 66 turned abruptly west to begin its long traverse to Barstow, I saw two girls from my high school class at the stop sign on River Road. They were waiting for a break in the 66 traffic. I gave the air horn a tap and waved, but they didn't wave back. I suppose I couldn't blame them. I was pretty unpopular with my classmates.

The previous November, my best friend Johnny Quentin, his girlfriend Judy McPhearson and I accidentally burned down an abandoned house out in the river bottom: the legendary House of Three Murders. We were unaware there were two people inside. One was Sixto Morales, a local bad guy who had been shot in a robbery. The other was a young Mojave Indian man, Charlie Merriman, who had been hog tied by the wounded Morales.

Charlie, who had just been in the wrong place at the wrong time, was railroaded by an overzealous, politically ambitious prosecutor and a bigoted judge in Mohave County, Arizona. It looked like he was headed for a long prison term. But the evidence faltered after the death of the main witness.

Charlie managed to trade a promise to join the army for having the charges dismissed and not going to trial. It was still a raw deal.

Judy McPhearson's father, a very rich man, had whisked his daughter out of the country to Switzerland so she wouldn't have to testify. Johnny Quentin was heartbroken. He wanted out of Smoke Tree. He joined the Army on the buddy system with Charlie Merriman.

With Johnny gone, I was besieged with relentless questions from my classmates about the whole affair. Did Judy's dad get her out of the country because she was pregnant? Had Johnny left because he was afraid of Judy's mysterious and powerful father, a man with reputed underworld ties? And exactly what had happened the night we burned down the house?

My response was to withdraw. I kept to myself at school and refused to answer questions. As the months went by, I became more and more isolated. I spent all my weekends hiking in the mountains of the Eastern Mojave, trying to come to terms with what had happened. I didn't even attend graduation with my classmates. I suppose that was the last straw.

As I began the long climb to the west, I couldn't get the heavily laden truck much over forty miles an hour. Switching from propane to gasoline helped a little, but not much. Before I had gone two miles, I could see the traffic piling up behind me. The big semis looked like railcars behind a slow-moving locomotive, but I couldn't pull over onto the shoulder to let the traffic go by. During the daylight hours in June on Route 66, there wouldn't be a long enough break in traffic to get the overloaded truck back on the highway.

The Sacramento Mountains rose to the southwest. The Dead Mountains to the northwest. Directly to the north, the broad expanse of Paiute Wash spread out beyond the highway. It was filled with the ghostly white smoke trees that gave our town its name

The highway began to rise even more steeply as I approached South Pass. My speed dropped lower. I knew I would have to shift to second gear if I stayed on 66. That would drop my speed into the thirties and create a longer line of frustrated travelers. I decided to take the highway 95 cut-off north to old highway 66, the mostly unused remnant of the original alignment of the Mother Road.

Before I started the turn, the Mohave Valley of the Colorado River spread out behind me in my rear view mirror. I could see the large "X" formed by two old, mining roads crisscrossing on the flanks of the Black Mountains near Oatman, Arizona. Directly behind me, on the California side of the river, were miles and miles of low desert filled with creosote, white bursage, saltbush, and bitterbush.

The river itself provided contrast with the sea of brown. There was a narrow swath of green edging the beautiful, blue waters of the Colorado. But in the Mojave, even green can be deceptive. This was the green of mesquites: dense, thorn-laden trees that dominated the river bottom.

I took northbound 95 at the cut off and passed through Klinefelter, where an old motor court, abandoned after the highway 66 reroute in the 1930s, was collapsing in on itself inside a circle of salt cedar trees. I came to Arrowhead Junction where the Santa Fe tracks crossed over highway 95. Just before the crossing, I turned west off 95 onto old 66. There was an ancient gas station at the intersection.

As I passed the station, I looked for the owner, an old man who somehow eked out a living from the lightly-traveled highway. Early mornings, Mr. Stanton could often be found sitting on the enclosed porch directly behind the service island, watching the sun rise over the Dead Mountains. After sunup, he liked to sit on a wooden rocker beneath the overhang that shadowed the pumps.

His rocker was empty. The only thing in front of the station was a bundle of rags. As I completed the turn, I realized it was no bundle of rags I had seen. It was Mr. Stanton!

I pulled the truck onto the shoulder, careful not to shift the load in the soft sand, and started running back to the station. I began calling his name. He did not respond. When I reached him, he was lying face down in the dirt, his long-billed, green cap beside him.

I turned him onto his side.

Mr. Stanton was part Chickasaw Indian, but his usually brown face was almost colorless. I put my fingers to his throat to search for a pulse. His skin felt cold and clammy. I found a heartbeat, but it was light and irregular.

I realized in all the years I had known him, I had never seen him without his cap. Even though he was over eighty five years old, he had a full head of thick, black hair. There was dirt and gravel stuck to the side of his face and spittle on his chin. His eyes were open, but he didn't seem to see me. I had no idea how long he had been lying in the direct noonday sun, but buzzards were already circling high overhead.

I had to get him into the shade. I was worried I wouldn't be able to lift him without injuring him, but he was as light as a burlap sack of small sticks. I carried him across the driveway. When I took him carefully up the wooden steps, I could feel the cool air from his swamp cooler blowing through the screen door. I pushed through it and onto the porch.

The big, glass display case was filled with candy, cheap cigars and cigarettes. Everything was covered in a light coat of dust. An old-fashioned cash register sat on top of the display case. Tacked to the wall behind the register was a Santa Fe calendar from 1944, with a picture of a steam locomotive pulling into the depot at Gallup, New Mexico. I could hear the compressor laboring in the ancient Coke machine in the corner. I carried Mr. Stanton behind the display case, through the open door, and into his living quarters.

I had never been in his house. It smelled of coffee, bacon grease, pipe tobacco and desiccated wood. The walls were bare and painted the mustard yellow of a Santa Fe reefer car. There was a couch covered with some kind of badly-faded, stiff brocade pushed against one wall. One of the legs on the couch had been replaced by a brick. On the other side of the room, I saw a large, console radio with a-walnut cabinet. Next to the radio was an overstuffed chair.

I eased Mr. Stanton into the chair. As I let go of him and stepped back, he stirred and moaned softly. His eyes were still open, and by the way they suddenly widened in surprise, I could tell he was seeing me.

"Hello, Mr. Stanton."

He tried to speak, but his words were so badly garbled I had no idea what he was saying. He tried again, but I still couldn't understand him.

"I'll be right back Mr. Stanton."

I hurried through an open doorway into his small kitchen. On one wall was a metal sink with the plumbing visible beneath it, a two burner stove of a design I had never seen before, and an old refrigerator. There was a black skillet full of congealed grease on one of the burners and a coffee pot on the other. A wooden table and one chair were against the other wall. An oilcloth cover had been tacked to the top of the table. A phone book and a heavy, black telephone sat on the oilcloth.

There was an empty glass in the sink. I filled it with water and took it in to him.

"Can you drink some of this, Mr. Stanton?"

He seemed to think about it for a long time. Then he nodded his head slowly.

As I held the glass to his lips, he opened his mouth. He made no attempt to lift his hands and hold the glass himself. I tilted the glass. Some of the water ran down his chin, but some of it went into his mouth. He got it down without choking. After he swallowed, he nodded his head slightly. I tilted the glass again and he began to take small sips, all the time keeping his eyes fixed on me as if he were trying to parse my identity.

It took almost five minutes, but he kept sipping until the glass was empty. When I pulled it away, he sat with his mouth open, still staring at me. With his black eyes and open mouth he looked like a baby bird.

"Can you tell me what happened?"

He tried to say something but was unable to talk. He shook his head slowly.

I went to the kitchen table, opened the phone book and found the number for the Sheriff's Department. Someone answered on the first ring.

"Smoke Tree Sheriff's station."

"My name is Aeden Snow. I'm calling from Arrowhead Junction. The man who owns the service station here has had some kind of an accident. I found him laying in the dirt. I brought him inside and asked him what's wrong, but he can't talk."

"Is he conscious?"

"Yessir, he's sitting in a chair, and he drank some water."

"Good. Is he there by the telephone?"

"Nossir. He's in the other room."

"I want you to put down the phone and do something for me. Go ask him if he can lift both arms over his head."

I went back to the chair.

"Mr. Stanton, I don't know if you can hear me. But if you can, would you lift both arms up over your head?"

For a moment, he continued to sit motionless. Then it seemed like he gathered his energy. He started lifting his arms. The right arm went all the way up, but the left one barely rose at all.

"Thank you, Mr. Stanton. I'll be right back."

I went back to the kitchen and picked up the phone.

"One arm went up, but the other one hardly moved."

A different voice came over the phone.

"Aeden, this is Lieutenant Caballo. The dispatcher is sending a car out your way. Shouldn't be too long before it gets there. I'll be right behind him."

Just hearing Lieutenant Caballo's voice calmed me down.

91

"It sounds like Mr. Stanton has had a stroke. I don't know how severe it is, but it's a good sign that he can understand you and tried to do what you asked.

I need you to stay with him until my deputy and I get there. Can you do that?"

"Yessir.

Is there anything else I should do?"

"Try to keep him comfortable, and try to get him to talk if he can.

I'll see you soon."

"Please, hurry."

I took the kitchen chair into the sitting room and put it beside him.

"Someone is on the way, Mr. Stanton."

He did not respond.

We sat there side by side for a long time. Every now and then I said something to him, but he did not speak. His eyes were open, and he was staring straight ahead at a bare wall. I had the feeling he wasn't seeing the wall, but whatever he was seeing demanded his full attention. I didn't think it was something pleasant.

Suddenly, he shook his head and sat up straighter. He turned to me, blinking rapidly.

"Aeden. Aeden Snow. What are you doing here?"

"I was driving by the station a while ago and saw you laying on the ground in front of the pumps. I brought you inside."

"Why was I out there?"

"I don't know, Mr. Stanton."

"I remember I was sittin' in my rocker, and all of a sudden I didn't feel good."

He struggled to get to his feet.

I stood up and put my hand on his shoulder.

"Maybe you'd better sit here a bit. Help is on the way."

"Help? What kind of help?"

"I called the sheriff's department. A deputy is coming, and Lieutenant Caballo is too."

"Horse is coming out here?"

"Yessir. Should be here soon."

Then, as abruptly as he had started talking, he stopped. He turned his head away from me and closed his eyes, sinking back into his chair. He sat motionless for another few minutes, then sat up straight again, raised his right hand to his head and turned to me.

"Ade, I've lost my cap."

"It's okay, sir, your cap is outside."

"Don't want to lose it. Them long billed caps is hard to find. Have to order them special from Monkey Ward."

He sat silently for a few more minutes before he spoke again.

"You say I was layin' in the dirt when you come by?"

"Yessir."

"Boy, howdy, I surely don't remember that."

I heard the wail of a siren rising and falling in the distance. I got up and walked outside.

A San Bernardino County Sheriff's car pulled off the highway and onto the apron in front of the station, raising a cloud of dust as it slid to a stop. The siren died.

A deputy got out.

"Aeden?"

"Yessir."

"Deputy Chesney. Where is he?"

"Inside."

"How's he doing?"

"Better. He's talking now."

The deputy hurried past the pumps, up the steps and through the screen door.

I noticed the wind had blown Mr. Stanton's cap over to the edge of the lot. I went and picked it up. I looked into the sky. The buzzards were gone. I followed the deputy inside.

Mr. Stanton was talking to Deputy Chesney.

I heard another car pull up outside. A moment later, Lieutenant Caballo came into the room.

"Hello, Mr. Stanton. How are you feeling?"

"Hello there, Horse. I'm fine, just fine. I was just talkin' to your depity here."

"Mr. Stanton, we're going to take you down to the hospital in Smoke Tree."

"Oh, I don't know about that, Horse. Don't much take with them places. My pappy went into one once. Never come out. Hadn't never been sick a day in his life afore he went in there, neither."

"Sir, I'm afraid you might have had a stroke. We need to have a doctor take a look at you."

"What about my place?"

"I'll stay and lock up for you and bring your keys to the hospital. Where are they?"

"On that hook yonder, by the door.

Lock her up good, Horse. The back door too. And get all them winders. Some rough types come by here time to time."

"I'll take care of it. Don't you worry.

Andy, go get the door open on your unit.

Mr. Stanton, I'm going to lean forward, and I want you to put you arms around my neck. I'm going to lift you out of the chair and carry you to the car."

"Oh no, sir. I can get there under my own power."

He put his hands on the arms of his chair and tried to rise. He could not. He sat back with a puzzled look on his face.

"Now don't that beat all? Cain't seem to get up.

Maybe you'd best help me after all."

Horse was over six feet tall and slender, but strong. His body was so hard he looked like he had been carved out of a chunk of agate. Once the lieutenant got Mr. Stanton out of his chair and onto his feet, he picked the old man up as if he weighed no more than a child.

I moved ahead of Horse and pulled the screen door open. The lieutenant carried him down the steps. He and the deputy got him into the front seat of the patrol unit.

The deputy sped out of the parking lot and onto 95.

Horse turned to me.

"How'd you happen to find him, Aeden?"

I explained all that had happened

"Mr. Stanton's lucky you came by.

"It scared me when I saw him. Do you think he'll be okay?"

"If I had to guess, I'd say the stroke was mild. When I leaned down, he managed to put both arms around my neck. When I talked to you on the phone, he could only lift one. And it's a good sign he was talking by the time we got here."

"Well, sir, I'd better get back on the road. I've got a delivery to make in the Mid Hills.

But I'd like to ask a favor."

"Go ahead."

"Can I call when I get home tonight and ask about Mr. Stanton?"

"Sure Ade.

Here, I'll write my home phone number on the back of my card.

Call me, no matter how late you get back."

"Thank you, sir. I'm real fond of Mr. Stanton."

"I can tell.

And thank you. You did a good turn here today."

When I got to the truck, it seemed like days since I had left it beside the road and gone running back to the station. I checked the ropes securing the load, trying to shake off a feeling of unease.

I pulled onto old 66 and headed up the road toward Goffs. The raised bed of the Santa Fe tracks loomed forty feet above me to my right, covered with creosote and bursage. The broad expanse of smoke-tree-filled Paiute Wash spread away to my left. As I drove, I could not get what had happened out of my mind. The shock at seeing Mr. Stanton lying there. The feeling of helplessness when he did not respond. The terrible sense of inadequacy because I had no idea what to do.

I reached the section of the highway that wound and twisted as it crossed through Paiute Wash itself. I passed the old railroad trestle spanning the wash where it ran beneath the tracks, carrying the run-off from the slopes of the mountains to the north. As I had many times in the past, I slowed and looked up the wash to the other side of the trestle where a narrow dirt road, once a wagon track, led out of the ghostly smoke trees and off through the low hills to the ruins of Fort Paiute on the old Mojave Trail, abandoned in the 1800s

Then something inexplicable happened. I saw soldiers, dressed in wool flannel uniform blouses and drab-colored cavalry hats, traveling on the wagon track. I heard voices in the rising wind that suddenly began scouring sand and grit out of the wash. I heard the sound of shod hooves clicking against rocks as the mounted column, saddle leather creaking, equipment rattling, moved up the hillside behind the troop guidon.

Some months before, I had dreamed I was running the ancient Mojave Trail, which stretched all the way from the Colorado River to the Pacific Ocean, with Charlie Merriman and other Mojave Indians. They were barefoot, and I was wearing rough shoes of mesquite wood lashed to my feet with yucca fibers. But that was a dream. This was a full-blown hallucination in broad daylight under the glare of a desert sky so clear it was almost washed of color. A hallucination so vivid it made me wonder if I were going insane.

I started to shake. I pushed in the clutch and stopped the truck in the middle of the road. My hands were trembling when I lifted them off the wheel and held them up in front of me. When I turned my head and looked up the wash again, the troop was gone, as were the sounds of its passing.

I had driven up that road to the fort many times and poked around the ruins. But for the first time I realized in a visceral way that living men had soldiered there almost a hundred years before. Men with daily concerns. Men with friends and families somewhere. Men who were all dead and gone. And the awful truth about mortality struck me like a physical blow. Oh, I knew people died. I had been to funerals, seen caskets lowered into the ground, seen dirt shoveled on top of them while relatives wept, but this was different.

It was different because of the way Mr. Stanton had sat staring at the poorly-painted wall in his barren house while I waited for help to arrive. I had wondered what he was seeing. Now I believed he had been staring down a desolate, deserted road carved through a blasted, bleak landscape to a desert destination where buzzards dropped deftly from an ominous sky, pinions creaking, eyes shining, beaks agape, in anticipation of the latest arrival to the place from which there is no returning. And it had scared him. Scared a self-sufficient man who had lived alone for many years. A man who had survived trench warfare in World War I, the dust bowl migration, and the Great Depression.

I also believed that if I hadn't happened by, he would have reached that destination and died in the dirt. I was struck for the second time in less than a year with the appalling randomness of life.

I'm not sure how long I sat there with sweat pouring down my face. Long enough that a car, horn blaring, swerved around me on that poorly traveled stretch of road. Shaken, I put the truck in gear and drove slowly on. My head felt like it was full of cotton.

When I reached Goffs at the top of the grade, I pulled into the parking lot at the little store and sat there with my own thoughts for a long time before I got out. I checked the load again and made a few adjustments. Then I went inside for a Dr. Pepper.

"Howdy, Ade. Don't often see you out this way of a week day."

"Hello Mr. Sweeny. Taking a load from the lumber yard up to the Stonebridge place."

"Might want to take the long way 'round. Had us a pretty good rain Monday night. Some of the lads from the OX said the road through Von Trigger Wash is in bad shape."

"Then Watson's Wash is probably worse."

"Sure to be.

Ain't this something? Dryer than a popcorn fart out here for years and years, and then in 1959 we started to get some good rains. Now we're even getting rain in the early summer. Never seen that in all my years out here.

I'll bet you want a Dr. Pepper."

"Yessir."

I paid for my drink.

"So long, Mr. Sweeny. Thanks for the information. You saved me a lot of trouble."

"Any time, Ade."

I got back in the truck. I opened my Dr. Pepper and took a drink. And once again was struck by how odd life can be. Twenty minutes before, I had been sitting in the middle of the road with my hands shaking, thinking deep thoughts about mortality. Now I was drinking a bottle of pop.

I pulled onto the road and headed west, passing the turnoff for Lanfair Road and continuing on old 66.

With Hackberry Mountain looming large on the north, I started down the long rise of the vast Fenner Valley. The Fenner Hills were ahead of me and to my northwest. When I left the plateau, the valley spread out below me, a huge empty space that could have held all of the city of Los Angeles. A space inhabited by fifty people at the most

I could see two dust devils spinning across the valley floor. It was three o'clock in the afternoon, and the sun was tilting to the west. The ribbon of highway shimmered in the heat, mirages forming in the dips ahead of me. Miles and miles of barbed wire fence paralleled the road almost all the way to the bottom of the valley before veering off and cutting directly north, receding into the distance until it could no longer be seen. I passed the abandoned gas station at Fenner with its collection of slowly rusting, junked cars. Then the road bent southwest toward Essex where old 66 and new 66 would reunite.

When I reached Essex, a wide spot in the road with a service station, a post office and a tiny schoolhouse, I took Essex Road north out of town toward the Providence Mountains. The road was paved, if poorly maintained, past the Clipper Mountains and the Blind Hills. When it hit the Clipper Valley, the paved road veered west toward Mitchell's caverns. Black Canyon Road, broad but unpaved, led directly to the north. I took the unpaved road.

As soon as I left the pavement, a plume of dust, fine as butterfly glitter, began to billow hundreds of feet into the air behind and above the truck. The sound of the tires changed from a high pitched whine to a ripping noise. Below thirty miles an hour, the truck yawed and swayed. At forty, the ride smoothed out and the truck seemed to almost float on a fine layer of dust atop the roadbed, just at the edge of being out of control.

Every time a heavily washboarded section appeared, I would have to slow down to a crawl and suffer through a series of jarring bumps that made me clench my jaw to keep my teeth from knocking together. Then the road would smooth out again, and I could pick up speed.

When I approached a dip, I pumped the brakes to slough off speed, so the heavily laden truck would not bottom on its springs and fling the load off the back. Every time I slowed down, the dust behind me caught up and filled the cab with a silty, dry mist. I wished I had brought a bandana to tie over my mouth.

It was hot, bumpy, noisy, dusty, and frustrating.

I was in the middle of nowhere, out back of beyond. The main highway was now far, far behind me, and I knew if I stopped I would be surrounded by the incredible stillness of the Mojave.

As I climbed higher, the glaringly white sky of the valley floor gave way to one so blue and deep it seemed to draw off into the blackness of space. The character of the land began to change. Creosote and white bursage transitioned to blackbrush, cholla cactus, catclaw and yucca. There was desert willow in the washes. The sloping hillsides were littered with volcanic rock: some of it solid black and some brown. The brown rocks were covered with desert varnish, giving them a reddish patina.

Gradually, the air began to cool, and the hills showed a green tint from the recent rain. Canyon country rose on both sides of the road. Joshua trees, junipers, pinyon pines and scrub oak began to appear among the cactus.

I passed the turnoff to the 71L ranch in the bottom of a broad wash. The sand was very soft, so I had to sustain just the right speed. To slow down would leave me stuck in the sand, but moving too fast would make the back end of the truck begin to slew out of control. I realized I was gripping the wheel so tightly my fingers hurt.

I got through the wash and began climbing again, the bulk of Wild Horse Mesa on my left. I was afraid the load may have shifted while I getting through the wash, so I stopped near Hole-in-the Wall to inspect.

When I got out, I was wrapped in stillness. A stillness in which the unimportant and non-essential had been stripped away, leaving a quiet world waiting for sound. Every noise I made: the door opening; the crunch of my boots on the road; the sound of the cap unscrewing from the dripping, canvas desert bag; expanded into the stillness before being swallowed, leaving behind the barely audible wind and the thrum of the wings of small birds flitting from shrub to shrub

I stood for a long time, taking sips of the musty-tasting, lukewarm water from the bag and letting the stillness fill my head and slow my heart. I was home. Home in the place sacred to me: the mountains of the Eastern Mojave. The only place I felt I belonged anymore.

I thought again about the strange hallucination in Paiute Wash.

"Buddy," I said out loud, "maybe you've been spending too much time alone out this way."

As I stood there thinking about that strange experience, I realized there was another side to that story. Those soldiers had been patrolling the Mojave Road, patrolling to protect mail riders and white travelers from the Paiute, Chemehuevi and Mojave Indians. Indians who were the ancestors of Mojave and Chemehuevi kids I went to school with in Smoke Tree.

One of the old men in the Mojave Village near Smoke Tree, Webster Charles, had been born before Camp Cady, Camp Marl Springs, Camp Rock Springs and Fort Paiute had been abandoned in 1868. I wondered what he thought of the role the soldiers had played. I would like to have asked Mr. Charles about that, but my Mojave friend, Billy Braithwaite, once told me there was no way the old man would ever talk to me about anything concerning Mojave history and culture.

I got back in the truck and continued on my way. Table Top Mountain dominated the view to my north, and the strangely striated rocks of the Woods Mountains rose to the northeast.

When the road crested the Mid Hills, Round Valley spread out below me, filled with juniper, yucca, Joshua trees and blackbrush. To the northeast, I could see the Pinto Mountains, my destination.

At the bottom of the valley where Cedar Canyon Road and Black Canyon Road intersected, I drove past the dense stand of chamisa beside the road and turned east onto Cedar Canyon. The road began to rise. Table Top Mountain now turned on the southern horizon as I drove toward Pinto Mountain and the Box S ranch owned by John Stonebridge.

In a few miles, I turned north onto the road John's father had carved out of the valley floor. Because of the topography of Pinto Mountain, the road he cut could not climb straight to the large shelf halfway up the mountain where he built his ranch. Instead, the road wound around the base of the mountain and came in from the west, where a series of switchbacks led up the mountainside to the ranch.

Unless you've ever visited a working, desert ranch, it's hard to imagine the isolation of such a place. To coax a living out of such unyielding land is an amazing accomplishment. There are many easier ways to earn your daily bread.

Because I spent so much time in these desert mountains, I was familiar with most of the ranches spread throughout the vast area: the OX, Valley View, Kessler Springs, Gold Valley and 71L. None of them had buildings that were completely finished. There was usually a tumbledown addition or two attached to the main building. There were middens out behind the main buildings full of glass bottles, tin cans and other detritus. And there were junk yards filled with abandoned vehicles and farm equipment of all sizes and descriptions.

The Stonebridge place was the exception. The main ranch house was a large, elegant, whitewashed adobe with a red tile roof. There was a good barn on the place. Perhaps not one that an Eastern or Midwestern farmer would envy, but one that was functional and in good repair, although the rough boards that covered the exterior had almost turned black under the multiple coats of creosote protecting them from the desert sun. The barn was not home to any farm animals. The barn's purpose was to provide cover for pieces of ranch equipment and the rudimentary machine shop required to keep the equipment running.

There was also a solid, wood-frame bunk house. In the heyday of the ranch, it had housed as many as ten full-time hands. Now there were only two, but sometimes more were hired when there was extra work.

Mr. Stonebridge had a substantial corral. No flimsy structure of pinyon and juniper posts; this was a well-constructed corral of almost five acres, outlined by railroad ties cemented into the ground and tightly strung with barbed wire. The gate was made of two-inch pipe, welded together, supported by cross struts and hinged into a railroad tie.

But the best thing about the Box S ranch was its location. Mr. Stonebridge's father had built the ranch into the side of Pinto Mountain. It must have taken a tremendous amount of work, but he had enlarged an existing flat area three quarters of the way up the mountainside by blasting and cutting into the mountain until he had the site the way he wanted it.

When he was done, he had stunning views. From his living room window he could see the sun rise over the Black Mountains. In the evenings, he could sit on his veranda and watch it color the sky as it set over the Marl Mountains.

The gleaming white adobe came into view as the International labored up the final switchback. There were no steers in the corral at this time of year. But there were five horses. They all turned to watch as I drove by. I pulled the truck to a stop on the flat hardpan.

I stepped down from the cab and stretched my back. It had been hammered hard by the washboarded roads. I pulled the water bag off the front of the truck and was getting a drink when I heard a voice behind me.

"You don't have to drink that warm water. Come inside and get something cold."

I turned around. A beautiful woman was walking toward me. My mouth probably fell open because the look on my face made her smile.

She was Asian and no more than five feet tall. Her black hair, cut in a page boy, framed a face with almond eyes, a delicate nose, and bright white teeth. She was wearing a pink T-shirt tucked into a pair of Levi's cinched to a tiny waist above narrow hips.

The only Asian person I had ever known was Mr. Lee, the Chinese owner of the Jade Cafe in Smoke Tree. I didn't know much about Asian people, but I was sure this woman with walnut-colored skin was not Chinese.

As she continued toward me, I saw movement off to her right. It was a Mojave Green rattlesnake coiling to strike.

"Stop!" I yelled.

As I yelled, the Green rattled.

An alarmed look came over her face. I was afraid she would move out of fear and be struck, but to her credit she didn't panic. She stood perfectly still.

"Okay, don't move. Don't even turn your head. The rattler is off to your right. He may be close enough to strike."

I dropped the water bag in the dirt.

When working in the heat, I wore long-sleeved, khaki shirts because they were actually cooler than T-shirts. I quickly unbuttoned my shirt and moved off to the right of the snake.

The ominous rattling stopped as the snake turned its head toward me and considered its options.

I talked as I walked and removed the shirt.

"It may seem like its safe now, but it's not. The snake is looking at me because I'm moving, but it can turn and strike faster than you can blink. Please, stay where you are."

As I approached the green, it began to rattle again, its tongue flicking in and out to pick up my scent.

"In a minute, I'm going to throw my shirt at it. When I do, run to your left."

With both hands, I pitched the shirt underhanded. The rattler struck at it. The Asian woman moved.

The shirt settled over the snake. It didn't like it one bit. It slithered out from under the shirt and began to move toward some rocks.

I picked up a stone and threw it.

The snake stopped, coiled, and rattled again.

"Get me a long-handled spade. Hurry!"

The woman headed off toward the barn at a run.

Two more times the snake started toward the rocks, and two more times I threw stones at it, making it coil and rattle. I was determined it would not get away.

The woman came running back with a spade. She gave the snake a wide berth.

I took the spade from her and closed the distance between the snake and me.

When I pushed the spade forward, the snake struck it twice so fast I couldn't actually see the strikes – only feel them.

I pulled the spade back. The venom showed white against the rusty metal.

I got between the rocks and the snake and began to herd it away from the pile. It gave ground reluctantly, buzzing angrily.

When I got it out on flat ground, I swung the spade high over my head and brought it down on the snake's body. Even injured, it still tried to strike, but it was stretched out now, and from a safe distance I smashed its head and then cut it off with the edge of the spade.

The woman and I stood looking at the remains of the snake. Even without its head, the body continued to writhe and twist in the dirt. She seemed to be badly shaken by what had just happened, so her next words surprised me.

"Did you have to kill it?"

"Yes ma'am. I usually don't kill rattlers; just let them go on their way while I go mine. But this one is way too close to the house. Even if I drove it away, it would be back. It probably lives in those rocks over there and hunts wood rats in the barn.

If it had struck you, you would have died."

She gave a small shudder.

"Really? I've heard people can survive rattlesnake bites."

Depends. The venom from most rattlers attacks muscles and organs. Adults can survive it. Mojave Greens are different. Their venom attacks your respiratory system. You go into seizures and stop breathing."

"Isn't there anti-venom?"

"In Smoke Tree. Anyone struck way out here would die before they could get to the hospital."

We stood for a moment while she absorbed what I had told her.

"You're shook up. Maybe you should sit down."

She shook her head.

"No, I'll be fine."

We stood there a few minutes longer before I broke the silence.

"Ma'am, I'm from Smoke Tree Hardware and Building Supply. The stuff on the truck is for Mr. Stonebridge. Is he around?"

"He was expecting you quite a bit earlier. When you didn't show up by two o'clock, he thought you probably weren't coming today."

"I know I'm late. I stopped to help someone."

She held out her small hand.

"I'm Kiko. And I'm being rude. I was inviting you in for something cold to drink before you saved my life."

I took her hand.

"I'm Aeden. Everyone just calls me Ade.

I don't think I saved your life. You would have stopped on your own when you heard the rattle. Even people who have never heard that sound understand it's bad news.

"Well, Ade, I'm pleased to meet you. And if it's not too much trouble, do you think I could have my hand back?"

I dropped her hand as if it had burned me.

She smiled again.

"My goodness, I've made you blush? I didn't know that was possible under all that tan.

Now, come on up to the house for that cold drink."

I followed her across the yard. Her gait was athletic, her stride energetic.

I followed her into the adobe. It took my eyes a moment to adjust to the dimmer light inside. We walked through the front part of the house and into the kitchen where Kiko gestured at a table.

"Sit down, Ade."

She opened the door to a small, propane refrigerator. From where I was sitting, I could see bottles lying flat on the bottom shelf. When Kiko bent over to see what was there, her Levi's stretched tight. I had to force myself to look away. If she had turned and caught me staring at her body, I probably would have died of embarrassment.

She straightened and turned to me.

"We have Coors, Pepsi and Nehi grape."

"A grape drink, please."

She bent over and pulled two bottles out of the refrigerator. Once again, I had to force myself to look away.

She came to the table with two bottles of Nehi grape and a bottle opener. She snapped the caps off, put one in front of me and sat down facing me. I took a huge swallow.

"So, Ade, you need to find John."

"Yes ma'am."

"I'm not a 'ma'am,' Ade. I'm a Kiko, and I'm not much older than you. So let's drop the ma'am thing."

"All right.

Kiko, I thought maybe Mr. Stonebridge or one of the hands could help me get the stuff off the back of the truck. And I have to have Mr. Stonebridge sign for it."

"John and the hands went over to Bathtub Springs. They took the jeep and the pickup. If you want to go get him, you'll have to take your truck."

"I'd have to go through Watson's Wash. With the truck so loaded, I don't think I could get through. I know the spring. I'll take hike over the hill."

"You know this area that well?"

"I spend a lot of weekends at Lee's Camp up in the New Yorks."

"I don't know where that is."

"As the crow flies, about twenty miles. A lot farther by road.

I'm know the springs because I hunt there in the fall."

Kiko wrinkled her nose in distaste.

"You shoot animals?"

"Yes."

"That's disgusting."

I finished my drink and stood up.

"Well, I'm sure some people agree with you.

But if you'll excuse me, I'd better get started."

I was dying to know where she had come from and why she was at a desert ranch on the side of the Pinto Mountain, but I didn't want to pry. I also didn't want to have any more discussions about hunting.

She followed me as I walked out of the house.

In the yard, I turned to her.

"Nice to meet you, Kiko."

"Likewise, Ade. And thanks again for saving me from the snake."

"Well, you're the first person I've ever met who likes snakes."

"Like snakes? I hate them. They scare me to death."

"But you didn't want me to kill it."

"I don't like it when people kill animals. They're just trying to live their lives. They have as much right to be here as we do."

"I see.

Well, I'm off."

I turned and walked around the house and along the hillside. I came to a steep draw choked with pinyon pine, juniper and yucca. Staying on the east side of the draw was easier than walking through the bottom of it. Safer too. With the draw so overgrown and filled with rocks, it was a great place to run into rattlers beginning to hunt now that the tilting sun had put the bottom of the gully in shadow.

Because the desert mountains of the Eastern Mojave had received unusual rains in the late spring, I could see the tiny, bright red blossoms of hummingbird bush. Farther down the slope a lot of lavender verbena was still blooming. There was white thistle in the disturbed soil ahead of me. As I climbed, the orange blossoms of desert mallow appeared. There was desert holly in the rocks. The rain had turned the plants a deep green.

I watched the ground in front of me for snakes. I couldn't get the picture of the coiled Mojave Green or the sound of its rattle out of my head. It didn't help that there was a big crop of brown, desert grasshoppers. Every time one of them whirred off the ground it front of me, it sounded for an instant like a rattler.

The mountainside was steep. I was sweating heavily when I reached the top of the ridge. The ground leveled out, and there were more pinyons than junipers. I found a big rock half embedded in the ground and surrounded by the bright green of Mormon tea and the purple blossoms of paper bag bush After checking all around it for snakes, I sat down to catch my breath and take in the view of the Pinto Valley stretching out below me.

As I sat there, I thought about the woman back at the Box S.

Who was she? What was she doing at the Box S? How did she get there? She was like no one I had ever met. Like all the other teenage boys in Smoke Tree, I had fallen in love with Nancy Kwan in *The World of Suzy Wong,* but this was a living, breathing, real person. It seemed impossible such a woman would be out here in the middle of nowhere.

I got off the rock and went on.

The north flank of the mountain fell steeply away below me, and walking through the badly eroded, unstable scree created a series of small emergencies as I tried to keep my feet. I scrambled down the steep mountainside in a series of cautious zigzags. I was careful not to step on any of the basketball-size rocks. They were unstable ankle turners that could easily send me pinwheeling down the side of the mountain. When I finally reached the bottom, I turned toward the narrow, west end of the valley and Bathtub Springs.

Bathtub Springs got its name from an actual bathtub. The Taylor Grazing Act of 1934 required ranchers who grazed cattle on public lands to improve multiple water sources, so a rancher with a sense of humor hitched a porcelain bathtub to his horse and dragged it to the bottom of the shallow draw. Then he rigged up a series of pipes to feed water to the tub from the artesian spring on the hillside.

I walked past the ranch pickup and a jeep. As I got closer to the springs, the area above and below the tub was full of catclaw acacia, desert willow and seep willow. There was water on the ground, enough to grow algae. Very unusual for a place where above-ground water was rarely seen. The bush muhly, indigo bush and arrowweed looked healthy next to the tiny flow, and Mojave asters bloomed in the shade close to the willows. There were wild honey bees buzzing through the blossoms and working the edges of the seep. I saw John Stonebridge and his hired hands, Chaco Hermosillo and Phil Fernald, farther up the draw.

Mr. Stonebridge turned when he heard me coming. He was fair-skinned, with sandy hair and the gray eyes of a sharpshooter. He was tall and very thin. The belt holding up his faded Levi's was tightened to the last notch, and the dangling end trailed down the front of his pants, but he was still in danger of having his jeans slide over his narrow hips. He had on both a long-sleeved, cowboy shirt buttoned to his neck and a broad-brimmed cowboy hat to protect his fair complexion from the desert sun. In spite of that, his face bore the tiny scars of surgeries to remove skin cancers.

"Hello, Mr. Stonebridge."

"Hello, Ade. Thought maybe you weren't coming today."

"I know I'm late. I stopped to help Mr. Stanton at Arrowhead Junction. I was driving by and saw him laying on the ground in front of the station."

"What was wrong?"

"Turned out, Mr. Stanton had a stroke. I got him inside and called the sheriff's department. Horse asked me to stay until help got there. Horse and the deputy took him to the hospital in Smoke Tree."

"That's too bad. Sure hope he's going to be okay."

"Me too.

107

Horse told me he thought the stroke was a mild one."

"Good. Known Mr. Stanton since I was a young man. Always like to stop and visit with him."

Mr. Hermosillo and Mr. Fernald had joined us during the conversation.

"You know the hands, right?"

"Yessir."

I addressed the two men: "Mr. Hermosillo, Mr. Fernald."

Both men nodded.

"Ade, didn't you just finish high school down in Smoke Tree?"

"Yessir."

"Well then, I think it's time you stopped calling all of us 'mister.'

I'm John. This is Chaco and that's Phil."

"All right sir, but that will be hard for me to get used to. I'll probably forget now and then."

"John, not 'sir'."

"Yessir."

"I didn't hear a vehicle. How'd you get here?"

"Walked. Truck's over at the ranch."

"Well, let's go over and take a look.

Chaco, Phil, I'm going to go back to the house with Ade. Bury the new pipe down here in the wash."

"Got it, boss."

As we walked down the hill to the vehicles, I asked John what had happened to the old pipes.

"Vandalism. Some idiot shot them full of holes. We're seeing more and more of that kind of thing. It was a .22. Probably some kid. I never thought I'd see the day we had to bury irrigation pipe, but I guess we have to.

We got in the jeep. There was no road in the west end of the valley, so we drove off over the rugged terrain in first gear and four-wheel-drive.

After we had been grinding along the valley floor for a few minutes, he turned to me.

"Go ahead and ask, Ade."

"Sir?"

"John, remember."

"Sorry. Ask what, John?"

"About the Japanese woman at the ranch.

You met her, right?"

"I did."

"So you know her name is Kiko."

"Yes.

"Don't you want to know where she came from?"

"I don't want to pry.

"I met her in Baker."

"She lives in Baker?"

"No, she's from Salinas."

"Where's that?"

"Up the coast near Monterey."

"How'd she come to be in Baker?"

"I was over there on a Friday night in March to get a part coming in on the late bus from L.A. After I got the part, I went down the street to the Bun Boy to get something to eat before heading home.

Kiko was sitting in a booth. I couldn't help noticing her. She was dressed in a black, evening dress. It was cold that night, and she didn't even have a jacket.

She's beautiful, isn't she Ade?"

"She really is."

"Anyway, she was trying to eat a burger, but some college boys, at least they looked like college boys, fraternity or football types, were bothering her.

Seems they were on their way to Vegas and had decided she should go with them. She told them politely she didn't want to go, but these boys had been drinking and wouldn't take no for an answer.

She got more emphatic in her refusals, but they wouldn't leave it alone. She got up and walked out.

They followed her out the door. I thought I'd better go see if she needed help.

Their car was parked pretty close to my truck, and when I got to it, one of them had her by the arm and was trying to drag her to the car.

I yelled at them to leave off.

They didn't take kindly to it. One of them called me "pops," and the one holding her called me something much less pleasant.

While he was distracted, Kiko bit him on the hand, hard."

Mr. Stonebridge smiled at the memory.

"He hollered and let go of her. She ran toward me with those boys after her, the big boy she bit leading the pack."

"What did you do?"

"I reached in the truck and pulled my .30-.30 off the rack.

It's astounding how the sound of a cartridge being levered into a carbine brings everything to a halt. Those boys stopped cold. I swear, one of them slammed on his brakes so hard he skidded in the dirt and almost fell down.

Anyway, they fussed and blustered a bit, but they did it while they were retreating toward their car. In a minute they were gone.

Sure raised a cloud of dust when they shot out of there.

I asked her if her car was in the lot. She said she didn't have a car.

She told me she had spent the last of her money on that hamburger she didn't get to eat.

I told her I was going to go inside and get some burgers and fries to go, and she was welcome to wait in the truck for me or go on her way.

When I came back out a bit later, she was still in the truck, leaned up against the door, fast asleep.

She woke up when I opened the door, and we talked a bit."

"How did she get to Baker?"

"She was not forthcoming on that, and I didn't push her. She was pretty shook up, and I don't think it was just because of those college boys, so I let it be.

I told her Baker wasn't a very good place for a young lady with no money in her pocket, and she agreed.

I invited her to come home with me to the ranch."

110

"She asked a lot of questions about the place. I had the feeling she was afraid someone was going to show up in Baker looking for her. When she understood how far off the beaten path the ranch was, it was like she weighed everything in her mind and decided that even though she didn't know me from Adam, it couldn't be worse that whoever might be coming for her.

She said she'd like to come back with me

We drove home eating burgers and fries and drinking chocolate malts. She's been here ever since. Took to the place like a duck to water.

She likes the horses and has a nice rapport with them. Likes to curry them and feed them treats. She rides them too, but only near the house. She won't go off the hill. And you wouldn't think a woman that small could get a saddle on a horse, but she can."

"Did she ever tell you more about how she came to be in Baker that night?"

"No, she hasn't. And she's made it pretty clear she doesn't want to.

But I'm glad to have her on the place. She's smart, she's good company, and she seems inclined to stay a while. You know, it's been lonely in that big house since Father died.

So, that's what the supplies are for. I'm going to build a little addition onto the house for her. Place where she can have a sitting room to read and so forth.

You know, Ade, unlike people in town, people out this way don't gossip much. They pretty much respect each other's privacy, although they're quick enough to help others if asked.

Still and all, I don't want anyone to get the wrong idea. I put her stuff in my bedroom and moved my stuff into my dad's. It's sat empty ever since he died.

But I think having her own room, a room made just for her, puts a different stamp on it for everyone. And I think she'll like it."

I realized this was no casual matter for Mr. Stonebridge.

"You think she's going to stay?"

"Would be fine with me if she did, but it's hard for me to imagine a young woman staying out here for too long, especially with just me and the hands for company. But even if she doesn't stay, I'd like her to know she's always got a place here if she wants to come back to stay or just visit."

"I can't image you'd meet a person like her in Baker."

111

"Well, she's not the first unusual person I've met there. Take Phil, for example. His full name is Philippe. He's from France. I met him in Baker one day. Told me he was hitchhiking around the United States. He had come over after the war. Told me he wanted to meet the country that produced the people who saved his country from Hitler. He's tried hard to blend in. I think he's completely lost his accent.

Now if he's just brought Charles De Gaulle with him, our countries might get along better. Anyway, Phil told me he'd always dreamed about being a cowboy. I asked him if he knew anything about cattle. He said not much, said he'd been a farmer before the war. Heck, didn't even know how to ride a horse."

"And you hired him?"

"Of course. Anyone who's been a farmer is used to hard work. Never deny a man a chance to fulfill his dream by working hard for low wages!

That was fourteen years ago, and Phil's been with me ever since."

We crossed the north end of Watson's Wash and drove up the opposite hillside before turning south on a road that was little more than a meandering track. The high desert scent of sage grew stronger as the jeep's hot muffler dragged over the brush that had grown in the middle of the road. We passed a huge cottonwood tree with bright green leaves blinking in the sun beside a windmill. There was a stock tank and a few scattered boards: all that remained of a homestead. The windmill was cranking briskly in the wind kicking down the wash from the north.

When we reached Cedar Canyon Road, Mr. Stonebridge turned west, and we drove down into the broadest part of the wash. There was no real road anymore – just sand, rocks, gravel and uprooted sagebrush and chamisa, but I could tell the jeep tires were making contact with the hardpan below the washout. That meant I would be able to get my truck, with its big dual wheels, through the wash.

Mr. Stonebridge was silent as he maneuvered through the sand and gravel.

When we started up the other side, he continued.

"I think she loves it out here. She's outside with her coffee in the morning to watch the sunrise, and she never misses a sunset.

She's not allergic to hard work, either. Pitches right in and helps me and the hands."

"Does she talk about Salinas?"

"A word or two from time to time. But she never says much. If I ask questions, she clams up. I suppose she'll tell me in her own good time. Or she won't. Either way is fine with me.

Something dangerous happened that dumped her in Baker that night. She's still very fearful. All she had when she got here was that black dress, so I wanted to take her to Barstow to buy some clothes. She wouldn't go. Didn't want to leave the ranch. She gave me the sizes and I bought the stuff. Downright embarrassing buying bras and underwear."

As we turned off Cedar Canyon onto the ranch road John's father had carved out of the desert all those years before, the setting sun slipped below the horizon, flaring crimson and gold in the west as only desert sunsets can. Bats and nighthawks were appearing in the evening sky. Venus was already visible.

When we climbed the last of the switchbacks and turned toward the ranch house in the twilight, I realized the truck was not where I had left it. Kiko had driven it over by the barn and parked it parallel to the barn doors, which were propped open.

Almost all of the building material was already off the truck. Kiko was dragging the last fifty-pound sack of cement off the flatbed as we drove up. All the concrete blocks were stacked neatly beside the truck.

She took her gloves off, put them both in her right hand, and stood in that slightly akimbo stance you often see with ballet dancers or figure skaters.

Mr. Stonebridge and I got out of the jeep and walked over to her.

"How'd you get all that stuff of the truck? Took me half the morning to get everything on there."

"I guess that excitement with the snake got my adrenalin flowing. Had to do something to work it off."

"What's this about a snake?"

Kiko told him what had happened. In her version of things I was quite a hero.

"Good Lord, Ade, it's a good thing you were here."

"I just saw the snake before it rattled. She would've stopped when she heard it. It's not something you have to teach people."

"I've heard rattlers before, and I still think you saved me."

Mr. Stonebridge looked at her in surprise.

"Out here, on the place?"

Kiko hesitated.

"No, somewhere else. A long time ago."

I think Mr. Stonebridge wanted to ask her more, but he could tell she wanted to drop it.

He turned to me.

"You're coming back tomorrow, right?"

"Should be here before noon."

I got in the truck and started it up.

Kiko and Mr. Stonebridge waved at me as I turned the truck toward the road.

When I reached Watson's Wash, I had to turn on the headlights to make my way carefully through the sandy, rock-strewn bottom. I managed to dodge the biggest rocks while going fast enough not to bog down.

When I rose up the other side, the Joshua trees next to the road looked menacing and bizarre in the headlights, their branches reaching into a velvet-black night sky. It would not be long before Orion crept briefly over the horizon.

I reached Lanfair Road, turned south, and hurtled along under the inky sky all the way to Goffs.

Once I got back to the pavement of old 66 and picked up speed, the insects that filled the night smashed against my windshield. As I drove, I thought about my strange day. Finding Mr. Stanton lying on the ground. The vivid, unsettling hallucination in Paiute wash. The incident with the Mojave Green at the Stonebridge ranch. I thought about Kiko and what Mr. Stonebridge had told me about her

I was sure there was far more to her story than she had told Mr. Stonebridge. But if he wasn't going to press her for more details, I certainly wasn't.

But that didn't keep me from wanting to know.

It was almost nine o'clock by the time I parked the truck outside our house. I took a little walk to stretch my legs. I crossed the last street on the west side of town to a raised berm that marked the boundary between the houses and the silent desert. I climbed up and stood there, taking in the Great Bear over the distant Dead Mountains. I looked up into the night sky to find the inverted "W" of Cassiopeia and the Pleiades before I went inside.

I was a little hesitant to bother Lieutenant Caballo so late in the evening, but I was anxious to know how Mr. Stanton was doing. I dialed the number the lieutenant had written on the back of his card.

A woman answered on the first ring.

"Caballo residence, Esperanza speaking."

"Sorry to bother you so late, ma'am. It's Aeden Snow. Lieutenant Caballo said I could call when I got home to see how Mr. Stanton was doing."

"Oh, you're the young man who saved Mr. Stanton's life."

"Ma'am, you're the second person today who thinks I did more than I really did."

"Well, I don't know who the first one was, but Carlos told me if you hadn't stopped by, things could have gone very badly for that kind, old man.

He told me you would probably call. I'll get him to the phone."

In a few seconds, the Lieutenant came on the line.

"Evening, Aeden."

"Evening, sir. I apologize for calling late. How's Mr. Stanton."

"He's fine, Ade. As we thought, he had a stroke, but it was a very mild one. He wanted to turn around and go home as soon as he got to the hospital, but they kept him overnight for observation. The doctor says he has the heart of a forty year old. Mr. Stanton should be back home by tomorrow afternoon."

"I'm glad!

I've got another load to deliver up in the Mid Hills. I could ask my boss if it would be okay to drop Mr. Stanton at his station on my way by."

"Kind of you to offer, but that won't be necessary. I'm going to take him back myself. I want to check around his place and make sure nothing was disturbed while he was gone."

"Thanks for letting me know about him."

"You're welcome, and thanks for all you did."

A wave of relief washed over me. I realized again how much I looked forward to my visits with Mr. Stanton.

I hung up and went into the living room. As usual, my mom was on the couch reading a book. She told me Dad had caught a trip east and wouldn't be back until morning.

I visited with her for a while, telling her about my day and what had happened with Mr. Stanton. I didn't tell her about Kiko. I thought I'd better ask

115

Mr. Stonebridge if it would be okay. He seemed so protective of her. Before long, I couldn't keep my eyes open.

I excused myself, took a quick shower and collapsed into bed.

CHAPTER 8

Smoke Tree, California

And the mountains

Of the Eastern Mojave Desert

June 9, 1961

Aeden Snow

The next morning, I got to the hospital early. I was told I would have to come back during visiting hours. I went on to work, even though the store didn't open for another hour. I unlocked the gate, drove the truck inside and locked everything up again. I had most of the order on the truck by the time the Halversons arrived to open up for the day.

Mr. Halverson came out to the lumber yard. I gave him the paperwork Mr. Stonebridge had signed to acknowledge delivery. I also told him about what had happened at Arrowhead Junction.

"You know, in all the years I've driven by that place on the way to Vegas, I've never stopped. I've seen the old man you're talking about puttering around out there a time or two. So that's Mr. Stanton?"

"Yessir. Hugh Stanton. He owns the station.

I went to the hospital this morning to see him. They said I was too early, so I came ahead over to start loading this order. I told Mr. Stonebridge I'd be there before noon to make up for yesterday. Stopping at Arrowhead Junction made me real late to the Box S. And I had to go the long way around because Mr. Sweeny at the Goffs store told me Von Trigger and Watson washes were both a mess. Didn't want to take a chance on getting stuck or losing the load."

"You're certainly getting an early start today.

I know this load isn't quite as big as the one yesterday, but you've got some expensive stuff on there. That knotty pine isn't cheap. So, just like yesterday, don't rush."

"Yessir. I'll be real careful."

When I reached Arrowhead Junction, I pulled the truck under the overhang at Mr. Stanton's station. I checked around the building to see if anyone had broken in. I didn't know what I would have done if they had, but everything was okay.

I got back on the road.

When I reached the spot where I'd had the vivid hallucination the day before, the images were still vivid in my mind. I pulled the truck off onto the shoulder and got out. I walked up the wash and under the trestle to the other side.

I knew it was stupid, but I scuffed through the rocks and gravel in the wash, looking for horse droppings or signs of shod horses. Of course, there were none, just tire tracks from some kind of vehicle, wandering off through the broken volcanic rock, bayonet yucca, barrel cactus and creosote. I went back to the truck and pulled onto the highway.

I was about halfway between the wash and Goffs when I saw someone walking west along the shoulder of the highway. As I drove by, I saw a slender man of medium height with jet black hair wearing a blue flannel shirt, Levi's and work boots.

Although it was only nine thirty in the morning, the temperature was already well on the way to a one hundred plus degree day. In spite of that, the man wore no hat: only a red bandana tied around his forehead.

I had not seen a vehicle of any kind parked along the road, so he was not leaving a breakdown. I couldn't imagine why he was walking along a desert highway, but by the time my curiosity got the better of me, I was already a hundred yards beyond him. I tapped the brakes a few times and slowly brought the truck to a stop, careful not to shift the load. Looking in the rearview mirror,

I could see he had broken into a trot. He had a canteen over his right shoulder. It banged against his hip as he ran.

I slowly backed up. In a few moments, I was beside him. He pulled open the door and looked in at me.

He was not a young man. Forties was my guess, although he was an Indian and I was not good at gauging the ages of adult Indians, or any adults for that matter. My perception of the world of grownups was pretty much limited to adult, somewhere in the middle, and real old.

"Thanks for stopping."

"I was surprised to see someone walking out here.

Where you headed?"

"Caverns in the Providence."

"Mitchell's caverns?"

"People charge admission call them that."

"What do you call them?"

"Suuparva i'nip."

"Could you say that again?"

"Suuparva i'nip."

"And that means?"

"Gather-together spirit."

"What language is that?"

"Chemehuevi."

"I'm headed to the Mid Hills to deliver this stuff. If you don't mind riding along, I'll take you where you're going when I'm done."

"Beats walking.

Help you unload. Earn my ride."

"Deal!"

He climbed in.

I held out my hand.

"Aeden Snow."

He touched it lightly.

"Joe Medrano."

"Pleased to meet you, Mr. Medrano."

He nodded.

When I stopped at the Goffs store for a Dr. Pepper, he didn't come inside with me. When I brought one out for him, he said, "Obliged."

That was the sum total of our conversation until we got to the turnoff for the Box S.

"Stonebridge Place."

"Do you know Mr. Stonebridge?"

"No."

We climbed the switchbacks to the rock-lined driveway that led to the ranch. I pulled the truck up next to the barn where Kiko had unloaded the supplies the day before. When I got out of the truck, Mr. Stonebridge was already walking toward me.

"Morning, Ade."

"Morning, John. Here's everything else."

"I'll help you unload."

"No need. I picked up a rider on the way. He said he'd help."

Joe Medrano was already out of the truck and untying the ropes securing the delivery.

John walked over. "John Stonebridge. Welcome to the Box S. Good of you to help."

He held out his hand.

Joe touched it lightly, as he had mine.

"Joe Medrano."

"Well, if two of you can do it quick, three of us will be even quicker."

We worked steadily for half an hour before we had everything inside the barn. When we were done, John checked the unloaded materials against the invoice and signed for the delivery.

"I've got my supplies. Now all I need are better building skills."

Joe spoke.

"Ask what you're building?"

"Going to put an addition on the northeast corner of the house."

"How big?"

120

"Twelve by sixteen."

Joe looked over at the house.

"Shouldn't be hard."

"Not for someone who knows what they're doing. I doubt if you could make one decent carpenter if you put me and both my hired hands together."

"Match the adobe?"

"That's way beyond me. Not even going to try. I'm just gonna stucco the addition."

"Shame. Won't look right."

"Do you know anyone who can build with adobe?

"Me."

"How about carpentry work. Any good at that?"

"Some say."

John stood staring at Joe for a moment.

"I'm sorry, I'm a little slow.

You must be Chemehuevi Joe. I've heard Keith Halverson talk about you. Says you're a heck of a carpenter."

"Kind of him."

"How'd you like to build this addition for me?"

"Depends on the pay, Mr. Stonebridge."

"I'm sure we can work something out."

"One other thing."

"What's that?"

"Won't let me match adobe, won't build it."

"I'd be pleased if you could match it! How long would it take?"

"Couple weeks to cure adobe bricks.

Build your addition while they dry. Put the roof on. Face it with adobes when they're ready. Faster that way. Underneath the adobe, plywood. Then insulation, then drywall. Knotty pine on top"

"I like that.

Could you match the roof?"

Joe walked closer to the house.

121

"Long-barrel tiles. Can't buy them. Can make them. Kiln to fire them. Hole side of that hill would do.

Need hot-burning wood. Pine won't do. Mesquite or cottonwood."

"There are some big cottonwoods over by government holes. Lots of branches on the ground."

"Nothin' burns hotter."

"Where are your tools?"

"My place. Long way.

Any on the ranch?"

"Come look at what's in the barn."

We walked back to the barn. Joe looked through the old tools.

"This stuff has all been on the ranch for years. I don't have any power tools."

"Don't like 'em. Hate the noise."

He sorted through the collection of old tools.

"Most everything I need right here. Couple things from my place. Special saw, hammer, couple wood tools."

"Joe, I don't even have a cement mixer."

"Big wheelbarrow there. All I need.

Plenty of straw for adobe."

"When can you start?"

"Have to do something. Back tomorrow."

"Come on down to the house. We'll get something cold to drink and come to an agreement on a price for the job."

Although it was hot on the hillside, it was cool inside the thick walls of the adobe.

The house had been cleverly designed. When the screened windows high up on the north wall were opened, they caught the down slope breeze coming over Pinto Mountain. Each of the rooms within the house had a row of rectangular openings near ceilings of their north and south walls. Those openings matched the ones on the north, exterior wall. At the front of the house, the screened windows high up on the south walls were carbon copies of those on the north.

Built in air conditioning. Efficient and effective. The ventilation was controlled by opening and closing shutters on the north wall.

As we moved into the hallway that ran down the center of the house, John called out, "We'll be in the sitting room, Kiko."

He led Joe and me through a doorway into a large room on the west side of the house. As we entered, I saw two large, mullioned windows set on either side of a river rock fireplace on the west wall. In front of the fireplace were eight leather chairs lined up on two sides of a long, low, narrow table of highly-polished dark wood. Between the chairs were small tables of the same dark wood. On every table were large, copper oil lamps with tall, glass chimneys. A large chandelier, also fitted with lamps, hung from a heavy, black chain. The chain ran through a sturdy eyelet set into one of the open beams on the ceiling. The chain passed through a similar eyelet set into the wall, so the chandelier could be lowered to light the wicks or refill the lamps with oil.

Sunlight streamed through the two large windows, and dust motes danced and swirled in the light.

"Please, have a seat."

John and I sat down on opposite sides of the low table. I could smell saddle soap and neatsfoot oil, which explained the supple feel of the leather.

Joe wandered around the room inspecting the workmanship of the furniture.

"Good work. Close fits. Flush dowels. No nails."

"My father had this furniture shipped here from Spain in the '20s. This has always been one of my favorite rooms in the house."

Kiko came through the doorway carrying a large pitcher of Kool-Aid and four glasses on a wooden tray.

I stood up.

"Hello again, Ade. Please, sit down."

As I sat, I glanced sideways at Joe Medrano. He was standing so perfectly still he could have been carved from stone. His eyes were fixed intently on Kiko. He looked for all the world like a hunter who had just seen an eight point buck walking toward him from a stand of pinyon pines.

"Kiko, this is Joe Medrano. He's a well known carpenter around Smoke Tree and Parker.

I'm trying to hire him to build the room addition."

Kiko put the tray on the table and straightened up to look at Joe.

She noticed the piercing stare. Her greeting seemed strained.

"Hello, Mr. Medrano."

Joe nodded his head almost imperceptibly.

"Ma'am."

They stood looking at each other. Kiko looked away first. Then she looked back.

"I hope you don't mind me asking, but you're Indian, aren't you?"

"And you're Japanese."

"Have you known many Japanese people?"

"No women."

"But men?"

"South Pacific. World War Two.

Lost friends in that war."

Kiko's voice hardened.

"And I lost two older cousins."

"What island?"

"Not on an island. Hill 140, outside of Castellina in Italy. They were in the 442nd Regimental Combat Team."

Joe visibly relaxed.

"Tough outfit. Brave men."

There was respect in his voice. Kiko's voice kept the hard edge.

"I miss my cousins. I miss them all the time.

I will never, ever, ever understand why they wanted to volunteer. They were in an internment camp. The government arrested us, all of us. Gave us one week to sell the family farm my father and my uncle had owned for years in Salinas. People who had been our neighbors for years got it for almost nothing.

So, Joe, can you help me understand why my cousins would fight for a country that did that to us? Because I don't think anyone who's not Japanese-American can understand what that felt like."

Joe shrugged.

"Some can."

"I don't see how."

124

"In '32, government broke its treaty with my tribe. Took our reservation. Drowned our homes under Lake Havasu. Grandparents are buried under that water. Some nights I hear their voices all the way over the Chemehuevi Mountains."

"You believe that?"

"Not to believe or not believe. Just is."

"Mr. Medrano," I interrupted, "are you saying when I go fishing for crappie under the light at the end of the Scott Atwater dock at Site Six, I'm fishing on top of your drowned reservation?"

"Yes."

The look on Kiko's face changed from defiance to chagrin.

"That's just up the river from where we were in the camp."

"Poston?"

"That's right.

You know it?"

"Built on Colorado River Tribes land. Tribes didn't want it there. Government did it anyway.

You in camp one, two or three?"

"We didn't call them that. We called them Roasten, Toasten and Dustin. We were in Roasten. A hundred and fifteen degrees in the summer in wooden buildings with tin roofs and no insulation. No heaters in the winter.

There were seventeen thousand of us inside the fence around the three camps. Nobody cared we were out there."

She stopped for a moment and shook her head.

"Lord, I can't believe I'm talking about this. My parents taught me never to bring this up in front of white people."

"Two white people here. Two white, two brown. Standoff.

Finish what you started."

Kiko took a deep breath and turned to John.

"John, you've been very kind to me, and you're a good man. But I have to ask you something I've never asked a *gaigen* before."

"What's a *guy jen?*"

"White person.

Why did your government do that to us? They didn't lock up the Germans or the Italians Just the Japanese. And most of them were Nisei and Sansei."

"Two more words I don't know. What's a *née-say* and a *san-say*?"

"Second and third generation Japanese-Americans. Nisei were born in the United States to parents who had emigrated here and become naturalized citizens. Sansei, like me, were born to the Nisei."

"Kiko, I hate to disappoint you, but you're not going to get much of an answer from me.

It wasn't my government then. I was born in England and lived there until my father brought me here when I was eleven. When England declared war on Germany in '39, I went to Canada and joined the Royal Canadian Air Force.

I was in England in the Canadian First Squadron flying Hurricanes off British soil when I heard about the camps. At first, I didn't believe it was true. And I never heard about the one in Poston until I got home from the war.

Drove down there once to look at it before they tore it down. Still couldn't believe it. Ugly place. Reminded me of P.O.W. camps in Europe."

"So can you see why I couldn't understand why my cousins joined?"

She turned to Joe.

"Mr. Medrano, maybe if you'd tell me why you signed up, I'd understand my cousins..."

"Don't know that's so. Was in Georgia, Pearl Harbor happened. Headed home to join."

"But why? You didn't owe anyone anything."

"Get what the government owed us, had to serve. Come back after, fight for what is ours."

"And did that work?"

The corners of Joe's mouth turned down.

"Not yet. But won't stop."

Clearly uncomfortable with giving out this much personal information, Joe turned the conversation."

"Mr. Stonebridge, you in England the whole war?"

"No. After D-Day, my squadron flew Spitfires off a field in Normandy.

126

Can't tell you how happy I was about that. First, we were taking it to Jerry all the way to Berlin. And second, Hurricanes were no match for the ME-109s. I had to be fished out of the channel twice because of those damned Hurricanes. But those Spitfires! Grand airplanes."

Kiko spoke again.

"But you're a U.S. citizen now?"

"Yes. I knew I was going to live here for the rest of my life. Thought I might as well vote. I became a citizen after the war."

Kiko turned to Joe again.

"Mr. Medrano, do you know what's at Poston today?"

"No wood buildings. No fence. Old adobe high school. Contractor ran out of lumber. Tribes use high school. Offices and such."

Kiko shuddered. "I never want to go there again."

"How old were you when your family was taken there?" asked John.

"I was seven. Eleven when we left."

Throughout this entire exchange, I sat transfixed.

Kiko had been in an internment camp? With seventeen thousand Japanese-American citizens? In Parker?

We had learned about the concentration camps in Nazi Germany in history class. But I had played football and run track in Parker for four years in high school and never heard anything about Poston. Ever.

I realized John was looking at me. He seemed to sense my dismay.

"Kiko, you have every right to be on your high horse, but climb off it for a minute and sit down. You're talking to two veterans and a young man who has obviously never heard about Japanese-Americans being rounded up and put in camps.

Have you, Ade?"

"Never."

"Well, you weren't even born when it happened, and you were only two or three when it ended."

"Mr. Medrano. I'd appreciate it if you would sit, too."

Joe eased into a chair.

"Ade, you look like you've been smacked with a baseball bat.

Is there something you'd like to ask?"

"This happened?"

"It most assuredly did."

"And this place Kiko and Mr. Medrano are talking about was only forty miles downriver from Smoke Tree?"

"That's right."

"We studied World War Two. The man who taught my history class was a veteran of the war. He never mentioned any internment camps."

"Well, Ade, by the time you studied about the war, people were so embarrassed by what they had done to Japanese Americans they didn't want to talk about it. Not least because the 442nd was the most decorated unit in the War, and they were volunteers from the camps, like Kiko's cousins.

In fact, the older generation, the one your history teacher is part of, wants to just forget all about the whole thing."

"But that's crazy."

"All the more reason to try to forget it. Because there's no excuse for it. Oh, there are explanations: war hysteria, national paranoia, righteous anger, mob mentality. But explanations are just that: explanations. They are not justifications."

"But Kiko said they didn't lock up the Germans and the Italians."

Joe spoke in his usual manner, softly and without inflection.

"White people."

John nodded.

"I think you assessment is correct, Mr. Medrano."

"I won't forget it. Not ever."

"No, Kiko, I'm sure you won't.

Now, I think we have stripped a sufficient number of scales from young Mr. Snow's eyes for one day. He needs to think about this before we speak of it again.

I am hopeful his generation will not have the experiences Joe and I had with war. I think this new president is pretty level-headed about ill-advised military adventures. He certainly avoided that mess the CIA tried to stick him with at the Bay of Pigs. And maybe he'll take to heart President Eisenhower's advice on avoiding land wars in Asia.

Anyway, let's have a glass of Kool-Aid and talk about something much more mundane, like room additions."

That broke the mood.

Joe asked Mr. Stonebridge for a paper and pencil.

After a few minutes of calculations, Joe handed John the paper with a price on the bottom.

"Joe, this is not enough for all the work you're going to do."

"Enough for me. Feed me, give me a place to sleep."

"You can bunk with the hands. Plenty of room in there. And you can take your meals with us, if you don't mind company."

"Don't mind."

John stood up and reached out his hand. Joe rose and touched it briefly.

"Then we've got a deal."

Joe and I thanked Kiko for the Kool Aid and left the house. John caught up with us just as I was opening the truck door.

"Ade, you still spending a lot of weekends over at Lee's Camp?"

"Yes. I'm off on Sundays and Mondays. Mr. Halverson says Saturday is too busy to miss."

"Will you be up this Sunday?"

"I will."

"Then I'd be glad if you'd join us for dinner on Sunday evening."

"That would the great."

"Let's say about five o'clock?"

"I'll be here. Thank you."

Joe and I drove down the stone-lined driveway and started down the switchbacks on our way to Cedar Canyon Road.

"Mr. Medrano, do you think Mr. Stonebridge is right about Americans wanting to forget about what we did to the Japanese?"

"Lots for Americans to forget about."

"But you're American."

Joe was silent while I slowed to make the turn from Cedar Canyon to Black Canyon Road. Then he turned his head to look at me.

"I'm Chemehuevi. Chemehuevi run over by Spain, Mexico, United States. Nobody asked what we thought about it. Were we Spanish? Were we Mexican? Are we Americans?"

Neither of us said anything else as we drove the long stretch to the spot where the paved road to Mitchell's Caverns swung off to the west. I slowed to turn onto the pavement.

"Stop here."

"I'll take you up."

"Rather walk."

"Mr. Medrano, I'd like to ask you something."

"Ask."

"Those caverns, are they important to the Chemehuevi?"

"Sacred."

"Do they charge you admission when you come here?"

Joe Medrano gave me the briefest of smiles.

"Thanks for the ride."

After I left Joe at the fork, I continued on to Essex to get back on old 66. The forlorn, childless swings on the deserted playground of the tiny elementary school were rocking in the hot wind,.

I joined Old 66 and drove across the broad, flat floor of the Fenner Valley. This was classic low desert: nothing but widely-spaced creosote shrubs, white bursage, stunted cactus and tiny clumps of desiccated grasses.

At the wide spot in the road that had once been Fenner, old 66 began to rise, paralleling the Santa Fe tracks that were just to the south of the road. Near the top of the grade, Goffs Butte rose to the south. Shortly afterward, I could see what remained of the town of Goffs, once a major stop for the Santa Fe Railroad. In the old days, locomotives that had helped push the freight trains up the grade from Smoke Tree were disconnected, shunted onto a siding and turned around to return to Smoke Tree. Locomotives that would continue to take the train west would replace water that had been used getting the steam engines up the grade. Now the railroad's presence was reduced to a huge pile of railroad ties, their creosote coatings glistening in the sun.

I passed the turnoff to Lanfair Valley and the now-abandoned, Spanish-style schoolhouse, one side of its tile roof collapsing. I crossed the tracks and drove past the tiny store and gas station. When I reached the top of the climb to the east of town, I reached down and switched the fuel supply from gasoline to propane, then turned downhill until I came to Arrowhead Junction.

I pulled off the highway to check on Mr. Stanton. I found him sitting on his rocker in the shade under the station's overhang. He waved when I got out of the truck.

"Hiddy, Ade."

"Hello, Mr. Stanton. How are you?"

"Right as rain and happy to be home. I didn't like that hospital."

"I'm glad you're back. I stopped by on my way to the Mid Hills this morning and checked your place. Everything looked okay."

"Thanks. Horse looked around too when he brought me home.

He's a good 'un, is Horse. Not many lawmen woulda took time out of their day to run a old man home."

"I guess not."

"Ade, I want to thank you. Horse said I might not have made it if you hadn't stopped by."

"He probably made it out to be more than it was. I didn't know what to do when I found you."

"You did just right, Ade. Yessir, just right."

"Well, good to see you home sir. I best get down the road."

Mr. Stanton thanked me two more times before I could get back in the truck.

When I got back to town, I told Mr. Halverson about picking up Joe Medrano along the road and about Mr. Stonebridge hiring him."

"Now we know the job will get done right. Chemehuevi Joe is a heck of a carpenter. None better."

"Interesting person."

"I don't know that much about him."

"Does he live here in town?"

"Lives way out on the desert, somewhere down toward Vidal.

He's never told me exactly where."

More deliveries had piled up while I had been gone, so I went right to work. But all that day and the next, Kiko and John and Joe rarely left my mind.

131

On March 11, 1961, President John F. Kennedy approved the departure of a four-hundred-man Special Forces group to help train South Vietnamese soldiers. On June ninth, 1961, President Ngo Dinh Diem requested additional troops to help train the fledgling Army of the Republic of Vietnam. President Kennedy agreed to the request and sent another one thousand troops. He also agreed the United States should finance an increase in the number of soldiers in the South Vietnamese army from 150,000 to 170,000. None of these events were reported to the public because they violated agreements made at the 1954 Geneva Convention.

By the end of 1962, there would be 12,000 U.S. advisors in South Vietnam. Johnny Quentin, and Charlie Merriman, both Army Rangers by that time, would be among the 12,000.

Chapter 9

Smoke Tree, California

And the mountains

Of the Eastern Mojave Desert

June 10, 1961

Aeden Snow

I thought Saturday would never end, but six o'clock finally rolled around. I headed for home. I packed up enough food for two days. I got a blanket from the closet. I picked out a couple of good books and put them in the trunk with the food box, the bedroll, the tank of compressed air, the small pick and the Army entrenching tool.

I went back in the house and made a salami, cheese, peanut butter and cabbage sandwich to eat on the way.

Dad wasn't home, but that was not unusual. A freight conductor on the Santa Fe, he worked odd hours. He was usually only home for the mandatory twelve hours of rest before he marked back up on the extra board to catch the next job going east or west from Smoke Tree.

Mom was on the couch reading a book.

"I'm off, Mom."

"Be safe, Ade.

Watch for snakes."

"I will.

See you Monday night."

I got back in my '39 Plymouth. The fuel pump hadn't vapor-locked during the drive home from work, so the straight six started on the first crank, always a pleasant surprise. I made my way down Jordan Street hill. After a long wait, I managed to turn left across Route 66. In a few minutes, I was out of Smoke Tree, just another piece of the flotsam and jetsam caught up in the steady eddy of traffic headed toward the California coast.

I took the same route I had taken with the second delivery until I reached Cedar Canyon Road, but this time I stayed on Lanfair until it turned into Ivanpah Road. I turned off Ivanpah onto the road into the New York Mountains.

It was deep twilight when I reached the OX Cattle Company stock tank and windmill and turned up the faint two-track into Carruthers Canyon. I turned off that onto what was more of a rumor than a road into a side-cut canyon. I turned on my headlights. A few cottontail skittered across the road in front of me.

My dad's best friend, Lee Hoskins, owned an adobe deep in the side cut. Lee built the house himself. It was next to the mining shack his father had lived in while he worked a vein of silver. The vein played out in the early 1900s but earned Lee's father title to all the land inside the claim.

I had been coming to the adobe with Dad and Lee since elementary school. When I was old enough to drive, Lee gave me keys to the padlocks on the heavy doors. He told me I could use the place anytime I wanted. The only rules were: clean up before leaving and bring in wood from the stack outside to replace any I had burned.

I got out of the car and took in the high desert perfume of sagebrush, juniper and pinyon pine. The canyon smelled more like home to me than the town of Smoke Tree.

After I unloaded the car, I lit an oil lamp and made myself a sandwich for dinner. After I ate my sandwich, I read by the light of the lamp for a while. When I started getting sleepy, I dragged a cot outside. I unrolled my bedroll on the canvas, took off my boots and lay down. The narrow band of velvet sky directly overhead was filled with stars.

It had been a long week. I was very tired, but for a while. I lay there thinking about Kiko and Dad's friend, Mr. Stonebridge. I thought there must be something between them. After all, he was building a special room just for her.

I stopped turning things over in my head and listened to the coyote chorus out in the main canyon. I was trying to locate the Pleiades in the sky when I fell into a deep and dreamless sleep.

I was awakened at first light by a flock of pinyon jays as they passed overhead. Their cries echoed down the canyon. I discovered I had pulled the blanket over myself in the night. Although it was summer on the Mojave, Lee's camp was at six thousand feet. The hours just before sunrise were chilly.

I pushed the blanket aside and got to my feet. I felt good, and I was happy. I had a whole day of hiking and dinner at the Box S to look forward to.

As I always did my first morning at Lee's camp, I scrambled up the south side of the steep, side-cut canyon. By the time I got to the top, the sun was climbing above the Black Mountains in Arizona. Beyond the Black Mountains, I could see the Hualapais, purple in the early light. In the distant south were the Old Woman Mountains, then the Turtle and Whipple Mountains to the west of Lake Havasu.

In the near foreground to the south, lay Pinto Mountain and the completely flat expanse of Table Top Mountain jutting over 5,000 feet above the floor of Gold Valley. To the southeast, I could see Hackberry Mountain, the Paiutes, the Dead Mountains, and the Sacramentos outside Smoke Tree.

A huge expanse. Millions of acres. Most of it trackless. Filled with mystery. Filled with emptiness. Filled with solitude. The home of very few people. I picked my way down the steep side of the canyon.

I didn't want to heat up the adobe for the rest of the day by firing up the wood-burning stove to cook breakfast. I had a cheese, smoked ham and peanut butter sandwich washed down by lots of water from the artesian well behind the house. Before I left, I brought in the washtub from the back porch and filled it with water from the hand pump in the sink. It would go from ice cold to room temperature by the time I got back.

I decided to hike to what remained of the group of buildings at the old settlement of Barnwell on the lower northern flank of the New York Mountains and then down into the southern Ivanpah Valley. It was a wonderful day on the desert. There was not a single cloud in the deep blue sky. In the wind that carried the scent of sage and the rank smell of cheesebush, the long, gossamer webs of balloon spiders glistened in the bright sunlight.

On my hike, I made a lot of stops to poke around abandoned mines and buildings. When the sun began to tilt, I hightailed it for home so I wouldn't be late for dinner.

When I got in the tub back at the adobe, the water was refreshingly cool but not cold. When I was done, I dumped a lot of dirt-clouded water off the back stoop.

I toweled off and put on a long-sleeved, electric-blue cowboy shirt with mother of pearl snap buttons, my very best one. I tucked it into dress jeans: Levi's that had never been seen the inside of a washing machine but had only been rinsed in cold water and line dried so they would retain the original indigo color.

When I stepped into my quarter boots, I was ready to drive to the Box S for dinner.

What followed was a wonderful evening.

The hired hands had not yet returned home from Searchlight where they were gambling away their wages at the tiny casino or visiting the lovelies who worked out of the motel across the street. There were only four of us for dinner: John, Joe Medrano, Kiko and I.

Kiko had cooked a meal of cheese enchiladas, chicken with mole sauce, and black beans and fresh nopales seasoned with onion, garlic, oregano, chili powder and cumin.

"You don't grow up in Salinas without learning about good Mexican food," she explained.

After dinner, we moved out to the veranda with flan and coffee to take in the amazing sunset flaming above the Marl Mountains and the purple twilight that followed. As the remaining color began to leach from the western horizon, bats and nighthawks appeared overhead in the darkening sky.

Although the ranch was over a mile high, it was still the Mojave Desert in June. It had been a hot day. But once the sun went down, the earth began to release its heat. Then a strong, north wind, born in the Great Basin Desert of central Nevada and coming all the way down through Austin, the Great Smokey Valley and Tonopah, came ripping over Pinto Mountain. The wind seemed to shred the little light remaining from the sky. Complete darkness descended.

In the dark, the wind blew hard for another ten minutes or so and then stopped as suddenly as it had started. In its aftermath, the temperature dropped ten degrees. A total calm settled across the vast desert landscape that surrounded us. The dry, desert air was soft and perfect.

John Stonebridge got up and went inside. There was no electricity in the adobe. He blew out all the oil lamps in the living room, dining room and kitchen. He brought the remaining carriage lamp outside from the hallway and extinguished it after he sat down. In the desert that rolled away from us on all sides, there was not one light visible.

Within fifteen minutes, the velvety sky was crowded with uncountable stars. The Milky Way formed a glowing, opaque highway against a backdrop of the evening stars from the southern horizon to where it was blocked from our view by the veranda roof. The handle of the Big Dipper was almost directly overhead, its sweep pointing the way to brightly shining Arcturus. Although I couldn't see it from where I sat, I knew that somewhere behind Pinto Mountain the bowl of the dipper poured out the path to the North Star and distant Las Vegas. There could not have been a greater contrast between that garish city and the peaceful place where we sat staring outward into the dark and inward into ourselves.

I heard the clink of somebody's spoon against a bowl. Otherwise, all was silence until, from off to my left, Kiko's soft voice floated out of the darkness.

"John, I have to ask. How in the world did an Englishman end up in the middle of the Mojave Desert?"

"Well, it's a convoluted tale, and a long one."

"I would like to hear it."

"All right, but stop me if you get bored.

My father, Benton Stonebridge, came from a fading but still secure aristocratic family. Then, in a move that added to the family fortune, at the age of thirty he met and married my mother, Elizabeth Wainwright, a woman eleven years his junior, the daughter of a successful merchant.

Father's family was wealthy in land and assets, but its wealth was eroding. The cost of keeping up appearances was nibbling at the edges of the once-large estate. As my grandfather struggled to maintain the great house at its center, he began selling pieces of the property.

Grandfather Wainwright was a merchant whose wealth was measured in pounds sterling, stocks, bonds and lucrative contracts. He and my grandmother were assaulting the bastions of the British upper class with floods of money. In essence, they were trying to buy their way into London society because, in spite of all their money, they were considered upstart *nouveau riche*. They knew they would always be looked at that way until they married my mother into a titled family. So my father, who would eventually inherit Grandfather's lands and minor title, was just the ticket.

How Father ever met Mother is a matter of mystery. He was rarely in London, preferring the quiet acreage of my grandfather's estate to the cacophony, smoke, fog and dirt of England's capital."

As John's voice rose and fell in the night air, I realized I was in the presence of a great storyteller. His voice conjured images of a lush, country estate, round hills and rushing streams, as well as grand balls and drawing rooms in a London filled with the rattle, roar, fog and filth of the teeming, cosmopolitan city.

"Grandfather Bucyrus Stonebridge, a widower with mutton chop sideburns and an actual monocle, was pleased his son was forging an alliance with a family that had both the wherewithal and the desire to support the Stonebridge Estate and great house in order to enhance its standing in society.

In 1911, Mother and Father wed.

Mother, who was delighted by the splash she had made in London society with her marriage, was not keen on relocating full time to an estate in the distant, barbaric countryside, regardless of how grand. To placate his young bride, Father bought a fashionable house in the city, so Mother could move back and forth between the estate and London society.

A year later, an heir to the Stonebridge family name was produced. That, by the way, would be me.

And so, Mother and Father began to live a life similar to many couples of their class. Father was rarely in London, and Mother was but an infrequent visitor to the countryside manor."

Kiko's soft voice came again.

"And where were you?"

"My mother refused to give birth at the estate with only the services of a country doctor at hand, so I was born in the London house. After my birth, I remained in London with a wet nurse and two other nurses: one for the daytime hours and one for the night. Father returned to the country.

As soon as I was weaned, Mother took me back to the estate, bringing a nanny and one of the nurses with her. When I was settled in and a suitable routine established, she left for London. My contact with her, which even in the city had been limited to one visit after breakfast and one before bedtime, ceased almost entirely.

I don't know how long I would have remained at the estate, but in 1914, the Great War broke out. As was expected of titled men of substance, Father accepted a commission and went off to fight the Kaiser's boys on the continent.

Much to Mother's chagrin, I was moved back to the house in London. Of course, the nanny came along. Before the war had ended, a governess was added to the staff of the town house.

Father experienced all the horrors of the first modern war. Those horrors included the boredom and wretched conditions of life in the trenches interspersed with the terror of the heavy bombardments that preceded every attack by the enemy. He never said much about his experiences, but I gleaned from Grandfather that on many occasions he led his men 'over the top' as they called the nearly suicidal frontal assaults on the enemy positions. On those occasions he was fearless, leading by example, screaming like a demented man, urging his troops forward in a pointless gambit to gain a few yards of dearly-bought ground that would often be re-taken within a fortnight."

Mr. Stonebridge paused. I heard him take a sip of his coffee, which must have been cold by then.

Nobody spoke.

I don't know what the others were thinking, but I was recalling scenes from movies about that war and marveling that I was listening to a man whose own father had been there.

He continued.

"Because he survived every one of those exercises in futility and sanctioned insanity without so much as a scratch, Father gained a reputation among the soldiers as a charmed man. So many of his men tried to stay as close to him as possible during those frontal assaults that it must have looked to the enemy like they were advancing single file in their frenzied dash across No-Man's-Land."

As if he were trying to marshal the exact words needed to tell the next part of his tale, John paused again

In the stillness, I heard a match pop off a thumbnail and I smelled sulfur as Joe Medrano held the flame to a cigarette he had somehow managed to roll in the complete darkness. In the sudden light, his skin had the appearance of rawhide stretched over sticks and dried in the sun, so pronounced were the contours of his face with its high cheekbones and deeply set eye sockets. In that moment, he could have been one of his aboriginal ancestors from centuries past. The acrid smell of tobacco cut the night air.

The companionable silence settled around us once again as we waited for John to resume his narrative. It was so quiet, I could hear the crinkle of Joe's cigarette paper as it burned.

John's voice had an emotional quaver when he spoke again.

"Then his unit was gassed in the trenches. If he hadn't rushed to help a wounded corporal who could never have put his mask on alone, he might have escaped injury once again. After he made sure the badly injured man was protected, Father got his own mask on. He was a little late. He had inhaled a small amount of the mustard gas. The gas cored into his lungs like an insidious canker.

When he was evacuated to England, the war was nearly over. His luck, which had been so good, had deserted him. The medal he received meant little to him, but he was always proud of having saved the life of one of his soldiers. Especially since the lives of so many of his men had been forfeit.

When he was released from the military hospital, the doctors told him he would never survive the damp climate of England. His only hope, they explained, lay in seeking out dry, desert air.

In his teens, he had been fascinated by romantic stories of the American West. After long discussions with my mother, discussions during which she adamantly refused to leave London, he made plans to travel to the United States. He hoped that once he was settled and established there he could persuade her to join him.

But in the winter of 1919, before he could set out on his journey, Mother fell ill during the Spanish Flu pandemic that was sweeping the world. It is entirely possible her crowded social calendar, which brought her into contact with so many people in close quarters, led to her exposure. Father was at the estate. As soon as he heard she was ill, he left for London. He arrived in time to remain by her side as she struggled in vain against the illness. It's a wonder he didn't contract it himself. With his damaged lungs, it certainly would have killed him if he had.

After the funeral, Father took me, the nanny, and the governess back to the estate, then left for the United States, leaving me with Grandfather Stonebridge.

He stayed in New York only long enough to buy train tickets to Los Angeles. Arriving at Union Station, he went straight to the Los Angeles Public Library and began to sift through back issues of the Los Angeles Times for information about land in the desert. He discovered stories about the Stock Raising Homestead Act of 1916. The act allowed the homesteading of six hundred and forty acres of land in the Mojave Desert. No cultivation was required: only the construction of a structure and the purchase of a few head of cattle. Although Father was a citizen of England, all he had to do to qualify for the land was sign a statement saying he intended to become a U.S. citizen at some unspecified, future date.

Before the sun went down over the Pacific Ocean, he had paid four hundred dollars for a new, Model T Ford stake bed pickup and headed east on National Old Trails highway. Late that night, he was in a hotel in Barstow. The next morning, he set out for the Eastern Mojave on what soon turned into a narrow, graded dirt road through the desert.

Father often told me that he felt better the instant he reached the desert. At Goffs, he turned off the graded road onto a bumpy track through Lanfair Valley, passing ramshackle homes and buildings built by homesteaders. He drove through the area, many times on primitive wagon trails, looking for a suitable place. He considered Carruthers Canyon but said he felt hemmed in. He wanted wide open spaces. He also had no interest in having his ranch headquarters close to the operations of the Giant Ledge silver mine. Gold Valley would have suited him perfectly, but there was already a ranching operation there.

Then he found this place. He drove past it several times on the Old Mojave Road before he realized it was just what he was looking for. He parked his car down there on what is now Cedar Canyon Road. With his damaged lungs, it took him a long time to get to the top of the mountain. But it was worth the climb. He arrived short of breath but satisfied. He saw wide open vistas to the south, east, and west, and plenty of grazing lands on both sides of the Pinto range: south of him through the Mid Hills and north though the Pinto Valley. There were a few homesteads in the Pinto Valley, but most of them looked like they were on their last legs. And even if they weren't, there was enough water throughout the area that he knew he could create stock ponds to water his herds without coming into conflict with the farmers.

On the advice of one of the locals, he hired an old Timbisha Shoshone woman from near Death Valley to witch him a well. Who better to find water than someone who had spent her entire life worrying about having enough of it? He watched as she worked with her desert willow dowsing stick on the hillside for several hours. She moved in ever narrowing circles until she came to the spot where the well is today.

"Right here," she told my father.

"Drive a stake in the ground."

He did.

She told him when the drilling company came to make sure they set up the rig right where they were standing and to make sure the bit went into the ground right exactly where the stake was. Not two feet or even a foot away. She told him there was a big sheet of solid rock right under their feet, but there was a crack in the sheet and the drill would slide right through into a big pool of water beneath.

That's exactly what happened. The well they brought in has never failed nor flagged.

Then father had this house built, and the barn and the bunkhouse and the corral. It took almost a year. While he supervised the construction, he lived in a tent over by where that last switchback turns into the driveway. He told me it was one of the best years of his life. Said he woke up feeling better every day. Said he went from being an old, sick man to being a young, healthy one in that year.

When the house was done, Father came back to England. He conferred with Grandfather Stonebridge on the kind of cattle operation he should run on the desert. He told grandfather most of the ranchers out here ran calf and cow operations. Grandfather convinced him a steer operation had potential for larger profits. Since Father had plenty of capital, the occasional bad year would not be a problem.

Once that was settled, Father spent a month on the continent, mostly in Spain and Italy, buying the furniture and other furnishings that are still in this house today. Had everything shipped through the Panama Canal to Los Angeles, and then to Goffs on the Santa Fe and then onto a siding off the Searchlight spur just by where Lanfair road and Cedar Canyon Road intersect.

Then he returned to England for me. We came to America, just the two of us. Father left the governess behind. I remember she cried when we left. I cried too. I was ten years old.

At first, that trip was a glorious adventure. First by ship and then by train across the American continent. It was late summer, and I was astounded by the endless miles of wheat and corn on the prairie. I had never seen anything remotely like that.

But then, as we traveled farther west, I started to worry. By the time we hit New Mexico, I knew I was in trouble. The land grew more barren and brown, the sky almost totally cloudless, the horizon more distant and the vegetation more sparse. When we got off the train in Goffs, I thought there had been a terrible mistake. Everywhere I turned, the landscape seemed dead and abandoned. Mountains made of black rock without a blade of grass on them. Sinister looking plants. Dust devils spinning across what might as well have been the face of the moon.

We stood together on the platform at the depot, a man in formal clothes and a boy in short pants. Father pointed at the Goffs schoolhouse on the other side of a dirt road and said I would be enrolled there in the coming week. I practically wept! But I was determined to be brave the way Grandfather Stonebridge told me Father had been brave in the war. Surely the ominous looking world spread out before me was not as bad as No-Man's-Land.

By Christmas, I loved the desert and felt like I had lived on it my whole life."

Kiko's voice came again.

"But it must have been quite a shock, coming from a life of wealth and privilege in the green fields of an English country estate to this place."

John laughed.

"Well, it was a little rough and tumble at first. I was in school with the sons and daughters of homesteaders, ranchers, miners and gandy dancers."

"What on earth is a gandy dancer?"

"Sorry. A worker on a railroad track maintenance crew.

Anyway, there I was with my upper-class British accent and perfect diction, which many of my schoolmates interpreted as evidence I considered myself superior to them. They picked on me and made fun of me. Naturally, I came right back at them.

I was often scuffed up and the worse for wear when Father picked me up in the Model T after school, so he taught me to box and grapple. He'd learned a lot of that in the army. It wasn't long before I was holding my own in the schoolyard. After awhile, I was just one of the gang."

"Mr. Stonebridge ... I mean, John, what was the Lanfair Valley like back then?"

"Well, there were a lot more people here then, that's for sure. Probably a few hundred of them, counting the Negro families in Dunbar."

"What was Dunbar?"

"Negro people from the South started coming west when they heard about the Homestead Act. Many of them were sharecroppers, a miserable life, and they had long dreamed of owning land of their own. The first few who got here sent word back to Mississippi and Alabama and Georgia.

Soon there was a whole little community. I'm not sure why it was called Dunbar, but it even had its own post office."

"Was it separate from the other homesteaders?"

"Well, in a way, I guess you could say that."

"Did the Negro families and the white families get along?"

"I never heard about any serious problems.

No, the real trouble was between the cattle operations and the homesteaders."

"You mean like in *Shane* with Alan Ladd?"

"Just like that.

The Rock Springs Cattle Company was the biggest problem. They were the most established operation. They ran over ten thousand head, and they were used to their cattle grazing on open range all through the valley. But then the homesteaders came and planted wheat. You can imagine what a field full of wheat would look to a steer that had been getting by on white bursage, big galleta and blackbrush. The homesteaders had to put up fences to protect their crop, and sometimes the fences kept the ranchers' cattle from getting to water sources they were used to using. All hell broke loose.

You know how hard it is to set a fence post in desert ground? Especially a crooked post chopped out of cedar or pinyon? Well, a fence that took weeks and weeks to put up could be pulled down by a few cowhands in one night."

"What did the law have to say about it?"

"What law? There was no law to speak of out here in those days. San Bernardino County had one deputy in Smoke Tree, and even if you could persuade him to come all the way up here, he didn't like to get his Model T off the main roads.

No, we were on our own out here."

"Who won?"

"There was an incident with gunfire and injuries across the valley there at Government Holes, but I don't know what would've happened eventually because in the end, the weather won.

The wet years came to an end, and the place remembered it was a desert. Also, grain prices took a dive after World War One. Put all those things together: less rain, lower yields, lower grain prices, and one by one the homesteaders gave up and drifted away.

Father helped the ones in the Pinto Valley, and those along the north end of Watson's Wash, so they could get their five years of improvements and farming in to qualify for title to the land. Then he bought their parcels at fair prices. At least that way they had something to show for the backbreaking work they had put in all those years."

John was quiet again for a moment.

"In the days when the homesteaders were active, if you stood on top of Hackberry Mountain and looked out over the valley, the place was almost crowded. At least crowded for the Mojave Desert. There were scores of one hundred sixty and three hundred and twenty acre parcels. They all had small farmhouses. That was required. Some had a little barn or at least some storage sheds. And they all had cleared acreage.

Even now, if you walk out through the Joshua trees, you will find squares of nearly vacant land that had been completely cleared of vegetation and planted with crops."

"I've seen those. Desert plants haven't grown back after all these years?"

"Not much. Wounds on the Mojave are very slow to heal.

Let me give you a great example. Take a hike northwest of Arrowhead Junction sometime. In a few miles you'll come to a place where General Patton's boys bulldozed and leveled the desert for an airstrip before World War Two. You could land a plane on that airstrip today and not run over anything over two inches tall."

"You said Lanfair Valley was full of homesteads. I don't see any buildings out there now."

"Patton's boys, again. Those were cold winters when the troops were out here training. There were ten thousand soldiers scattered over the desert living in unheated tents. They tore down all those abandoned buildings and burned the lumber to keep warm.

And one more thing you would have seen from the top of that mountain in those days. The railroad. From the late 1800s until 1923, the Nevada Southern, which was later bought out by the Santa Fe, ran through the valley all the way to Barnwell and then on to Searchlight."

"How big was Searchlight?"

"Fifteen hundred people lived there and worked the mines, mostly copper, but then everything played out. The Santa Fe abandoned the line, and the town died."

"Aeden," said Kiko, "you spend a lot out time out here. I'll bet you'd like to see the place the way it once was."

I thought about that.

"I'd like to see it, but I like it better the way it is right now."

"Why?"

"I like it without a lot of people. Besides, I think a lot of those people never really left. Maybe they're wandering around out here."

"What a strange idea."

"Sometimes, when I'm walking at sunrise, especially on a cold, winter morning when the wind is blowing hard, I think I hear voices from just over the hill or up the draw somewhere. But when I go to look, there's no one there."

"You're a strange boy," said Kiko. "You might want to try to give up that kind of thinking. The white jacket people may come looking for you. If I thought I heard voices of dead people, I'd go the other way as fast as I could."

"Voices, what do they say?"

"I can never make out what they're saying."

Joe took another puff of his cigarette. By the movement of the glowing ember, I could tell he was nodding his head.

"Chemehuevi voices. Mojave, Southern Paiute. Spirits everywhere out here. Not for you to understand."

"Maybe so, Mr. Medrano.

And sometimes, it's more than a feeling. The other day ...."

I realized I was about to describe my hallucination in Paiute Wash. I knew if I did, I would sound like a real nut case. I clamped my mouth tightly shut to keep the words from coming out.

"The other day what, Aeden?"

"Never mind."

I tried to laugh but it came out more like a cough.

Joe put out his cigarette with his fingertips.

John leaned down and struck a match. The sudden light seemed very bright after the darkness. He lifted the chimney on the carriage lantern and lit the wick.

The veranda came into view all around us. The spell was broken.

I didn't want to overstay my welcome. I got to my feet.

"Thank you for inviting me to dinner. And for the story about the old days. I love hearing about that stuff."

When I walked off the porch and headed for my car, Mr. Stonebridge came with me.

"Nice to have you join us this evening. I think it's good for Kiko to have someone close to her own age around. You come by whenever you can, Ade. Don't be a stranger this summer."

"If you don't mind, I'd really like to be around while Mr. Medrano builds the new room. I could learn a lot by watching him. I'll help if he'll let me. I'd like to learn to build."

"If you really want to do that, come by in the morning. Say around seven? Joe and I are going to plan out the room. You can be in on it from the very beginning."

"All right."

"One more thing I forgot to talk to you about the other day. Who have you told about Kiko being here?"

"No one, yet, John. I didn't know if it was okay to."

"Good lad. Go ahead and tell your mother and father. You shouldn't have to keep secrets from them. But ask them to please not to tell anyone else in town. I know your folks. I know they can keep something to themselves."

"All right. I'll tell them you don't want it to get out."

"Appreciate it.

Kiko's not ready to tell me what happened. Maybe she never will be. And that would be okay with me, but I think there's something she wants to get off her chest. Sometimes, when we're sitting at the table, she looks like she's just about to spill it, but then she holds back.

Anyway, see you in the morning if you want to come by."

"See you tomorrow."

A few minutes later, I was on Cedar Canyon Road heading back to Lee's camp. As I drove, I thought about the marvelous story Mr. Stonebridge had told us about the old days. But it wasn't long before I was thinking about what Kiko's mysterious secret might be. And I realized I wasn't ready to tell Mom and Dad about her yet. When I did I was going to ask what they knew about Poston. I wanted to be sure I knew exactly how to ask before I started down that road.

I turned on the radio. It was permanently tuned to KOMA in Oklahoma City, the only radio station playing rock and roll that could reach the middle of the Mojave. The Coasters were singing "Searchin".

I came up the driveway the next morning at exactly seven o'clock. John and Joe were standing beside the house where the addition would be built. I joined them.

"Good morning, Aeden."

"Good morning John. Mr. Medrano."

Joe nodded.

Joe had a tablet. He sketched as they talked. It was fascinating watching not just the room but its underpinnings taking shape.

When Joe was done sketching, we went inside and sat at the kitchen table. John and I talked while Joe arranged the pages in a "start to finish" order. He made some sketches of small details which he inserted at various places. When he was done, I looked on as he and John went through the pages one by one.

As they went, John asked for some minor changes here and there. Joe made them. John apologized for asking for changes.

Joe almost smiled.

"Change your mind again. Don't worry. Always happens."

When they were done, I thanked them for letting me sit in.

"I've got to get down the hill. I'll be out next Saturday night. See you next Sunday morning, if that's okay."

"Glad to have you, Aeden."

"Ask a favor?"

"Sure, Mr. Medrano."

"Catch a ride?"

"Certainly."

He turned to John.

"Finish something in Parker, pick up couple tools. Back next Saturday, get started."

"That sounds good."

"We went out and got in my car. We drove all the way to Smoke Tree without saying a word.

I broke the silence when we got into town.

"Where do you want out?"

"South end."

"How are you going to get to your place?"

"Hitch."

"I can take you."

"Hitching's fine.

Another favor?"

"Sure."

"Ride back with you next week?"

"Where should I pick you up?"

"Klinefelter."

"I'll be coming through in the early evening."

"Pull in under the big salt cedars. Meet you."

I drove through Smoke Tree to the south edge of town, and Joe got out.

"Thanks."

He was already walking down Highway 95 toward Parker when I turned around and headed home.

Mojave Desert Sanctuary

Chapter 10

Smoke Tree, California

And the mountains

Of the Eastern Mojave Desert

June 17, 1961

Aeden Snow

On Saturday evening, I was on my way out of town before sundown, but not by much. By the time I reached Klinefelter, twilight was settling over the desert. I pulled off the road and parked next to the two large salt cedars where the southeast corner of a little cove created by the low hills cupped a decaying motor court.

I didn't see Joe. I waited for a moment with the motor running but he didn't appear.

I switched off the engine and got out. The twilight desert air was like warm water. There was no wind at all. There were no cars passing on 95 and no trains on the Santa Fe tracks. Highway 66 was too far away for the sound to carry to where I was.

As much as I was enjoying the stillness, I did want to get on up the road. I didn't know whether to walk back over the hills toward the spring and see if Joe was there or just drive away. I was trying to make up my mind when I heard a quiet voice.

"Ready?"

Startled, I turned quickly.

Joe was leaning against the fender of my car, not five feet from where I was standing. I had not heard him coming. Not a sound.

He had a canteen slung over one shoulder and a canvas knapsack over the other. I could see the handle of a hammer sticking above the flap.

"Scared me, Mr. Medrano."

"Ready when you are."

We got in the car pulled onto the highway in the gathering darkness. Once again, neither of us spoke during the drive.

When we reached the turn off for Cedar Canyon Road, I began to slow.

"Going Carruthers Canyon?"

"Yes."

"Drop me here."

"I'll take you all the way over, Mr. Medrano."

"Rather walk."

I stopped the car.

"Can I ask you something?"

"Ask."

"Did you hitchhike to Klinefelter?"

"Walked."

"Through town?"

"Base of the Sacramentos."

"Didn't you get thirsty? You've only got that little canteen."

"Water there, know where to find it."

"So, you walked all that way and now you're going to walk again?"

"Rested while you drove."

He got out of the car.

"Tomorrow."

I noticed he didn't walk down the road. In a few moments he was swallowed by the Joshua Trees.

On Sunday morning, I was up well before dawn. I fired up the Coleman lantern and started a fire in the wood-burning stove. I filled the blue porcelain coffee pot with water, set it on the stove for cowboy coffee and mixed up a big batch of buckwheat pancake batter. While I waited for the stove to get hot, I sat at the kitchen table reading "To Kill a Mockingbird," the book that had just won the Pulitzer prize.

When I could feel heat from across the room, I got up and cooked a big breakfast. I put everything on a platter and carried it to the table, along with a cup of coffee. By the time I finished my breakfast and two more cups of coffee, I had been so completely drawn into Harper Lee's world I had to force myself to close the book.

I washed my dishes and banked the fire before I left.

There was a hint of light in the sky above the cut canyon as I drove off. I was climbing the last of the switchbacks to the Box S as the sun rose, ready to get to work. I hoped I wasn't too early.

I needn't have worried. Joe Medrano was outside hammering two by tens into forms that looked like book cases. I parked and walked over. He handed me a saw, and I went to work. After Joe finished nailing together four of the forms, he stood up, pointed at the wheelbarrow and spoke for the first time.

"Make adobe in there. Pour it in the forms."

"Make it from what?"

"Come on."

We got into the ranch pickup, a nearly new Ford, and drove down to the edge of Watson's wash. Joe got out and dropped the tailgate. There were two shovels in the back.

"Could use dirt up the hill. Sand, clay and straw mixed are better."

We spent all that morning shoveling sand and hauling it up to the ranch. By noon, we had a substantial pile. We covered it with tarps. Didn't want to have to chase our sand back down the hill if the wind came up.

As we were piling rocks on the tarps, Kiko called us in the house for sandwiches, potato salad and iced tea.

We heard the Jeep pull up outside. John Stonebridge came in and joined us at the kitchen table.

153

"That's quite a pile of sand out there."

"Done with sand," said Joe. "Need clay."

"Where do we get that?"

"Ivanpah Valley."

"That's a long way."

"Best clay."

We thanked Kiko for lunch and drove the pickup west on Cedar Canyon Road. When we rose out of the canyon, we could see the hump of Cima Dome to the west. We drove down the hill through the Joshua trees, creosote, sage and yucca until the road crossed the Union Pacific tracks. We turned right on Kelso-Cima-Road and then took Morning Star Mine Road down into the Ivanpah valley.

It was harder work getting a load of clay in the back of the truck than getting a load of sand. When we had shoveled in all we could fit, we covered the bed with a tarp, tied it down and drove back to the ranch.

By the time we finished unloading, it was late afternoon.

Joe spoke for the first time since lunch.

"Need more clay, but make some bricks now."

He picked up a shovel and explained as he worked.

"Six shovels sand, two shovels clay, couple handfuls straw.

Keep doing it."

When the big wheelbarrow was three quarters full, he poured in some water and handed me a hoe.

"Your turn."

I started mixing while Joe kept adding water. It wasn't long before we had a batch of very thick mud.

"Shovel into the forms."

When I had filled two of the forms, Joe took a piece of wood and smoothed the mud.

Kiko came out of the house with a pitcher of lemonade. She was backlit by the reddish tint of the sun sinking behind the Marl Mountains.

"Made twenty four bricks," I told her."

"How many do you need?"

154

"Nine hundred eighty eight more," answered Joe.

She poured us each a glass of lemonade.

After we finished our drinks, we pulled the forms off the adobe and knocked the leftover mud from the forms with trowels while Kiko watched.

Joe stood up and pointed his trowel at me.

"Adobe man now.

More tomorrow?"

"Sure."

At John's insistence, I stayed over for dinner. After coffee and desert, I headed back to Lee's camp. I was so wiped out when I got back, I didn't even take my clothes off. Just lay down on the cot and fell asleep.

I was stiff and sore when I got up in the dark to start a fire in the stove. After breakfast, I headed back to the Box S. We hauled clay from the Ivanpah Valley until lunch and then set about making bricks in earnest.

By the time the sun went down, we had hundreds of bricks spread over the hardpan. But we needed hundreds more.

"Next Sunday?"

"I'll be here."

"Okay."

I drove back to Lee's camp. I removed the hot coals from the stove, dumped them behind the outhouse and poured water on them. Then I packed up all my stuff and locked up the house.

As I drove down the Lanfair Valley toward Goffs in the darkness, my arms, shoulders and back all ached. I was going to be stiff and sore again in the morning.

Some days off!

When I got home, I left my boots on the patio. Mom and Dad were watching Tales of Wells Fargo. I was glad to see Dad home. Between his unpredictable schedule and my work, we hadn't been home at the same time for quite a few days.

Mom told me there was leftover roast beef in the refrigerator. I made a huge sandwich and ate it standing at the sink. When I was done, I went into the living room and sat down on the asbestos tile floor, careful not to touch the furniture or lean on the walls.

Dad got up and turned off the television.

"Looks like you got in a tussle with a mud puddle. Looks like the mud puddle won."

"I was helping Joe Medrano make adobe bricks at the Box S."

"Joe's working at the Stonebridge place?"

"Yessir. He's building a room addition."

"Why in the world does John need another room? He's been rattling around in that big house ever since his father died."

"He has a guest. A young woman. He's building the room for her. Says he doesn't want people getting the wrong idea."

"Wrong idea about what?"

"About why she's there. That's the way he explained it."

"Does this young woman have a name?"

"Yes, Mom. Her name is Kiko Yoshida."

"That's Japanese?"

"Yes ma'am."

"And John knows her from where?" asked Dad.

"He met her in Baker."

"She lives in Baker?"

"Nossir, she was passing through."

"When was this?"

"In March."

"And this Japanese woman has been at the Box S ever since?"

"Yessir. And Mr. Stonebridge would like to ask a favor of you and Mom. He wants you not to say anything about her being there."

"Did he say why?"

"He says when he met her, she was on the run from something or someone. She hasn't told him what it is, but he says she's very afraid. He wants as few people as possible to know she's at his place."

"But he's building a room for her so people won't get the wrong idea? This is confusing. Can you tell us more?"

I related the story John told me about meeting Kiko in Baker and bringing her home with him. I also told Mom and Dad about Kiko's unwillingness to go to Barstow with John to buy clothes.

When I finished, Dad said, "Very mysterious. But he told you it was okay to tell your Mother and I about this person?"

"He trusts you to keep it a secret. He doesn't want anyone else in Smoke Tree to know about her. Says he's not worried about people out his way, but he thinks town people gossip too much."

"Well, he's right about that.

We'll keep this between us, but I hope she isn't on the run from the law."

"Mr. Stonebridge doesn't seem to think so."

"What's this woman like?" asked Mom.

"She's very nice. And she's beautiful."

"Son, when you're eighteen years old, all beautiful women seem nice."

"Judy McPhearson didn't."

Dad laughed. "I stand corrected. Too bad Johnny Quentin couldn't see that. He'd be getting ready to go off to college on scholarship like you."

I hesitated, unsure how to proceed.

"Dad, I've got a question for you."

"Shoot."

"Did you know there was a Japanese internment camp near Parker during the war?"

"Yes, I knew about Poston. Everyone in Smoke Tree and Parker knew about it."

"Did you think it was right, what the government did to those people?"

"*Those people* attacked us at Pearl Harbor, Aeden," said Mom.

"No, no they didn't, dear. We were attacked by the Japanese nation, not Japanese-Americans. The people at Poston were citizens. Most of them were born in this country. I never thought we had any right to put them in prison camps."

"Dick, prison camp is far too harsh a term."

"What else can you call a place with barbed wire fences, police dogs and gun towers?"

"A relocation camp."

"And if those people had tried to relocate themselves to someplace else?"

"Well, I suppose they would have shot them. They couldn't just let them roam around the country loose. They could have sabotaged things."

"If that was the case, why didn't we relocate all the Germans and Italians in this country? After all, we were at war with Italy and Nazi Germany too."

"Well, if you want my opinion, I think if we had rounded up all those darned Italians, we wouldn't have this big Mafia problem in this country today."

"And the Germans?"

"Well, they were, they were..."

She hesitated.

"Is the phrase you're looking for 'more like us'?"

"Yes. There, I've said it. And I don't apologize for saying it."

"As you can see, Ade, your mother and I disagree about this."

"I can tell.

Can I ask you another question? One I feel funny asking you?"

"I have an idea what it's going to be, but go ahead."

"Since you thought it was wrong, did you say anything about it?"

"To my shame, I said nothing."

"Why not?"

"When the war broke out, I was twenty five years old. I was working as a butcher at Milner's. Your mom and I had only been married two years. I was trying to get a job on the railroad, but the country was slipping back into the Depression and I couldn't get hired.

Right after Pearl Harbor, Lee Hoskins and I went down to enlist. When I took my physical, the doctor said I had a heart murmur. The army wouldn't take me. I went to Las Vegas and tried to sign up there. I failed the physical again. So my best friend went off to the war, and I stayed here. Thank God, Lee survived the war. I don't think I could have lived with myself if he had died while I was safe at home.

158

I've always felt guilty about not serving. I don't think the heart murmur is anything serious, but it kept me out of the army. And because so many young men were signing up or being drafted, the Santa Fe needed trainmen. In ordinary times, the Santa Fe doc would have disqualified me because of my heart. But there was nothing ordinary about those times. The company waived my condition and put me to work. I've had this good job ever since.

I benefited twice. While other men lost their lives, I didn't go to war. And, I got this job That's why I didn't think I had any right to speak up. I kept my mouth shut. It was that simple. I should have had the courage to speak up anyway because I knew what was going on was just flat wrong, but I didn't."

"I'm not trying to criticize, Dad. I'm just trying to figure out what happened and why I never heard about it. I mean, this was in our back yard and everybody just forgot about it? Like it had never happened?"

"Aeden, you're going to find that Americans are very good about forgetting things they don't want to remember."

Chapter 11

Las Vegas, Nevada

June, 1961

Eddie Mazzetti's phone rang at five o'clock in the morning.

"Eddie here."

"Send a car."

Eddie recognized that voice. A voice he really didn't want to hear.

"Send a car where, Thomaso?"

"The airport, stupid. Christ, you think I'm in the lobby?"

"Sorry. Half asleep here."

"And I haven't been to bed yet. Send somebody."

"I'll have a car there right away."

"I brought someone with me."

"Good looker?"

"You think Salvatore Lupo's good lookin', that's your problem."

Eddie was silent for a moment.

"Thomaso, you think it's a good idea to bring a guy the law's lookin' at real hard to the Serengeti?"

Thomaso's voice dropped to a whisper.

"You questionin' my judgment here?"

"No, Thomaso, of course not, but..."

"But nothin'. And fix us each up with a suite."

"It's Saturday mornin', Thomaso. They're all full."

"So, kick some people out."

"These are high rollers. Guys who drop fifty, hundred yards a day in the casino. You wanna kill the goose lays them golden eggs?"

Thomaso's voice dropped so low Eddie had to strain to hear him.

"Listen, goombah, I'm tired. I flew out here to clean up a mess you made. See why you can't find one miserable little slant-eyed whore. Already I have to tell you what to do. Now, I know you keep them showgirls out there in the best rooms so the big spenders can get a rod just watchin' them walk by. So, kick a couple of them out."

"Woman who directs the show will have a fit. High-strung French broad."

"Yeah? You want I should have Sal pay her a visit, unstring her?"

"No, no. That's all right. Car will be on its way as soon as I hang up."

"Be in your office when I get there. And have them suites ready. I need to get some shuteye after we talk."

Forty minutes later, Eddie was in his office when Thomaso Cortese and Salvatore "The Wolf" Lupo walked in.

Eddie stood up.

"Hello, Thomaso."

Thomaso nodded. "Eddie, you know Salvatore?"

"Never met him. Heard of him."

"Young man on the rise. Got *forza!*"

Eddie extended his hand to a big man with a smirk on his face.

"Eddie Mazzetti, Salvatore."

Salvatore waved his hand dismissively.

"Yeah."

Thomaso turned and stared at the young man.

Salvatore didn't say anything at first, but as the silence stretched on, he got uncomfortable.

"What?"

Thomaso slapped him hard on the back of the head.

"Show some respect, you little *stronza*. This man worked with Al Capone. Capone went to jail. Eddie didn't. Maybe you could learn somethin' here.

Now, get out until I call for you. I'm gonna talk with my associate."

Thomaso waited until Salvatore was out of the room.

"All right. Why can't your crew do one simple thing? I shoulda smacked you instead of Salvatore. Almost three months you've had to find the little Jap killed Frankie, and you got nothin'."

"We're not the only ones can't find her. All the families are lookin' for her. You got a contract, ten large on her. What's anybody come up with?

Same as us. Nothin'."

"There's a difference, Eddie."

"What's that?"

"You're sittin' out here fat, dumb and happy. You don't gotta hear the remarks when the Commission meets. How the Chicago Outfit let a tiny little woman kill Frankie "The Whale" and walk away.

I'm tellin' ya, Eddie, we're losin' respect. Losin' respect is dangerous in our business."

"I'm sorry, Thomaso. Believe me, we're doin' the best we can."

"Yeah? Not what I hear."

Eddie was very still.

"Who'd you hear it from?"

Thomaso gave Eddie a long, appraising look.

"You know, Eddie, there's always people lookin' to get ahead in the organization. And sometimes they got guts go over your head, come right to me. Even if they know you'll hear about it."

"*Madone!* Fiore Abbatini, that *figlio di puttana*! I'll have his ass for this."

"No, you won't. Was right, come to me. Tell you the truth, Eddie, he didn't complain about you. Not in so many words. Complained one a your top guys."

"He bitched out Clemente?"

Thomaso laughed. It was not a pleasant sound. "Not even Fiore's that crazy.

No. Tells me was times Guido didn't push hard enough. Let some chances get away."

"Get away how?"

"Fiore says Guido's losin' it. No fire in the belly no more. Hell, Fiore says he let some old man run him off with a shotgun. Didn't go back, square it."

"Thomaso, Fiore's a hot head. His dumb moves already brought the law into my office. The kind of law I can't buy and can't control."

"Yeah. Heard you was fronted by some hick deputy from California."

"Alicia!"

"Hey, just lookin' for the best chance like everyone else."

"I'll give her a chance! She'll be humpin' drinks to quarter slot players by tomorrow."

"No, she won't. Just like Fiore, want her right where she is. I return favors with favors."

"You here to run the show?"

"Not the casino or the hotel. None a that stuff. That's still you and Meyer.

Here to make sure we find that girl."

"But why here? Why not run it from Chicago?"

Thomaso was silent for a moment.

"Tell you why. You always was a good thinker, Eddie. Always. Al went down; you landed on your feet. Now you got this gig. Good food, good broads, big house, new cars, all the money you need. And you're good at this thing. We got no complaints, your operation. Keep the money rollin' in.

But you're not hard enough, Eddie."

"So, you want tough like Fiore?"

"Nah. Fiore couldn't think his way outta a closet. For instance, thinks your idea is nuts."

"What idea is that?"

"About the girl goin' to ground out there somewhere." Thomaso waved his hand toward the desert.

"But I think you're onta somethin'. I think she's out there, laughin' her ass off. Waitin' for us to forget her. But Tommy Bones don't forget. Not ever. And no one laughs at Tommy Bones, stays above ground.

164

So, Salvatore and me, we're gonna be your guests for a while. I need a little vacation anyway. Take in some shows, squeeze some a them showgirls, play some golf. Cause I got a feelin' Eddie. Got a feelin' somethin's gonna break soon. And I trust my gut. When it breaks, I'm gonna send the guys with an edge after it. Fiore Abbatini and Salvatore Lupo."

His voice dropped to a whisper again.

"There won't be no more soft shoe. That little whore is goin' down."

Thomaso walked out of the room.

Eddie didn't like having Thomaso Cortese and Salvatore Lupo in his town. Eddie loved Las Vegas, and he was afraid they would ruin it for him. Eddie thought he was the luckiest man in the world to be the Casino Manager at the Serengeti and even own a small percentage of the operation. There was nothing like the feeling he got walking across the floor of his casino. The noise, the smoke, the excited faces of the gamblers, the flashing lights and clanging of the slot machines.

He loved watching the parade of fools. Loved to watch them come in, beaming in anticipation, eyes glistening with excitement. Hurrying to the tables. Hurrying to jam money into his slot machines. Hurrying to buy more chips from the very dealer at the blackjack table who had just taken everything they had in front of them.

Part of it was the light. The light inside his casino was deceptive.

When people came in off the street, it seemed dim inside. It took their eyes a moment to adjust, and then it seemed normal. The light was that way for a reason. It was designed to lull gamblers into an otherworldly, somnambulant state. A twilight state, somewhere between wakefulness and dozing. A state where chips were not hard-earned money but heavy, reassuring objects that felt good in the hand. Objects to be tossed with abandon in exciting games. Objects you had to have. If you lost them, you bought more. Bought more until you'd spent every nickel and found yourself outside again, dazed, unbelieving. Devastated. Trying to think of a way to get more money and buy more chips.

The light had no obvious source. It was soft, but it came from every angle. There were no shadows in Eddie's casino. No place to hide any kind of deceptive act. And the light was forgiving. Made the gamblers and the friendly dealers and the cocktail waitresses look good. The cocktail waitresses who brought the free drinks to help you loosen up and forget how much you were losing.

Eddie controlled the light and everything else about the world inside his casino. The gamblers existed in an air conditioned bubble, the smoke-filled air circulating and re-circulating. No way to know if it was hot or cold outside. No way to know whether it was day or night. No way to know what time it was because there were no clocks.

And the sound was different. The casino was noisy, but the loud sounds were baffled. The carpeting and the ceilings caught the sounds and kept them from bouncing back. Even playing the slot machines with their incessant beeping and ringing and coins rattling in the trays, it was possible to carry on a conversation in a normal voice with the person next to you. No need to raise your voice.

And beneath the noise of the slots, the croupiers calling for bets, the shouts from the crap tables, the sounds of roulette wheels spinning and cards being shuffled and dealt, was the sound Eddie loved most of all. It was the sound of desperation. A constant, sub rosa background murmur. Voices heard but never quite understood. An endless, repetitious mumble that never stopped. The sound that meant The House was winning.

All the risks he had taken in the Capone organization back in the old days in Chicago. Bringing in illegal booze. Selling it to the speakeasies. The times he had almost been arrested. The times he had almost been killed by rival gangs. All that was behind him now. A Nevada gambling license was a license to steal! Eddie was amazed it was legal.

Sometimes, he would have his driver take him up and down the strip at midnight or one or two in the morning. The streets jammed with cars, the sidewalks packed with pedestrians. You could live for years in Las Vegas and never once see the night sky because of the glare from the millions of lights. All those people under those bright lights. People who should have been at home in bed in West Covina or Peoria or Phoenix. All those people in an exquisite hurry to lose their money and go home and tell everybody they had won a few bucks. Or broke even. Or made enough to pay for their trip. Or any other lie to keep from admitting to themselves they were suckers.

Chapter 12

Smoke Tree, California

And the mountains

Of the Eastern Mojave Desert

June 25, 1961

Aeden Snow

When I arrived at the Box S at sunrise the following Sunday morning, there were hundreds and hundreds of adobe bricks lying flat on the hardpan between the barn and the house. Joe Medrano was already at work on the east side of the house, marking out an area with metal stakes and white twine. I pulled on my work gloves as I got out of the car.

He was finishing the task as I walked up.

"Ade."

"Mr. Medrano."

"Joe's easier."

"Yessir. Joe, then."

He gestured toward the bricks scattered all over the ground.

"Solid. Turn on edge."

We went to work. Because the bricks were ten inches thick, they stayed upright when we turned them.

When we had them all standing, Joe said, "Cure in a week, this sun. Foundation now."

We walked to the area Joe had marked. There were two picks and two spades leaning against the house.

"String's the inside edge. Need a trench foot and a half deep, foot wide."

Joe started on one side. I started on the other.

If you've never attacked desert hardpan with a pick and shovel, you've been spared a lot of frustration. The whole experience gave me an appreciation for prospectors and hard-rock miners. It was very slow going, and we often had to resort to a pry bar to get stubborn rocks out of the way.

Halfway between the house and the southeast corner of the planned addition, I came across a huge rock. I was getting nowhere with the pry bar, so Joe came over to help. Even the two of us together could not budge it. Fortunately, I only had another six inches to go to reach the depth Joe wanted for the trench, so I used a chisel and a hand-held sledge to create a foot-wide, three-foot-long groove in the massive rock. Part of the foundation was going to be very solidly anchored!

We were almost finished with the trenching when Kiko came out and invited us in for a lunch of cold tamales and fiery-hot salsa washed down with iced tea. We were back at work when John Stonebridge drove up the driveway and walked over.

"Joe. Ade."

We both nodded.

John walked inside the trenched area and stood staring toward where the north wall of the addition would be. He turned to Joe.

"Just realized. It would be nice if Kiko had a fireplace."

Joe nodded.

"Be good."

"If I order a factory-built fireplace, could you frame it into the north wall?"

"Other two are stone. Could build you one from stone."

"That would be great."

"Be hotter than the ones you have."

"How's that?"

"Make drafts?"

"Yes. The fires are pretty, but when it's really cold, you have to stand right next to them to get warm and then only one side at a time."

"Make a better one."

"How?"

Joe picked up a stick. He got down on one knee to draw in the dirt. John got down beside him.

Kiko came outside. She walked over to where Joe was kneeling and casually sat down on the other side of him with her feet flat on the ground and her arms on her knees. I had never seen anyone sit like that before, but I was sure there was no way I could ever get in such a position.

Joe sketched out a U-shaped design. He talked as he drew.

"Two of these. One each side. Threaded, three-inch pipe. Elbows for turns, elbows on top. Mesh screen spot welded on the outside elbow. Keep things out. Other elbow sticks up inside. Open end points to the fire.

Start a fire. Heat pulls cold air in from outside. Fire gets hotter. More air comes in. Fire gets even hotter. No air pulled across the floor. No drafts."

"Very clever. Never heard of it before."

"Iroquois hunting lodges.'

"You've visited the Iroquois?"

Joe nodded.

"Depression. Rode the rails. Visited lots of reservations. Kept me from starving sometimes. Indians never turn you away."

"Always good when people help each other."

Joe nodded.

"Need anything but the pipe?"

"Steel plate. Torch and a welder in the barn. Build a flue."

John smiled.

"Joe, is there anything you can't build?"

Joe thought for a moment.

"Cars."

John laughed.

"Okay. Give Ade the measurements."

John turned his head and looked up at me.

"Ade, I'm being presumptuous by assuming you're coming up next Sunday."

"I'll be here."

"Okay, bring what Joe tells you. I'll give you a signed check. Fill in the amount and bring me an invoice.

Anything else, Joe?"

"Rocks. Lots of rocks. Volcanic rock is best."

"Ade, can you haul some rocks?"

"Okay."

"Kiko, maybe you could help?"

"Sounds like fun."

I wondered if John realized how happy he had just made me.

"Joe, I'm going to have to pay you more to add this to the room."

Joe nodded.

"Put a price together.

And I'm adding you to the payroll, Ade. All your days off have turned into work days."

"I'm learning a lot from Joe. That's payment enough."

"I know you're learning, but I won't feel right if I don't pay you. We'll settle on an amount."

John turned and walked toward the jeep.

Kiko rose to her feet in one smooth movement and went with him. She didn't push off with her hands. Just uncoiled and was on her feet.

Joe caught me staring at her and almost smiled.

"Trenches for pipes now."

We dug the new trenches and then blocked them with wood to keep the cement from filling them in. We mixed concrete and created the foundation for the room. We put inverted bolts in the wet cement so we could anchor the sill plate for the framing. We weren't finished until after sundown.

I stayed over for dinner again. John barbecued steaks and cooked foil-wrapped, sweet corn in the coals. When we went out to the veranda for coffee, the gibbous moon was dipping toward the western horizon.

Joe drank his coffee quickly and took his cup into the house. When he came back out he said, "Many thanks," and walked off down the driveway. It was not long before he disappeared from sight.

Even though I had seen him walk away, I hadn't heard him.

"Does Joe usually sit and talk with you after dinner?"

"Joe mostly listens. It's pretty rare to get more than a word or two out of him. Only time I heard him say much was when Kiko asked him a question related to the war."

"What did you ask him?"

"I was curious about something. I've had some unfriendly reactions from men I assume were veterans of the war in the Pacific. And I know Joe is a veteran."

"Unfriendly how?"

"I'll give you an example.

When I was a freshman at Cal Berkeley, I was dating an upperclassman. He took me to the Stanford game. Steve told me we were going to meet his parents there.

We were already in our seats when they showed up. His dad took one look at me and turned around and walked back up the steps and out of the stadium. Didn't say a word. His wife tried to make excuses for him, but I had seen that look before. I knew what it meant. Then she left too."

"What did your date say?"

"Said his dad was in the Pacific during the war. Hated Japanese people. He didn't know Steve was dating me. Steve thought if his dad met me and got to know me, he'd be okay with it.

The week after the game, Steve and his dad got in a big argument. His dad said Steve had to stop seeing me. We went out a few more times, and I guess his dad heard about it somehow. When the next semester started, Steve didn't come back to Cal. His frat brothers told me he'd transferred to a college on the east coast because his father wouldn't pay Steve's tuition if he came back to Cal.

I never heard from him again."

Except for the sound of the evening breeze, we sat in silence for a while.

"What did you ask Joe?"

"I asked him why he didn't seem to have those kinds of feelings, especially after the way he looked at me the first day we met.

He said, 'well, missy,' that's what he calls me now, 'missy,' 'well, missy, your cousins joined up'."

"'Yes,' I told him, 'but I think there's more.' He gave me one of those Joe almost-smiles. Then he said, 'Chemehuevi believe the woman who created us brought us across the ocean and dropped us in the desert. Chemehuevi believe she came from somewhere near where your ancestors lived

So, maybe you're related to Ocean Woman someway.'"

"Joe must have talked himself out with that explanation," said John, "because he hardly spoke for the next couple of evenings. Most evenings he does what he did tonight. Joins us out here for coffee and then walks off into the night."

"Doesn't he go to the bunkhouse?"

"Chaco and Phil tell me they never hear him come in. If they wake at first light, he's just there, already dressed. If they wake up after first light, he's already left. At least that's what they think must have happened, but they're not sure. They think maybe sometimes he hasn't been in the bunkhouse at all."

"Where do you think he goes at night?"

"I think he walks. I think Joe hears voices in the night. Remember when you told us about hearing voices out on the desert sometimes and not being able to understand what they're saying? I think Joe not only hears them, I think he goes out there and talks with them."

"That's spooky," said Kiko.

"Not to Joe. As he said the other day, 'It just is.'"

The three of us sat and visited for a while longer, but it wasn't long before my eyelids began to droop in spite of the coffee.

I got to my feet.

"Thanks for the great dinner. I'll see you in the morning."

"Ready to go rock hunting?" Kiko asked.

I tried not to sound too eager.

"I'm ready."

I drove down the switchbacks and onto Cedar Canyon Road. As I rose up the steep hill out of Watson's Wash, I caught a fleeting movement out of the corner of my eye. It might have been a deer, or a coyote, or a bobcat.

Or Chemehuevi Joe.

The next morning, Kiko and I set out to get rocks. I knew just the place, and it wasn't too far. East of the intersection of Cedar Canyon Road and Lanfair Road were some north-facing, low hills covered with volcanic rock. Yucca, reddish-pink barrel cactus and blackbrush dotted the hillsides. What made the rocks so unusual was that so many of them were almost the same size.

The terrain was very rough just beyond the road. I couldn't get the truck very close to the hillside. We had to carry the rocks down the hill and over to the pickup. It was slow, hot work. When we had a layer of rocks that nearly covered the bed of the truck, we sat on the tailgate to take a break.

As soon as we stopped moving, the silence settled in around us like a blanket. The sky was the deepest of blues and lacked even the wisp of a cloud. Two red tail hawks were riding the thermals high above the valley. A slight breeze whispered in from the north, and the distant New York Mountains shimmered in the heat. Then a raven croaked from one of the nearby Joshua trees.

We sat quietly for a while. I don't know what Kiko was thinking, but I was trying think of a way to get her to open up about her past.

"That day I brought the first load from Smoke Tree, something about the way you stood made me think you were a dancer. Are you? Were you?"

Kiko didn't answer for so long, I thought she wasn't going to. Then, as if she'd made some kind of a hard decision, she spoke.

"Yes. I minored in dance and theater."

"What was your major?"

"Microbiology."

"That sounds hard."

"Not if you like it."

"Do you have a degree?"

"Yes, a Bachelor's and a Master's."

"Ever try to do anything with the dance stuff?"

"After graduation, my roommate and I went to New York to break into show business."

"That's exciting. Did it work out?"

"My roommate had some success. She's very beautiful and very talented."

"I think you're beautiful too, Kiko."

As soon as the words were out of my mouth, I could feel my face turning red.

"Oh, look. He's blushing again."

"It's true. You are."

"It's nice you think so, Aeden. But there's one thing I'm definitely not."

"What's that?"

"White."

Under the hot sun in the middle of the huge, quiet desert, the word hung between us like a limp flag of regret.

She spoke again.

"So, my friend's job was to sing and dance in the chorus line in a Broadway show. A job we had both dreamed about in our dorm room.

But my job? My job was to be a waitress and go to audition after audition and be turned down – sometimes as soon as I walked onto the stage. Before I had a chance to sing a note or dance a step or read a line. Just a quick, 'thank you very much,' or sometimes not even that. Sometimes just 'next'."

"But at least you tried. I bet a lot of people aren't brave enough to do that."

"Cold comfort, Aeden. Cold comfort."

It was obvious Kiko thought many of her problems were because of her skin color. Her exile to the internment camp, her family's lost property, the ugly scene with her date's mother and father, her failure to penetrate the elite world of Broadway musicals: all caused by the fact she was Japanese. And I realized there was no way I could ever understand what it felt like not to be white.

"What was it like living in New York?"

The look on her face changed from bitterness to despair. Something far more painful than her failure to get work as a dancer had just crossed her mind.

174

She pulled a bandana from her pocket and wiped her face. When she pulled the bandana away, the sorrowful look was gone, replaced by a look I couldn't read.

She stood up abruptly.

"Let's finish this load and get back to the ranch. See if the mysterious Joe approves of our rocks."

Not a word passed between us as we finished carrying rocks and stacking them in the back of the truck. By the time we had as many as I thought we could get up the steep switchbacks at the ranch, the sun was directly overhead and brutally hot. I eased the truck along the hint of a trail that had allowed us to get a little closer to the hillsides. I was just about to pull onto Lanfair Road when I realized there was a truck coming from the north. Lanfair Valley traffic jam.

The driver slowed to look at us. I could see "OX Cattle Ranch" on the door. As he turned his head, Kiko pulled her LA Dodgers cap lower and looked like she was trying to sink into the floorboards.

She spoke without lifting her head.

"Who is that?"

"Cowboys from the OX."

"Why are they slowing down?"

Her voice was tight.

"People are friendly out here. Curious, too."

"What's happening now?"

"They're pulling off the road."

"Let's get out of here!"

"Take it easy, Kiko. They're just stopping at the phone booth."

She lifted her head a bit and leaned forward far enough to peek past me out the side window.

"There's a phone booth over there?"

"Yes. Only phone out this way."

One of the cowboys got out and walked to the booth.

Kiko seemed to relax. I eased the truck over the graded berm and onto the dirt road.

When we got back to the Box S, Joe walked over.

175

"Good. Two more loads, enough for the fireplace and chimney. Can get cinder rock over on Cima Dome. Firebox, back wall."

"I'll get something together for lunch," said Kiko as she walked toward the house.

Joe watched her go.

"She okay?"

"I don't know. We saw a couple of OX cowboys drive by. Spooked her real bad."

"Woman's watching for something. Always watching. See her looking down Cedar Canyon Road."

"What do you think she's watching for?"

"Nothing good."

After lunch, Kiko and I drove back to the hillside. There was very little conversation as we worked. A number of times she stopped working and stared up Lanfair Road.

When we got back in the pickup, I was just about to start the engine when she put her hand on my arm. It was the first time she had touched me since we shook hands on the day we met.

"Ade, I'm sorry I got upset this morning."

"It's all right."

"No, it isn't. It doesn't have anything to do with you or John or Joe. I'm just jumpy."

"Maybe sometime you could talk about yourself. Your life in Salinas. And college and your time in New York."

"Maybe. Not today."

"Okay."

"And maybe you could tell me something about yourself."

"Not much to tell. Just a kid from a hick town in the middle of nowhere."

Kiko smiled.

"I'm not so sure about that."

"You will be after you hear about my boring life."

Back at the Box S, Kiko looked almost happy as she helped Joe and me unload the rocks. She made jokes, trying unsuccessfully to get Joe to smile. When everything was off the truck, she headed for the house.

Joe pulled a piece of paper out of his shirt pocket. He had written down all the measurements for the pipes he wanted me to cut and thread and the information about the piece of steel he wanted for the flue.

"I'll bring this when I come next week.

While I'm gone, maybe Kiko will tell you what she's watching for."

"Doubt it."

Chapter 13

Las Vegas, Nevada

Fourth Week of June, 1961

Eddie Mazzetti sat with Thomaso "Tommy Bones" Cortese in the Shores of Tahiti Polynesian restaurant on a busy Friday evening. Thomaso was drunk and getting drunker. Eddie didn't like being seen in public with Thomaso, drunk or sober, but when Tommy Bones said, "Come to dinner with me," you went to dinner with him, no matter the consequences.

Thomaso had been drinking steadily ever since they sat down, and the drinks had certainly loosened his tongue. Eddie had never heard him talk so much. He was also talking loudly and beginning to slur his words.

"Some show them hula broads put on! Talk about shakin' it! Bet they could give you a real ride in bed."

"The marks like it. Place has been a money maker ever since we opened the door."

"Gotta give you credit, Eddie. You get these losers drive across the desert this heat just to go home broke in a couple days. You've figured somethin' out."

"Know what really made the place take off? We got them naked girls in the Moulin Rouge Revue walkin' around out there with stupid stuff on their heads and their boobs hangin' out. They don't sing, they don't dance! Just walk around. But we fill that show up every night with horny old men get to stare at them 'cause they brought their dumpy wives along. Makes it all right to ogle somethin' they get slapped for lookin' at anywhere else."

"Well, whatever it is, you sure as hell pack 'em in.

Hey, have that girl bring me another one a them scorpions. I can't seem to get enough to drink out here in this heat."

"How about some iced tea?"

Thomaso's eyes went to half mast and he stared at Eddie until Eddie felt like squirming.

"I wanna iced tea or a ginger ale or a pink lemonade or some other goddamned sissy drink, I'll let you know, Eddie. Now, get me another one of these scorpions."

Eddie didn't appreciate being ordered around in his own place, but he knew better than to complain about it. He signaled the waitress. She was at the table in an instant.

"Another scorpion for our guest."

"Yes sir, Mr. Mazzetti. Coming right up."

As she turned to go, Thomaso grabbed her arm

"And tell the bartender no umbrella this time. Last one almost poked me inna eye."

He let go of the waitress and laughed. It was not a pleasant sound. He had already had five of the powerful drinks in less than half an hour. He had also waved aside Eddie's attempts to get him to order some food. All he seemed to want to do was drink and be obnoxious.

Eddie didn't mind Thomaso eating and drinking and partying on the arm at the hotel. That was the prerogative of anyone from the leadership of The Outfit who was in town. What he didn't like was Thomaso's habit of walking into the counting room anytime he felt like it and pocketing thousands of dollars.

Eddie plastered a smile on his face to hide his anger.

"So Thomaso, how much longer you and Sal gonna be with us?"

"As long as we want. You got a problem with that?"

Eddie held up his hands, palms out. "No, no. Always glad to have you visit."

"Just yankin' your chain, Eddie! Another week or so is about all I can take. I tried playin' golf, but I can't even get in a whole early round before that goddamned sun burns me off the course. By ten o'clock, too hot even lay out by the pool.

But Sal and I are gonna stick it out just a little longer."

"Thomaso, you know I got no problem with you. Never have, never will. It's that Salvatore makes me nervous. I hear the Feds is lookin' at him, and I don't like to bring that kind of attention to our operation here. This is a sweet deal for everyone, and I want it to stay that way."

"What Feds you talkin' about?"

"F.B.I."

Thomaso laughed again.

"Relax, Eddie. Don't sweat those guys. We got Hoover in our pocket."

Eddie looked around the room to see if anyone was listening, then leaned forward.

"You tellin' me we're bribin' the head of the F.B.I.?"

"Even better. We got proof Hoover's a *finocchio*."

"I've heard stories about that. Never knew if they were true."

"They're true. Our guy on the West Coast, Roselli? He got the gen on a time Hoover and a boyfriend was picked up down in New Orleans in the twenties for bein' sissies. The cops knew who Hoover was and called the local Don, Sam 'Silver Dollar' Carolla, try and score some points. Carolla sprung Hoover, made the charges disappear, but kept a copy of the arrest record."

"Carolla was that tight with the cops?"

Thomaso smiled.

"Remember the story about him and Capone when Al was just startin' to get big?"

"Not really."

"Well, Carolla was runnin' South Louisiana. Took over from Matranga, Matranga retired in '22.

This is where Capone comes in. Matranga had been doin' some small time bootleggin' but Carolla kicked it way up. Flat out went to war with rivals for the business. After a lotta guys wised up or disappeared, Sam bought the cops. From them on, he controlled the product comin' in off the Gulf.

So, in '29, Al took the train down to New Orleans to tell Sam he had to sell his bootleg hooch to The Outfit instead of Joe Aiello if he wanted to do business in Chicago. But see, Aiello was *Siciliano*. So was Carolla. Had no intention doin' business with anybody but Aiello in Chicago.

Anyway, Sam met Capone at the depot. Brought a buncha cops he had in his pocket. Cops told Al's bodyguards give up their guns. They didn't. Cops took their guns, threw them in jail for a few days."

"What did Al do?"

"What the hell could he do? Got on the train, went back to Chicago."

"Okay, so Sam got a piece of paper 'cause he had some cops on a pad. But even if he did, the story doesn't sound like enough leverage to hold off Hoover."

"Yeah? Try this. New Year's Eve, 1936, Stork Club in New York, Frank Costello seen J. Edgar holdin' hands with his faggot squeeze, this Clyde Tolson guy. Had a photographer at the club take a picture.

"Yeah, yeah, but does anybody have real evidence besides a story from New Orleans and a picture in a night club with a bunch of other drunk people?"

Thomaso leaned closer and dropped his voice to a whisper. His breath smelled like rum, pineapple and death.

"Meyer Lansky's got pictures of Hoover naked with this other guy. And they wasn't playin' leap frog, if you know what I mean. Don't know how he got 'em, but Hoover knows he has 'em locked up somewhere. Hoover don't know where. He's scared shitless of Lansky.

And *that's* why Hoover don't bother us. Hell, he even said we don't exist! Told Congress ain't no such thing as the Mafia."

"But what about this new Attorney General, this Bobby Kennedy? He's J.F.K.s brother, for Chrissake. He's makin' a lotta noise about organized crime."

Thomaso leaned back. There was a worried look on his face for the first time that evening.

"Yeah, that could be a problem. That Kennedy prick don't know how to repay a favor. You know The Outfit give Kennedy Chicago, right? Wouldna won without it. Now he acts like he don't know us. Already dropped the ball with that bastard Castro. Cost us millions in Havana. And now this little *pazzo* Bobby's after Carlos Marcello and Jimmy Hoffa. Don't look good."

Thomaso shook his head.

"That's why I'm worried, Thomaso. What if Kennedy orders Hoover to come after us? He's Hoover's boss, right?"

"Not worried about that. Goddamned Hoover's been tellin' presidents where to stick it for years. Bastard's got the goods on everybody in Washington, and we've got the goods on Hoover.

No, the people we got to worry about are those Treasury guys."

"Yeah, I remember how they took Capone down."

"We got no leverage with them."

"No?"

"No. Look over my right shoulder. See the guy in the blue suit with the glasses? Looks like an accountant?"

"Yeah."

"T-man. Spotted him yesterday. That's why I'm not stayin' much longer. But I don't want to leave just yet. I've got a feelin' somethin's gonna break loose about that little *mignotta*, and when it does, I'm gonna make sure she gets her buckwheats."

Eddie shivered. And it wasn't because he cared that Kiko Yoshida was to be tortured before she was killed. It was because of the T-man Tommy Bones had drawn to his casino. If Treasury ever found out about the skim, his good life in Las Vegas was over.

Chapter 14

Smoke Tree, California

And the Mountains

Of the Eastern Mojave Desert

Fourth Week of June, 1961

Aeden Snow

In Smoke Tree, the constant, blustery, cold north winds of February and March are irritating to the point of madness. They howl and moan all day and all night for weeks on end, taking the humidity to near zero, cracking lips, making noses bleed, shaking houses and rattling windows and doors. The sand driven before the unending winds pits car windshields, scars paint jobs and leaves piles of grit on windowsills, no matter how securely windows are closed.

But the harsh winds of winter give way to mild breezes out of the west in April and May. Those are wonderful months in Smoke Tree. Because the humidity stays low, days in the nineties and even one hundreds are pleasant, and the lows dip into the seventies at night.

Most years, the good weather lasts through the first two weeks of June, but in 1961, we were blessed with one extra week. But just when we had been lulled into the false hope of a mild summer, the terrible heat of the Mojave came down on us like a hammer.

On the very day of the solstice, the sun rose like the baleful, angry, blood-red eye of a dragon over the Black Mountains. By ten o'clock, it was already a hundred and ten under a cloudless sky. By noon, it was clear any hope of overnight cooling was gone and would not return until early October.

When I got in my car to drive downtown for lunch, I had to wrap a rag around the steering wheel to keep from burning my hands. Rolling the windows all the way down was no help either. The inside of the car was still like an oven. The hot air swirled around me and sucked the moisture out of my skin as I drove to Renée's drive-in for lunch.

I got my five burgers for a dollar and carried them to an empty table beneath the overhang. The thermometer wired to the pole next to where I sat read one hundred and fifteen degrees. As I ate, I watched the traffic streaming by on 66. None of the older cars had air conditioning. I saw lots of red, irritated faces. Most of the tourists who had just dropped down the hill from Kingman, Arizona had no idea what lay ahead of them on their way to the coast. Those who had made it across the Mojave and were headed east still had the drive from Topock through Yucca and Kingman before they could leave the worst of the heat behind. Sixty more miles of steady climbing that could destroy radiators, rupture hoses, overwhelm water pumps and vapor lock carburetors.

The previous summer, when I worked at the '76, I tried to keep an eye out for cars with young children as they pulled into the station. Unsuspecting parents sometimes let kids get out of the car barefoot to dash to the restrooms, unaware the temperature on the blacktop could approach one hundred and eighty degrees. If I was too late to warn them, I tried to scoop up the closest kids, their faces already contorted with the first shock of the horrible heat blistering their feet.

Heat. Mojave heat. Dangerous, relentless, brutal heat. It felt like the flaming hydrogen plasma blasting off the surface of the sun had hurtled through space with the specific intent of blistering Smoke Tree from sunup to sundown. Over a hundred and twenty some days. Always over a hundred at midnight. Dropping into the low nineties just before dawn. And then the blazing fireball would lift above the horizon and start the assault again. On the twenty third of June, the temperature reached one hundred and twenty degrees for the first time in the year. It would hover in the vicinity for the rest of the summer.

The low desert heat took a toll on the hardiest plants. The white bursage looked dead because it gave up its tiny leaves to conserve moisture. Even matchweed, skeletonweed, and scorpionweed, all tough plants, drooped in the heat. Only the resilient creosote, with its extensive root system, was capable of staying green for months without rain.

Not only shrubs, but even large cactus could not survive the summer heat of the low desert. The reddish-pink barrel cactus, staghorn cholla, teddy bear cholla and Mojave mound cactus did not grow around Smoke Tree. Instead, they kept to the hillsides at higher elevations. Only the very small, ground-hugging types clung to life in the sparse shade beneath the creosote.

Work was a challenge. Mr. Halverson pretty much kept to the hardware store, leaving Will Bailey and me to custom cut lumber as required and load the varieties of building supplies onto the truck. I made the deliveries while Will stayed back at the yard to deal with other orders that came in.

When I drove the delivery truck through residential neighborhoods, it was rare to see anyone outside. Dogs and cats stayed shaded up next to trees and under porches. No birds flew or called. Children stayed indoors, with the exception of those lucky enough to get dropped off at the high school swimming pool, the only pool in Smoke Tree, to spend the entire day in a cloud of chlorine for twenty five cents. Life seemed to hold its breath, waiting to see if this would be the day the world finally burst into flame.

Two sounds predominated in the otherwise deserted neighborhoods. First was the constant murmur of swamp coolers. The second was the shrill, insane trilling of thousands upon thousands of Apache cicadas. They were loudest in the hottest parts of the day, as if the sun had driven them mad. They were everywhere in town and in the river bottom. Hundreds on every tree and shrub. Easily alarmed, clouds of them flew when disturbed, squirting out the liquid they had sucked from plants and trees as they went.

At around four o'clock, when the sun finally angled to the west, the temperature would drop below a hundred and ten. Little League teams would show up to practice at the town's two ball fields. Children would re-appear in the neighborhoods. Birds emerged from the trees and sat on telephone wires. But the dogs stayed under the porches until after sundown.

By the end of my work day, I was always wiped out. The gallons of water I drank and sweated out seemed to leach all the energy from me. All I wanted to do was get to the Colorado River. From lunch on I dreamed about its cool waters.

The river ran along the east edge of Smoke Tree, but it was not easy to get to without a car. And it was not a place parents let younger children visit on their own. Because of the strong current, it was as dangerous as it was appealing. But the few teenagers who owned cars went there as often as they could during the heat of the day and even lingered into the night.

As soon as we closed, I would drive to Sunset Beach. Taking off nothing but my boots and socks, I would walk to the northernmost end of the boat dock and dive in.

Instant bliss! Even on the hottest days, the temperature of the river never rose above fifty five degrees. In the terrible heat, the water felt frigid. I would let the strong current carry me swiftly to the south end of the dock where a rope tied to a cleat stretched out in the water. I would hang from it, letting the cold water flow over me as I twisted and turned and ducked under the surface, letting the river pull the heat from my body.

When I felt like all the sawdust, cement, gypsum, sand and sweat had washed off me, I would climb onto the dock. Stretching out on the planks, I would be completely dry within fifteen minutes. Sometimes, before I left, I would stop by the Sunset Beach snack shop to visit with my former girlfriend, Linda Bergstrom. Although we didn't date anymore, we were still friends. She was working over the summer between her freshman and sophomore years at Westmont College in Santa Barbara. Linda was the only person I knew who was in college. I had lots of questions for her.

I never had much appetite after a day in the sun, so I usually put off eating anything until after my evening run. My track season had come to an end after the C.I.F. individual quarterfinals in May, and I took a break from training. But because I was due to report for freshman football practice at Cambria College in the middle of August, I knew I had to start running again to get back in shape

As I pounded through the streets of Smoke Tree not long after sundown, there were very few people outside. Occasionally, I saw an adult watering a lawn, or some kids playing tag or hide and seek, but mostly I saw the flickering blue lights of televisions and heard music and canned laughter. The sounds came all the way to the street because windows were left open so swamp coolers could do their job.

Three years earlier, if I had run through the same neighborhoods, I would have seen people outside visiting in the twilight. Three years before, there had been no television in Smoke Tree. Because of the town's isolation, television had arrived very late. We were too far from any large city for television signals to reach us. But in 1958, a group of locals formed a club to raise money to bring TV to Smoke Tree. By 1959, they had enough subscribers to put what was called a "'translator" on top of a peak in the Black Mountains. It pulled in VHF signals from distant Las Vegas, converted them to UHF and beamed them to the valley below. Suddenly, Smoke Tree residents could watch ABC, NBC, CBS, and a Las Vegas channel that mostly played old movies and had some pretty awful local shows.

Residents became addicted. It was if the people of Smoke Tree were trying to make up for lost time. TVs in many households ran from sign-on in the morning to sign-off at midnight. Having a commercial window on the world changed the town, but in a strange way. Instead of making us feel more connected to the rest of the world, it reinforced our isolation.

People in Smoke Tree had always had a sense of "otherness. They had long referred to driving to the coast as "going inside," as in, "heard you went inside last week" if someone had driven to San Bernardino or Los Angeles. For all that travelers, tourists and commerce had flowed through Smoke Tree for decades, both on Highway 66 and over the Santa Fe tracks, the impact of the outside world on Smoke Tree had been very small.

But with the availability of television, "inside" took on a more complex meaning. TV reinforced the reverse concept: our perception of ourselves as being "outside". Residents began to understand with greater clarity how little we had in common with the people in the big cities of America. Before, life in the cities had simply seemed far away, but when the networks brought it into our homes, we saw it as something alien and different from life in Smoke Tree. It was as if the wider world was another dimension. One we could perceive but not penetrate.

The one item people rarely missed on their televisions was the network news segment about weather across the nation. We waited anxiously for the segment pointing out the cities with the highest and lowest temperatures for the day. We watched to see if we had been the hottest place in the country, a designation that routinely rotated between Smoke Tree, Death Valley and the tiny town of Thermal in the Coachella Valley. When it had been Smoke Tree, residents felt a tiny bump of excitement because someone on television had mentioned our name.

After jogging the streets for a few miles, I would make my way to the high school. Out on the track, I did my speed work, a series of exhausting three hundred and thirty yard sprints. After I was finished, I would circle the track at an easy pace to shake the lactic acid out of my legs before moving to the bleachers to rest for a while before running home. Sitting there alone in the darkness, I would think about leaving Smoke Tree.

I woke up before dawn on Sunday morning at Lee's Camp. I was well rested. It had been cool enough in the night for a thin blanket, a blessed change after a week in Smoke Tree. When I walked outside after breakfast, the thermometer by the front door read fifty eight degrees.

I beat the sunrise to the Box S. The new room was taking shape. Joe had framed it, leaving space for a large window with a southern exposure and a bigger gap for the fireplace on the north wall. He walked over to the car.

"Bring the stuff?"

"Got it all."

I opened the trunk and pulled out the pipe I had cut and threaded. We slid the bottom pipes with the elbows attached under the foundation, then twisted the other straight pieces and elbows into place. They came up inside the form Joe had built for the hearth. We mixed a batch of cement and filled in the trenches holding the pipes.

We got the four foot by four foot sheets of cold-rolled, weldable steel out of the back seat of my car and carried them one at a time to the barn. Inside, we laid them flat on the ground. Joe marked the metal with a piece of chalk and then lit the acetylene torch. I watched as he cut the pieces for the flue out of the metal. Then he marked some more of the metal for the flap and handle for the flue and cut those.

He shut down the torch and got the generator running for the welder. I held the pieces in place with my gloved hands and my eyes averted while he welded the whole contraption together. The last bit of welding he did was to tack the metal hinges onto the flap and onto the box and then weld a rod and slider into place so the flue would open and close. He took off the welder's helmet and shut down the generator.

He picked up the chalk and wrote "Patent Pending-Joe" on his creation. We were just walking out of the barn when Kiko came outside and called us for lunch. We ate a big pan of cornbread, chunks of cheddar cheese and a four-bean salad. Throughout the meal, Kiko seemed her old self, smiling and trying to make Joe laugh.

As we were having coffee, I asked Joe what was next.

"Take a ride. Kiko, you come too?"

"Always ready for a ride with my favorite guys."

Joe filled a desert water bag and hung it on the front of the truck. He had Kiko fill three big canteens with water from the pump in the kitchen. She asked him why we needed so much water.

"Hot where we're going."

"Where are we going?"

"Hunting obsidian."

Kiko left a note for John. We climbed into the truck with her in the middle. We took Kelso/Cima Road to the Union Pacific Depot, then turned south on Kelbaker Road and crossed the Union Pacific tracks. As we crossed, I looked down the long row of salt cedars that stretched along both sides of the tracks to keep the sand from the Kelso Dunes from drifting across the rails. Mediterranean trees, thriving in the middle of the Mojave.

We climbed the blacktop road all the way to the pass through the Granite Mountains. I thought maybe we would stop there, but Joe kept going down past the Old Dad Mountains and on toward Highway 66. Now I knew why we had all the water. If there was anyplace hotter than Smoke Tree or Death Valley on a summer day, it was Bristol Dry Lake.

When we reached 66 and turned west toward Amboy, Kiko's posture changed. She pulled her Dodger's cap low and slouched down the way she had when the OX cowboys had driven by on Lanfair Road.

"Where are we going, Joe?" she asked in an anxious, tight voice.

"Down the road a ways."

She did not speak again.

We drove past both Amboy and Bagdad without stopping. A few miles west of the Cafe Bagdad and the service station, Joe pulled the truck onto the shoulder to wait for a break in the traffic. The flow was steady and we were still waiting when a highway patrol car pulled in behind us. I watched through the side view mirror as the patrolman got out and walked up to my side of the truck.

"You folks all right?"

"Fine."

"Thought maybe you had car trouble."

"Nope. Waitin' to cross the road."

"Where you headed?"

Joe turned to face him.

"Stedman."

The patrolman looked closer.

"Joe Medrano! Didn't realize that was you."

"Yep."

"Usually see you hitching. Never seen you drive before. Do you have a license?"

191

"Yessir," said Joe, reaching for his wallet.

The officer held up his hand.

"That's okay, Joe. If you say you have one, I know you do."

The patrolman looked at me.

"Well, Aeden Snow. How's your mom and dad, Ade? Haven't seen them in a while."

"Real good, Mr. Scarborough."

I was aware that Kiko had not looked up. I could feel the tension in her leg where it rested against mine. Her mouth was set in a thin line, and her right hand was balled into a fist. Even though the temperature in the already-hot cab had climbed even higher while we were parked under the blazing sun, Kiko looked like she was freezing. Her face was bloodless.

"Well, careful crossing the highway, Joe."

He turned and walked back to his unit.

Kiko kept her head down as she spoke.

"You know that man?"

"That's Stan Scarborough. Lives down the street from us."

She bobbed her head but did not look up.

The patrol car pulled out from behind us and merged with the westbound traffic. Kiko relaxed. She unclenched her fist and color returned to her face.

When there was a break in the traffic, Joe drove the truck across the highway and onto a dirt road that wound off to the southwest. After a few miles, the road began to climb, and we came to a fork in the road. A crude, bullet-riddled, wooden sign lettered "Bagdad-Chase Mine" pointed off to the west. In the distance I could see the raised roadbed of the abandoned Ludlow and Southern, a railroad that had once served the mines at Stedman. Joe took the southeast fork for another two miles and then turned off onto a barely discernible track that wandered south, paralleling the low foothills of the Bullion Mountains.

He turned off the track into a narrow wash, dropping the transmission into compound low. We crept along. The hillside on the south side of the wash was covered with lava rock, and in another half mile we came to the edge of the lava flow itself. Joe stopped the truck. We all got out.

Joe looked behind us. He stood listening.

Kiko, who seemed to feel better now that we had left the highway behind, started to say something, but Joe lifted a finger to his lips.

We stood there a while longer. The great stillness settled around us. There was not even the whisper of a breeze. The heat was stifling. It must have been close to a hundred and twenty. Nothing moved. Not a bird, not a lizard, not even an insect. Sweat poured off my face. Kiko looked faint. Joe didn't even seem to notice the heat.

He looked at me.

"Never tell about this place. Rock hounds clean it out."

He led us farther up the wash, now choked with boulders, creosote, bursage and a few struggling catclaw shrubs. Then, on the right bank, underneath the overhang from the edge of the lava flow, I saw something glinting. As we walked closer, it realized it was obsidian, shining like black glass in the sun

"What we're here for. Set this in the cement in the hearth. Reflect firelight for the missy"

We spent the better part of two sweaty hours selecting pieces of obsidian and carrying them to the pickup. When Joe thought we had enough, he said, "One more thing."

He led us back up the wash beyond the trove of obsidian. He stopped and looked around for a minute, then walked over to a large rock. Dropping to his knees, he dug into the sand and gravel with his hands and uncovered two objects the size of cannonballs. He handed one to me and set off toward the truck.

"How did you know those were there?"

"Put them there three, four years ago."

"What are they?

"Geodes. Rock people say none here. Found these. Thought I might want them someday."

"What are you going to do with them?" asked Kiko.

"Have Ade take them to the rock guy in Smoke Tree."

A brief smile appeared on Joe's face.

"One of the guys says none here.

Cut them in half."

"Why?"

193

"Full of crystals. Pretty."

It was late afternoon when we took the turnoff east of Amboy and headed for home. It was twilight by the time we reached the Box S. We were tired and hungry and thirsty. All three canteens were empty. So was the Desert Bag.

We could smell the smoke from John's mesquite barbecue fire when we stopped the truck. He walked around the house to meet us.

"I have potatoes on the grill. There's a big salad in the refrigerator. I'll put the steaks on and toast the garlic bread while you wash up. You look hungry."

"Could eat the hide steaks came in," said Joe.

We put in another long day on Monday. I learned a lot more from Joe about construction. We started by mixing concrete and pouring the hearth for the fireplace. While the cement was still wet, Joe set in place the pieces of obsidian. He used the geodes to make four depressions where he would mortar the halves in place at an angle once they had been cut. He did it all without hesitation. It was clear to me he had already planned where each piece would go while we were gathering the rocks. While we waited for the concrete to set up, Joe laid out the stones for the outside wall of the fireplace and the exterior chimney on the ground north of the addition. Then he did the same with the cinder rock that would make the firebox and the stones that would face the inside of the finished room.

Kiko came outside as he was finishing up.

"Looks like a puzzle."

"Sort of."

"What are you going to do next?"

"Tear out the wall."

We went inside the house and taped sheets of plastic over the section we were going to remove and then went back out and covered the damp cement of the hearth with more plastic. Once everything was in place, we began the process of removing the wall. It was messy, dirty work. As Joe had expected, the wall had been made with a double layer of adobe bricks. It was over three feet thick. No wonder the house stayed cool in the summer. It gave me an odd feeling to look at bricks someone had set into place all those years ago.

Partway through the job, we broke for lunch. We were so dirty we ate outside.

We went back to work. By late afternoon, we had finished removing the wall. I helped Joe nail up the plywood sheets and enclose the new room. We were pounding the last nails just before sundown when John drove up in the ranch jeep. Chaco and Phil climbed over the side and headed for the bunkhouse.

John came over and stood, examining our work.

"Looking like a room, Joe."

Joe nodded.

"Insulation, drywall next. Have a question."

"Go ahead."

"Conduit in the walls for electricity someday?"

"No. I'll not have some damned generator destroying the peace and quiet of the ranch."

He shook his head.

"You know, Joe, man gets electricity and pretty soon there's a radio blaring, and after that he's climbing up to the top of Pinto Mountain to stick up a TV antenna to try and pick up a signal from Las Vegas. No way! If the world ends, I want to be the last one to know."

Joe nodded.

"Good."

I walked up to the soapstone sink outside the bunkhouse and washed the worst of the dirt off before starting home. When I came back, Joe, John and Kiko were talking about something. John and Kiko were both laughing. They heard me walking up, and all three turned toward me. Something about the scene made me feel good in a way I hadn't in a while. I realized what it was. These people were my friends.

I thought maybe when old friends are lost, new ones appear.

I said goodbye to everyone and headed for my car. I was getting in when I realized John had come with me.

"Are you coming up next weekend?"

"Yes."

"I wasn't sure, since next Tuesday is the Fourth of July. I thought you might have other plans."

"No, I'd like to help Joe some more."

"Ade, you have been real hard at it. How about taking a day off on the Fourth and doing something for me?"

"Okay."

"I'd like you to take Kiko to the river."

"I'd like that. Do you she'll want to go?"

"Might take some persuading. The only time she's been out of this area was yesterday when you and Joe took her to hunt for obsidian."

"She got real nervous when we got to 66. And then we were parked on the shoulder waiting to cross the highway south of Bagdad, and Stan Scarborough pulled in behind us in his Highway Patrol car. I thought Kiko was going to faint."

"I'm sure that has something to do with who or what she was running from the night I brought her home from Baker. But I'd like her to get a little break from this place. I'm going to be in Barstow this week. I'll get her a bathing suit, and when I come back, I'll start getting her used to the idea she's going to the river.

Do you know a place where you wouldn't be likely to run into a lot of other people?"

"I know a few beaches below Bullhead you can only reach on dirt roads."

"Good. When you come up next week, get ready for a day off."

Chapter 15

Smoke Tree, California

And the mountains

Of the Eastern Mojave Desert

Last Week of June

And the

Fourth of July, 1961

The last week of June, the door to the Mojave blast furnace opened and stayed open in Smoke Tree. A hundred and fifteen on Tuesday, a hundred and seventeen on Wednesday and a hundred and eighteen on Thursday and Friday. After sundown, reddish-orange heat lightning flickered on the horizons like the darting tongue of some demented beast licking at the ridgelines. Because the almost unbearable heat continued day after day without relief, there was no way our overworked swamp cooler could cope. Temperatures in our house were still in the nineties when I went to bed at night. It was harder and harder to get to sleep. Even if I managed to nod off, I usually woke up drenched in sweat an hour or so later.

I was young and healthy, but the long days in the sun and the restless nights were taking a toll. At the end of each work day, I hung longer and longer from the rope at the end of the dock at Sunset Beach, twisting and turning in the cold current of the Colorado as I tried to leach the accumulated heat out of my body. The hot days killed my appetite. I began to lose weight. Weight I would need when freshman football started.

In the evenings, I had to force myself out the door for my workout. Running through the quiet streets of town before I went to the high school track for my speed work gave me lots of time to think. But I rarely thought good thoughts.

I thought about the events at the House of Three Murders the previous fall, turning them over and over in my mind. My pointless, obsessive analysis an endless parade of "what ifs." I thought about going away to college to a place I had never even seen. I worried about whether I would fit in there. My ex-girlfriend had described Cambria as the snootiest college on the west coast. That didn't sound good.

One night after I got home from my run, I was sitting in my room reading "Fear and Trembling" by Soren Kierkegaard. It was one of the books the admissions office at Cambria had sent. I was supposed to read the books and be prepared to discuss them at freshman orientation.

Sweat poured down my face in the stifling room as I tried to make sense of Kierkegaard's discussion of the difference between Abraham and Agamemnon. I couldn't see much. Abraham didn't want to kill his son and couldn't understand why killing him would please God. Agamemnon wanted to kill his daughter because he was sure it would please the State. So what? No matter what these two men thought about their situations, their kids were going to wind up dead. Old Soren didn't seem concerned about that. Seemed like a big deal to me.

As I tried to think of a coherent way to explain my concerns in some future group discussion, the phone rang. I heard my mom answer it and walk down the hall.

"Ade, it's Mrs. Braithwaite for you."

Mrs. Braithwaite was the reason I was going to college. I had never seriously considered it before she asked me to think about it. The only woman on the Tribal Council of the Fort Mohave Band of Mojave Indians, she was a very determined person. She had wrangled a scholarship for her son Billy to Cambria College because the school was seeking "diversification."

Billy was a classmate of mine confined to a wheelchair years before by polio. Once Mrs. Braithwaite had his scholarship in hand, her next concern was for Billy going off to college alone. She wanted me to go with him to be his roommate and help ward off the homesickness he would feel for the Colorado River, the ancestral home of the Mojave Indian Tribe. She was confident she could get me a scholarship because of my grades and athletic achievements.

After I thought if over for a few days and discussed it with my parents, I told her I was interested. She turned her efforts toward getting a scholarship for me. The poor people at Cambria College had probably never had a chance once she started pounding on their door. It wasn't long before I was filling out applications.

"Good evening, Mrs. Braithwaite."

"Good evening, Aeden. We need to get together and talk about transportation arrangements to get you and Billy to the college. I've talked to the people at housing and arranged for Billy to come to school with you early when you report for football practice."

"We'll drive up in my car. It's old and ugly, but it runs good."

"I see you haven't read all the way through your orientation packet."

"No, ma'am. I've been reading the books."

"I've read through everything. Freshmen at Cambria are not allowed to bring cars."

"Oh."

"We're going to have to make other arrangements."

I digested that bit of news.

"Mrs. Braithwaite, Dad's in Barstow, but he'll be back tomorrow evening. I'll ask him about getting us up there on the train."

"That would be good."

There was a long pause. Then Mrs. Braithwaite cleared her throat.

"Aeden, I'm not quite sure how to say this."

"Say what?"

There was another silence.

"Let me put it this way. Money is an issue for Billy and me. As in, we have very little of it."

I could sense her embarrassment and felt like an idiot for not realizing how difficult finances would be for her and Billy, even with a full scholarship.

"Let me talk to my dad. I'm sure he can come up with an idea."

"Thank you, Aeden.

Now, I think the three of us should sit down and talk. Could you come to our house this Friday evening?"

"What time?"

By the time Friday evening arrived, Dad had solved the problem. Trains were an expensive way to travel, but the sons and daughters of railroad employees could ride certain trains for free. Not the fancy ones like The Chief or The Super Chief, but slower trains like the Grand Canyon. Those trains were basically a few ancient passenger coaches and a mail car. The Grand Canyon could get us to Union Station in Los Angeles, and since my dad knew all the conductors, we could slip Billy on for free.

Getting up the coast, would be more challenging. The San Francisco Chief was another expensive train the children of employees couldn't ride for free. But Dad knew the conductors who worked that train too. Once we were sure what day we were leaving, Dad would talk to the conductor about letting us sit in the observation car without paying a fare. Of course, this meant we wouldn't have an assigned seat in one of the coaches because we wouldn't officially even be on the train. But that would get us to the central coast. Since the closest stop to Cambria on the Santa Fe was San Luis Obispo, Mrs. Braithwaite said she would research the cost of a bus ride from there to Cambria and the coordination of the bus and train schedules.

Billy was a gifted and determined student. He had already finished all the books and was starting through them again. We talked about what we had read and tried to figure out what would come up in the orientation discussions. Mrs. Braithwaite joined in. She had read them too.

It was even hotter at the Braithwaite's than at home. Their tiny house lacked even a swamp cooler. Also, some of the screens were ripped, and since Mrs. Braithwaite was saving every penny for Billy's expenses at college, she couldn't afford to replace them. Mosquitoes from the river bottom buzzed around the room as we talked. We laughed about the irony of three people in a desert town sweating and swatting mosquitoes while discussing a book written by a man from a rich family in frigid Copenhagen.

When I drove out of the Mojave Village that night, I tried to get used to the idea I would be leaving Smoke Tree. I had committed, and whatever I felt about it, I was going.

I arrived at the Box S on Sunday morning to discover Joe had finished the insulation and the drywall and fitted the knotty pine planks to the walls and ceiling. They gave the room a soft, comfortable glow.

On Sunday and most of Monday, we built the fireplace.

Let me clarify that. I carried rocks to Joe and mixed small batches of mortar while *he* built the fireplace. When he finished the part inside the new room, the volcanic rock contrasted beautifully with the varnished pine. It was going to be a wonderful room. I could imagine Kiko sitting in there on a cold, winter evening, reading a book.

By Monday afternoon, the fireplace was complete, inside and out.

I asked Joe what was next. He pointed at the subfloor of the new room.

"Make tiles for the floor. Molds for roof tiles."

We went to the mountainside behind the house and dug out an oven-shaped enclosure where Joe would fire the floor and roof tiles once they were made. When we finished, we drove over to Government Holes and gathered a good collection of downed cottonwood branches for the fire.

That evening, we had another wonderful dinner. A dish Kiko created from shrimp that John had brought home from Barstow. I didn't know there was anything you could do with shrimp besides deep fry them the way they did at the Jade.

After dinner we sat on the veranda, surrounded by the wonderful, velvet stillness of the desert night and talked and laughed while John and Joe and I alternated turning the crank on the ice cream maker. We had apricot ice cream with our coffee.

On the Fourth of July, I slept in for the first time in a long while. It was wonderful to sleep in a place cool enough that I could stay in bed late. And even though I had slept much later than usual, the sun still had not hit the slot canyon by the time I was ready to leave.

It was hotter out in Carruthers Canyon, but nothing like the heat down on the low desert. There was a soft breeze coming out of the south. It carried the scent of pinyon and sage into the car.

When I pulled into the driveway at the Box S, the adobe was in the full sun, the light splashing off the white plaster and bleeding into the red tile roof. The horses ran to the corral fence and watched me go by. There was nobody outside working. Looked like even the tireless Joe Medrano had taken the day off.

Kiko came out of the house wearing cut-off Levi's, a T-shirt, tennis shoes and her Dodger's cap. She was carrying a picnic basket and two towels.

I got out and opened the door for her.

"Good morning, Ade. John commanded me to go to the river with you today."

"I'm glad. I hope you like it."

We headed down the switchbacks.

"He also bought me a bikini. I told him there was no way in the world I was wearing that."

She laughed.

"Maybe a fourteen-year-old girl could wear the one he brought home, but not me."

When we turned east on Cedar Canyon Road, rattling down the heavily washboarded dirt road with the windows rolled down made conversation difficult. Very little was said until we reached the short, paved section of Lanfair Road just before we turned onto Old 66 and drove through Goffs.

As we drove the highway, Kiko asked a lot of questions about the desert around us. In the upper reaches of Sacramento Wash, she pointed at the pale trees.

"What are those?"

"Smoke Trees. This is the northernmost stand."

"They're beautiful."

"They look like ghosts under a full moon."

The temperature rose as we drove down the hill. When we reached Arrowhead Junction and stopped at the stop sign before turning north on 95, I pointed over at Mr. Stanton's station.

"The first day I came to the ranch I told you I was late because I had stopped to help someone. The old man who lives at that station was the person I stopped to help. Mr. Stanton was lying in the gravel in front of the station. Turned out he'd had a stroke."

"He's lucky you came by. Doesn't look like the kind of place where a lot of people would stop."

As we drove on, a broad desert tableau stretched around us. It was in the transition zone to low desert: filled with creosote, burroweed, bayonet yucca, rock, sand and sky. Inhospitable. Forbidding. Unforgiving. Beautiful.

When we reached a dirt road that stretched away to the northeast, I turned off the highway. After a few miles, we entered Nevada. There was no sign marking the border between the two states. To our north, the Newberry Mountains rose over five thousand feet above Lake Mojave and the Colorado River. The dirt road turned to blacktop just before we reached Davis Dam. By the time we drove across the dam into Arizona, we were in low desert. The heat was worse. We turned south on the blacktop paralleling the river.

Kiko stared at the river as we drove.

"This is only the third time I've even seen the Colorado. I saw it when we arrived in Parker and never saw it again until we left Poston after the war."

As we approached the service station and liquor store, the only two commercial buildings in Bullhead, I asked Kiko if she'd like a soda pop. She quickly answered, "No. Please, just keep going."

We drove past the buildings toward the low, rolling hills. Before we had gone too far, I turned off onto a faint track that wound through the mesquite trees and westward toward the river. The fine silt of the river bottom, the product of a million years of deposits laid down when the river had roamed all over the valley before it was dammed, blossomed into a cloud that ballooned up behind us.

The heat in the stillness of the mesquites was incredible: dense, palpable, an almost living presence. The thorny mesquites scraped the faded paint on my clunker as we approached the Colorado. The steadily increasing humidity made it feel like a steam bath inside the car.

When we broke out of the thicket, I turned south on the dike road the Bureau of Reclamation created after trapping the Colorado in a narrow channel. After half a bone-jarring mile, I pulled onto one of the revetments that jutted into the river, put in place to keep the river from eating its way out of confinement.

Below us lay a perfect, private beach. I turned off the engine. In the sudden stillness, the only sounds were the gurgle of the river as it swirled around the revetment and the high-pitched shrilling of millions of heat-crazed Apache cicadas calling from the mesquites bordering the dike road.

"What's that sound?"

"Cicadas, but everyone out here calls them locusts. The hotter it gets, the louder they get."

We carried our picnic basket and our towels down to the secluded beach that stretched between two promontories. The promontories and the riverbank itself behind the sandy beach were lined with a dense stand of tamarisk. Before I went back to the car to change into my swim trunks, I asked Kiko what kind of a swimmer she was.

"Okay. Not great. I used to swim in the ocean and Monterey Bay now and then."

"The current is very strong. Maybe you should wait until I get back before you jump in."

"Okay. But hurry! I'm dying to cool off."

As soon as I changed and climbed back down to the beach, Kiko took off her cap and waded into the river wearing her cut-offs and T-shirt. She turned and looked back at me.

"I didn't know it would be this cold."

She waded out a little farther. The river dropped off sharply and took her off her feet. She yelped in surprise.

I walked rapidly along the beach beside her, ready to jump in if she got too far out into the river, but she turned and swam to shore before she reached the next revetment.

She was laughing as she got out.

"That feels wonderful! It's so cold I've got goose bumps."

"You're gonna want to jump in again after a few minutes. You'll be burning up again. We call it 'ins and outs'."

"I could get used to that."

She peeled off her T-shirt. She had a modest halter top underneath.

I couldn't help wishing she'd worn the bikini. I was sure she'd look better in it than any fourteen year old girl.

She spread out a towel and sat down. I put the other towel down and sat beside her.

After a few minutes, she said, "I see what you mean about getting hot again so quick."

She ran and jumped back in the river. I dove in behind her. We floated to the end of the beach, got out and walked back to our towels.

After ten or twelve ins and outs, we were walking back up the beach when we heard a boat approaching from downriver. We couldn't see it yet. Kiko hurried back to her towel, pulled on the T-shirt, jammed on her cap and lowered her head as the boat came into view out in the middle of the channel.

There were two couples in the boat. They waved and I waved back. Kiko didn't raise her head until the boat sounded far away.

"What do you think those people are doing?"

"Looked like a ski boat. Big Mercury on the back."

Kiko seemed to be fine once the boat was gone.

"Hot already."

She took off her shirt and hat and we started ins and outs again, setting the tempo so we never got too hot or too cold. We were climbing out of the water when we heard the boat coming back. It sounded like it was moving very fast.

Kiko reacted the same way she had before.

The boat came into view, towing a skier on a single ski. The driver pulled her in circles in front of us. She was a very good skier and put on quite a show, jumping wakes and leaning over so far her pony tail touched the water.

Kiko kept her head down and saw none of this. After a few more circles, the boat sped off down river, the Mercury screaming at full throttle.

Kiko looked up as the boat receded but didn't take off her cap and shirt until the sound had died away completely.

"How about some lunch?"

While we were eating, Kiko said, "Aeden, you were going to tell me about your boring life. I'm very curious to know why you're off in the mountains every weekend and not back in town or at this wonderful river with your friends.

Don't you have a girlfriend?"

"Did once. Don't anymore."

Kiko laughed and punched my shoulder.

"Listen to you! You've been working with Joe so long you're starting to sound like him. Come on, spill it, what happened with your girl?"

"She's a year older than me. She went off to college last year and met someone new. Didn't tell me about it. Just stood me up for Homecoming. I had to hear about her new guy from her mother."

"That must have been hard for you."

I thought about it.

"It wasn't as hard as I thought it would be. I guess it wasn't that serious to begin with."

"Why didn't you find another one? You're a healthy, good lookin' boy. Must be girls who would go out with you."

"That's not the problem."

"Then what is?"

"It's a long story. You sure you want to hear about a bunch of teenagers in Smoke Tree?"

"Please, tell me. It can't be any worse than a bunch of teenagers in Salinas."

"Okay. Across the river there, way back in those mesquite thickets, there was an old place called the House of Three Murders. Some people were shot to death there a long, long time ago and the house was abandoned. Me, my best friend, Johnny and his girlfriend, Judy, ended up there one night last fall when we were supposed to be somewhere else."

I paused.

"You really want to hear this?"

"Don't stop now! You had me hooked at the name of the house."

So, I told Kiko about burning down the House of Three Murders and what happened after we did it. When I was done, Kiko didn't say anything for a while. I could tell she was thinking things through.

"Okay. Your best friend and this Charlie person joined the army. I'm sure you miss your friend, but that doesn't explain why you're off in the desert all the time."

"It didn't happen all at once. It really started even before that night. See, when my girlfriend went off to college I didn't want to date anyone else. I thought it was important to be loyal.

Linda and I and Judy and Johnny used to do stuff together, but after Linda left, it wasn't the same. I didn't want to tag along behind Johnny and Judy."

"Three's a crowd, huh?"

"That was part of it, but not all of it. Watching those two together was like waiting for an ax to fall.

As soon as Johnny fell for Judy, I knew he was in trouble. She was beautiful and smart and rich, but she was never, ever in love with my friend, and she was never going to be. She was only marking time until she could get out of Smoke Tree. She just wanted to have the guy all the other girls in school wanted. To prove she could.

He just wasn't the same after he found out what she was really like."

"Young love, huh?"

"That's what my dad said.

You probably think it's just some dopey kid talking, but I don't think Johnny will ever love anyone again."

She was quiet again for a while.

"I don't think you're dopey. But there's more to the story, right?"

"Yeah. Like I said, I was already off on my own a lot. I was spending my weekends over at Lee's Camp, and I could feel myself just peeling away from everybody else. Then, after Johnny left, everybody kept asking all the wrong questions."

"Like what?"

"Like were Johnny and Judy having sex? Was that why Judy's dad sent her away? Was Judy pregnant? Like that."

"So, the questions bothered you and you didn't want to talk about what had happened?"

"The worst thing was the question nobody asked. Nobody asked about Charlie Merriman. He was just a good guy in the wrong place at the wrong time, but he ended up in a trial on this side of the river because the robbery where Sixto got shot was at that liquor store we passed back in Bullhead. If it hadn't been for Lieutenant Caballo and a smart lawyer who took the case for next to nothing, he would've spent years in prison.

But nobody cared. They didn't care because he's Mojave. People in Smoke Tree don't care about the Mojaves."

"I can see why that would bother you. But at least he got to join the Army instead of going to jail."

"And my best friend thought it was so wrong he joined with him on the buddy system. Or at least that's why he told me he did it. I think Johnny just wanted out of Smoke Tree."

"So you're unhappy with your classmates."

"Yes."

She turned toward me.

"You're too hard on people, Aeden. You might think about cutting them a little slack.

Did you ever try to explain any of this to them?"

"No."

"So you just turned your back on everyone."

"I guess so.

Then I lucked into this good job at the lumber yard right before the school year ended. I had to go straight to work right after school every day, so I couldn't go to graduation practice. The rule at Smoke Tree is: no graduation practice, no graduation ceremony. So I didn't go to graduation. That iced it."

"I can see how it would."

By the time we finished lunch, the sun was directly overhead. We were being broiled. We did ins and outs for a long time, enjoying the cold water. When we were sitting on our towels again, I said, "I told you my story. Your turn.

I know about Poston. I know you have a degree from Cal. I know you went to New York, but there's a lot I don't know."

"Maybe you know enough."

"No fair!"

Kiko sat staring at the river for a long time before she seemed to come to a decision. She stood up quickly.

"Let me take another dip before I tell you. It may take a while."

She dove into the river and stayed underwater until she popped up at the far end of the beach. She walked back very slowly, as if she were turning something over in her mind.

"I hesitate to tell you this. I'm afraid you'll think less of me after you hear my story."

"I don't think so."

"Okay, here goes.

At Cal, I was dating a guy who was in his third year at law school when I was a senior. Like your friend's girl, he was from a wealthy family. We dated all year. I thought we were getting very serious."

She pulled her knees up and wrapped her arms around them.

"Here comes the hard part.

You have to understand, Aeden, this was before the pill. Birth control wasn't even close to a hundred percent effective.

We got physical. One of us wasn't careful enough

208

About a month before graduation, I found out I was pregnant.

I didn't know what to do. I don't know what I expected when I told Danny. I mean, I know I was a senior in college. And I was a biology major for heaven's sake. But in a way I was still naive girl from a very strict home in a small town."

"What did this guy say when you told him?"

"I'll never forget it. These were his exact words: 'A stiff dick has no conscience'."

I had never in my life heard language like that from a girl or a woman, but I wasn't embarrassed. I just felt bad for Kiko.

"I was stunned. I thought we were both in love. I was hoping he'd say, 'Let's get married'.

But the worst part was what he said next. 'You've got to get rid of it'.

'Get rid of it!' Not, 'let's talk about this and decide what to do'. Just, 'Get rid of it! As if it were a piece of meat that had gone bad or a faulty appliance.

I was such a fool.

I went home to ask Mother for advice, but of course, she told Father, and all hell broke loose."

"Did you ask her not to tell your father?"

"Yes, but that just shows how stupid I was.

My mother is a very traditional, obedient little Japanese wife, submissive and self-effacing. There was no way she was going to keep her daughter's secret.

If the father had been a Japanese boy, and we were going to get married before the baby was born, I think Father would secretly have been pleased. You see, he had been hoping I would get married right after high school to a Japanese boy I was dating.

Father never wanted me to go to college. Said it was not right. I was supposed to get married and be a dutiful Japanese wife and have babies. Preferably boy babies. My parents never contributed a penny toward my education. I worked on campus so I could buy my books and have a little spending money."

"So, the big problem was this guy wouldn't marry you?"

"No. That was the little problem. The big problem was this guy was a *Haku-jin*."

209

"Which means?"

Kiko smiled a brief smile.

"White boy.

Because of *that*, my father disowned me. Said I had brought shame on the family. Told me he didn't have a daughter anymore."

"What did your mother say?"

"She apologized to my father for raising such an unworthy daughter.

So, I left. There was nothing else to do. I went back to school and took my finals and graduated. And I told Danny I would get an abortion, but he'd have to pay for it. When he gave me the money, it was more than I would need for the abortion, and he knew it. And I knew it. It was buy-off money from his family. I was just an unfortunate, best-forgotten bump on the road to Danny's successful life.

But I took the money and went to New York with Allison."

We sat without speaking. The water swirled and gurgled around the end of the revetment, churning up sand that rose to the surface before it was pulled downstream in the current.

After a while, I broke the silence.

"Aren't abortions very dangerous? I mean, I've heard stories of women dying."

"I suppose they are, but I never for one minute intended to have one!

Allison and I rented a tiny place in New York and started taking dance classes and looking for work in a show. Any show. On or off Broadway."

She looked straight up into the sky.

"If I'm honest, I suppose I have to admit I was hoping all the hard training would take the problem out of my hands. If something had happened naturally, I suppose I would have been relieved.

But it didn't.

By the time I began to show, I was almost out of money, and there weren't going to be anymore dance lessons or auditions. I got a job as a waitress. When I got too far along to work, I went to what was euphemistically called a home for unwed mothers. An adoption mill, really.

I gave birth there."

"A boy or a girl?"

"I don't know. They took the baby out of the room as soon as they cut the cord. I never saw the child. The new parents picked the baby up a few hours later."

She looked out over the river.

"Somewhere out there is a little person, six years old now. A little person I think about every day, but one I'll never know.

But I hope that little person is a boy."

"Why?"

"If he was adopted by a Japanese couple, he will be pampered and spoiled and fussed over all his life. But if she's a girl adopted by that same couple, she'll be treated like a servant.

Even if she's adopted by a white couple, her life will not be as good as it would be if she were a boy.

I'm convinced that's true."

I felt like an insensitive clod. Here I had been going on and on about my stupid, teenage troubles to a woman who had experienced things that were ten times worse.

Still, I felt I had to say something.

"Kiko, I'm sure someday you'll get married and have children. And you'll be a wonderful mother."

"No," she said. "I will never have children."

I stumbled ahead when I should have kept my mouth shut.

"You might change your mind someday."

"It's not a matter of changing my mind. The people at the home were of a moralistic bent. In spite of the fact they had no qualms about making lots of money for their adoption services, they strongly encouraged us wayward girls to have a procedure so we could never get 'in trouble' again.

Believe me, I didn't need much encouragement. I let them sterilize me. I will not be giving birth to any children."

We were both sweating, so we started doing ins and outs again. But there was no joy in it, although I think it was a relief for Kiko that I couldn't tell whether her face was wet from the river or from her tears. Our day had turned somber. In spite of the blazing, desert sun, the sky seemed dark somehow.

We swam and sat and swam and sat without speaking until I asked a question that in retrospect I never should have asked.

"Did you ever try to talk to your mom and dad after that day you left?"

"I tried to call them a few times. Neither one of them would speak with me. I sent them a graduation announcement, but they didn't come."

"Have you tried since then?"

"What's the use? Kiko no longer exists for the people who live in the little house on the edge of an onion field in Salinas."

"Kiko, your dad sounds like a hard man. An unforgiving man. But what about your mom?"

"She will never disobey my father."

"Maybe not, but I'll bet she thinks about you all the time.

Do you think she loved you when you were growing up?"

"We were very close when I was growing up. That's why it hurts so much."

"So, she really doesn't know what became of you?"

"No."

"It's probably not for me to butt in, and you can tell me to mind my own business, but don't you think you should write to her? Even if it's just a little note to let her know you're okay."

"Father would never let her read it."

"Is he home when the mail comes?"

"Sometimes, but not often. He's usually at work."

"Well, there you go. Write her. She can either show him the letter or get rid of it, but at least you'll put her mind at rest. It must be torture for her not knowing where you are."

"Let me think about that, Ade."

Kiko seemed to brighten after that. We swam and talked until the sun began to tilt to the west, and the heat abated a little. We packed up and drove across the dam and on west until we left Nevada. We continued down the dirt road and then turned south onto 95.

I think the heat had taken a toll on Kiko. She fell asleep shortly after we got onto the highway, her head resting against the window, her Dodger cap low over her eyes.

When we reached Arrowhead Junction, I pulled off the road and drove under the overhang at Mr. Stanton's station. Kiko woke up. It seemed to take a moment for her to get her bearings.

"Why are we stopping?"

"I want to check on Mr. Stanton. I haven't seen him in a while.

Want to come in?"

"No, you go ahead.

By the time I got out, Mr. Stanton was coming down the steps.

"Hiddy, Ade. Haven't seen you in a coon's age."

"Hello, Mr. Stanton. Your lights are usually out when I go by. I don't want to bother you."

Mr. Stanton laughed.

"Never a bother, Ade. I'm usually up late listenin' to my radio. Just no need to keep the light on and waste all that 'lectricity.

You knock anytime, hear?"

"Okay.

So, how have you been?"

"Fit as a fiddle! Feelin' like my old self. How 'bout you?"

"Real good, Mr. Stanton. Real good.

Well, just wanted to make sure you were okay. I'd best be getting on. I'll stop next time I'm by if it's not too late."

"You do that. Gets a mite lonely out here at times."

We shook hands, and I turned and walked back to the car. Mr. Stanton followed me. He stopped at Kiko's door.

"Hello, young lady. Didn't know young Master Snow had a friend with him."

I could tell Kiko didn't want to talk, but she made an effort to be polite.

"Hello, Mr. Stanton. Aeden has told me about you."

"Did he tell you he saved my bacon?"

"He said he stopped to help you one day. He didn't make a big deal of it."

"Well, he's a good'un, Ade is. If he hadn't stopped that day, I'd be pushin' up daisies."

I was standing on the other side of the car with my door open.

"Mr. Stanton, this is Kiko Yoshida."

He doffed his cap.

"Charmed, I'm sure. Any friend of Aeden's is a friend of mine. Y'all stop by anytime."

"Thank you, Mr. Stanton. I'm glad to meet you."

I got in the car, leaned across Kiko and said goodbye. As we pulled out of the parking lot, I could see him in my rearview mirror. He still had his cap off as he stood watching us go.

When we crested the hill above Goffs, a crimson sunset was bleeding into the dark indigo of the early evening sky above the Providence Mountains. The dark shadow of the cinder cone southwest of the town bulked on the horizon. As we turned northwest and started down the hill toward the tiny town, a rocket arced into the darkening sky, followed quickly by two more. I pulled well off the road and shut down the engine. We sat for a while and watched as more small rockets went up, followed by Roman candles and fountains. Occasionally, we could see flashes from firecrackers, but we were too far away to hear the explosions.

As we sat watching the Fourth of July fireworks show in the Lanfair Valley, the last of the color leached out of the sky. Night settled around and over us. Kiko spoke out of the darkness.

"I've thought about what you said about my mother. I'm going to write her a brief letter as soon as we get to the ranch. Will you mail it for me?"

I smiled. "It was my idea! I'll be happy to mail it."

We sat in silence a little longer as the number of fireworks slowly dwindled.

"I have a question, Kiko."

"Yes?"

"Does it seem to you that John keeps trying to throw us together?"

"In a way."

"Why do you think that is?"

"I think he just wants me to have a friend a little closer to my own age."

I took a deep breath and forged ahead.

"Please don't take this wrong, but is there anything going on between you two? That is, well … what I mean is..."

Kiko laughed.

214

"I know exactly what you mean, Aeden. And no, there is no John Stonebridge-Kiko Yoshida romance."

"You can see why I would ask, can't you? I mean, he's building a special room at the ranch just for you."

"I know. I didn't ask him to do that. I even tried to discourage him because I don't know how long I'll be here. But now I'm glad he did it. I got to meet you and Joe, so now I have three good friends instead of just one.

But John is building me the room because he's a very lonely man. He's out on his mountain by himself, except for the hands. I think he just wants someone to talk to about books and music and other things in the evening. According to John, those things don't interest Phil or Chaco.

And Aeden, I love it out there. I've never felt so at peace in my life. I wish I could stay forever!"

"Why can't you?"

"I can't tell you that."

"Why not?"

"I just can't."

"Then tell me why you think John's so lonely? I mean, he's well-known, well-respected, seems to have lots of money. Why hasn't he ever found a wife?"

"You really don't know, do you?"

"Know what?"

"Let me put this delicately. John is not attracted to women in that way. Not to me, not to any woman."

I didn't respond.

"For goodness sake, John's a homosexual, Aeden. He's a wonderful man. He's just a little differently wired, that's all."

I was shocked. I knew there were homosexuals. I just didn't think there were any out our way. It would be years before I found out there were indeed homosexuals in Smoke Tree. Some of them had been schoolmates of mine, and I had never had any idea. I can't imagine how lonely they were while we were growing up.

"How do you know he's, uh, you know, that way? Did he tell you?"

"He didn't have to. I've been in San Francisco and the Castro District many times. Believe me, I don't have to ask. Nor would I ever ask such a thing.

215

I just know. And John knows I know. I can tell. And I think someday he may want to talk about it."

So John's not the only one waiting for someone to let go of secrets, I thought.

"Do you think anyone else knows?"

"Out here? In John Wayne land? Goodness no. And don't ever tell anyone what I suspect. It would destroy John's reputation."

"I can keep a secret, Kiko, and I will."

I thought for a minute, turning this information over in my mind. I decided it didn't make any difference whether Kiko was right or not.

That's when I realized the rockets, Roman candles and fountains had stopped.

I started the car, pulled back on the road and headed down the hill. As we drove, we could still see flashes from firecrackers.

As we got closer to town, I pushed down hard on the accelerator.

"Why are we speeding up?"

"You'll see when we go by the store."

As soon as we were past the store, I got on the brakes before we hit the railroad crossing.

"I don't get it. What was I supposed to see?"

"Did you see a bunch of guys tossing firecrackers?"

"Yes."

"Those were cowboys from the ranches out this way. They usually come to Goffs on the Fourth of July."

"So?"

"Were they standing next to something big? Something white?"

She thought a minute.

"Yes."

"That's the propane tank for the store.

The cowboys come down here and drink all afternoon. When it gets dark, they go out and light fireworks. Of course, they're pretty drunk by then, and it's not long before they start daring each other to light fireworks next to the propane tank."

"Oh, Lord.

What does the person who owns the store say?"

He says, 'Have another six pack, boys'."

When the pavement ended and we hit the graded dirt road, I slowed down. It wasn't long before Kiko fell asleep again, her Dodger's cap turned sideways as she leaned against the window. I don't know what had tired her most: sunlight, swimming or sadness.

She woke briefly when I slowed to turn off Lanfair onto Cedar Canyon Road. In the green light from the dashboard, she looked childlike and confused. After looking around for a moment, she smiled at me and went back to sleep. She didn't wake up again until we turned off Cedar Canyon onto the ranch road.

The house was dark when we topped the switchbacks and drove up the driveway. John had apparently been sitting in the darkness on the veranda because he lit one of the big carriage lamps and carried it out to the car as we came to a stop. He held it up for us while Kiko climbed out. I got the picnic basket and towels out of the back seat.

When we reached the veranda, Kiko took the lamp from John and went into the house. John and I sat on the comfortable chairs in the darkness with our feet propped on the railing.

For a while, neither of us spoke. There was no moon, and we sat looking at a million stars. The summer triangle was in the sky: Venus in the west, Cassiopeia, Mars and Scorpio to the south and southeast.

"Good day?"

"Yes. She liked the river. Wore her out. She fell asleep on the way home."

"Were the crazy cowboys at Goffs?"

"They were."

"Around the propane tank?"

"As usual."

John laughed.

"Cowboys! One of these days they're going to blow that place sky high."

As we sat enjoying the evening, I thought about what Kiko had told me about John and realized again I didn't care. I felt the same about him as I ever had.

"Do you think Kiko went to bed?"

"Nossir. I think she went in to write a letter to her mom. Let her know she's okay."

"Did you suggest that?"

"I did."

"Well, you've had more luck on that score than I ever have. Good for you."

After a while, Kiko came back out with the lamp. She was carrying a letter.

"Took me longer to find an envelope than it did to write the letter. That drawer in the kitchen is a mess, John."

She handed me the letter.

"Please mail this for me, Aeden."

"I will."

"You'll have to put a stamp on it."

"I think I can spare four cents."

I took the letter and started to the car. Kiko came with me. John stayed on the porch.

When I opened my door, Kiko put her hand on mine, stood on tiptoe, and gave me a peck on the cheek.

"Thank you, Ade, for being a friend."

"Anytime. When you want to go the river again, just let me know."

I got in and put the letter in the glove compartment.

As I drove slowly down the switchbacks, I turned on KOMA. The station jingle came on: "Might pretty, in Oklahoma City." I thought a commercial would follow, so I reached to turn it off, but the Shirelles came on singing "Will You Love Me Tomorrow?"

When I was almost to Arrowhead Junction, I remembered what Mr. Stanton had said about getting lonely sometimes. I thought I'd check on him. But as I was approaching the intersection, the crossing gates went down on the Santa Fe tracks. A headlight pierced the night. The engineer blew for the crossing, and I heard the deep, heavy thrum of the three big diesels as they strained to pull the long string of cars up the grade. I stopped and watched the train as it crossed highway 95 between the intersection and Mr. Stanton's station. The train was slowing down instead of speeding up as the uphill grade grew steeper. It was going to be a long wait. I was tired. I decided to visit Mr. Stanton next time through. I turned right and headed for home.

Would that I had stopped. A lot of things might have turned out differently.

Chapter 16

Las Vegas, Nevada

Smoke Tree, California

And the open desert

Between those two cities

July 8, 1961

Eddie Mazzetti called Thomaso Cortese's room at noon. The phone rang for a long time.

"Yeah."

"Eddie Mazzetti."

"This better be good, goombah. We was out real late last night. Feel like I just got to sleep."

"This is way better than good. The crumb we have in the post office in Salinas called."

"Yeah?"

"The Yoshida's girl's parents got a letter from her this mornin'."

"What'd she say?"

"Thomaso, this guy won't steal a letter. Afraid he'll lose his job"

"What's the return address?"

"Wasn't any. But he has a sample of her handwritin'. He says it's from her for sure."

"What's the postmark?"

"Smoke Tree."

"Sonofabitch, you was right! And I was right to come out here.

Meetin', your office, twenty minutes. I'll bring Sal. You round up Clemente and Fiore.

And Eddie?"

"Yeah?"

"Have some coffee, tomato juice and Danish sent up. My head's killin' me."

The moral depth of the five men seated at the table in Eddie Mazzetti's office could be represented by a flat line drawn with a number four pencil on the very bottom of a sheet of black paper.

Thomaso Cortese spoke with a mouth full of the Danish he was waving in his hand. Pieces of the flaky pastry flew out of his mouth.

"Eddie was right all along. This little *mignotta* is somewhere down in that crap town. And you two," he pointed at Salvatore and Fiore, "are gonna find her. And you're gonna take her out in the middle of nowhere and make her tell you what she done with that money. And then you're gonna cancel her ticket.

But you're gonna do it slow. Take one a them Polaroid cameras with you. I want pictures every step of the way, from the time she don't have a mark on her until the time she's dead."

"Are you sure that's wise, Thomaso?"

"Eddie, like I told you the other night, you're a smart guy, but you're gettin' soft. 'Wise' got nothin' to do with this. We need these pictures for a lesson, a whadyya call it," he snapped his fingers," a, a..."

He looked at Eddie.

222

"What's the word I'm lookin' for here?"

"Object?"

"Yeah! That's the one. A object lesson. A lesson what happens to someone takes down a made man, steals from The Outfit.

People who do that? They don't just disappear. That's too easy. They disappear ugly."

He pointed at Fiore and Salvatore with the remains of the pastry.

"Do I make myself real clear here?"

Both men nodded.

He looked at Fiore.

"I heard from Eddie how you did it in Smoke Tree the last time. With the gumshoe licenses and all?

None of that crap this time. Go in with detective badges. Say this girl's wanted for murder. Tell them she killed her roommate.

And you shake this broad loose."

"Got it, boss."

Eddie spoke up again.

"What about that deputy, came to my office?"

"What about him?"

"He gets wind of this while they're in town, Salvatore and Fiore could be in big trouble."

Thomaso's voice dropped to a whisper.

"Listen to me. I ain't worried about what some small town..."

"County, Thomaso, not town. County."

Thomaso closed his eyes. The room went quiet. Salvatore, who had been pouring himself another cup of coffee, stopped with the carafe poised above the rim.

When Thomaso opened his eyes, they were blazing. But his voice was a whisper.

"You wanna go along, Eddie? Maybe kiss this yokel's ass, he shows up?"

Eddie swallowed. He didn't trust himself to try to speak. He shook his head.

"Good! Salvatore and Fiore are doin' this. Doin' it today. Not lettin' this bitch get away again.

Fiore, you remember the places you checked last time?"

"Sure, Mr. Cortese."

"Don't bother doin' them again.

This is a little place, right?"

"Yeah. Real hick town."

"You wanna get businesses you missed last time, that's okay.

But I want somethin' else too.

First motel you come to? Stop. Send Salvatore in. They ain't seen him before. Have him get one a them chamber of commerce maps, you know, the ones have a buncha ads, show all the streets in town?

I want you to knock at one house on every block. Show the picture. Tell the story. Work your way through the whole town. Got it?"

"Yes, Mr. Cortese."

"And find the library. These smart broads? They can't stand to be without no books. Who knows, might have a library card."

He laughed.

"Wouldn't that be somethin'? Broad gets snuffed 'cause she has a library card."

The men laughed, glad to have the tension leave the room.

"Any questions?"

Both men shook their heads.

"Okay. Get after it.

And don't forget the camera!"

Salvatore and Fiore got up and started toward the door.

"Hey?"

Both men turned around.

"One more thing. Long time ago, my *Antonate* used to tell me stories about Italy before it turned into a dump. Back when there was Romans and stuff. Caesar and them guys, you know?

Anyway, *Nonno* said they had a thing they told them legions, sent them out to fight. Said, 'Come home with your shield or on it.'

224

You know what that means?"

The two men looked confused.

Thomaso's voice dropped to a whisper again.

"Means don't come back here and tell me you couldn't find her, don't know where she went. Believe me, you don't wanna do that!!"

When Salvatore Lupo and Fiore Abbatini drove east out of Las Vegas on the Boulder Highway, it was not long after noon. Their car cast no shadow they could see. But when they turned south onto Highway 95 at Railroad Pass, their shadow appeared beside them, so sharply delineated that Fiore could see the window openings and the profile of his head flickering by on the slightly raised shoulder of the empty road.

It was not long before the road turned more sharply downhill. As they descended, the vegetation around them began to dwindle. Soon, even the Creosote was gone. The sandy soil was full of alkali creosote could not tolerate and sulfates even alkali-loving plants could not accommodate. Soon a wasteland devoid of anything but sand stretched out before them, the heat shimmering above the expanse and forming the false promise of a mirage above the blacktop far below them.

A few miles ahead, they could see a small billboard of some kind beside the road. Lone evidence of the hand of man for miles in any direction. When they got close enough to read the lettering, Salvatore shook his head.

"Slow down a minute."

Fiore brought their speed down from eighty to twenty miles an hour. It felt like they were crawling.

Salvatore read the sign aloud.

"'No Fishing 1,000 yards'? The hell that mean?"

"Dunno."

"How far's a thousand yards?"

"A little more'n half a mile."

"Stop, you get that far."

Fiore watched the odometer roll up the tenths. Then he came to a stop.

Salvatore opened the door, stepped out, and stood looking in all directions. He got back in the car.

"Turn around."

"Why?"

";Because I hate a smart ass. Take me back to that sign."

"Sal, we're a long way from this place we're goin'. Every place out here, far apart. Should keep movin'."

Sal ignored him.

Fiore shrugged, made a 'K' turn and drove back up the highway. When they drew parallel to the sign, Salvatore said, "Stop here.

Got extra rounds, these guns?"

"Glove compartment."

Salvatore opened it and looked inside.

He slammed it shut and opened his door.

"C'mon."

The sign was twenty yards off the road. As they walked over the bare terrain, Fiore could feel the sand coming over the tops of his loafers and filling his shoes.

When they reached the sign, Salvatore looked up and down the highway. Save theirs, there were no cars visible. He suddenly drew his .45 and fired into the left hand post until the slide locked back. A wisp of smoke drifted from the chamber. The sign tilted slightly. The sound of the shots rolled off into the desert and was swallowed as if it had never been. The smell of gunpowder and cordite hung momentarily in the air and then drifted away in the hot wind, leaving little trace of its passing. Salvatore turned to Fiore and spoke in an unnaturally loud voice, as people momentarily deafened often do.

"Gimme the clip outta your gun."

Fiore swallowed and tried to clear his ears, but he was still half deaf.

He popped the clip out of his .45 and handed it over. Salvatore walked to the other end of the sign, slammed the full clip into his gun and emptied it into the post there. The sound rolled away as before. Was swallowed as before. The smell of gunpowder and cordite hung monetarily in the air and then drifted off leaving little trace, just as before.

The sign still stood.

Salvatore ejected the clip and put it in his pocket along with the other empty magazine. He put the gun back in his shoulder rig. Sweat was pouring off his face and running down his torso. He shook his head. Sweat flew off his nose. It evaporated the instant it hit the hot sand.

He stepped up to the post and leaned against it.

Once again, he spoke in a loud voice. "Gimme a hand here."

Fiore put his hands against the other post.

"Push."

They put their considerable weight and leverage into their effort. Slowly at first, and then all at once, the sign toppled.

When it fell to the ground, the two men walked to the car, got in, turned around and continued on their way. Salvatore was already thumbing replacement rounds into the magazines.

"Jesus," said Fiore. "I can't believe we just killed a sign."

Behind them, the sign lay flat on the sand, the letters etched sharply against the white background in the glaring sun. Before the car was out of sight, a dust devil kicked up and blew across the sandy expanse. It obliterated the footprints the men had made. When the dust devil blew off into the distance, there was a sheen of sand and grit on the sign.

A raven neither man had seen circling high above them landed next to the shiny shell casings and pushed at them with its beak. It picked one up and lifted off into the air.

A half hour later, they were coming up on Arrowhead Junction. Fiore nodded toward the service station there.

"Old man lives there? Stuck a shotgun in my face. This job is done, comin' down here some night, paint the walls with the sonofabitch."

They drove on.

Nothing was said until they were almost to Smoke Tree.

A building beside the road just outside of town had a sign that read, "Rock House."

"Didn't get this place last time."

He pulled the car off the highway and into the parking lot. There were no other vehicles.

It seemed very dim inside the store after the glare of the sun. There was an old man standing behind a glass counter.

"Help you gentlemen with something?"

"We sure hope you can," said Fiore. "I'm Detective Blake, and this is my partner, Detective Kinston." Both men held up the shields. "We're from the Las Vegas Police Department."

He took the picture of Kiko out of his inside pocket.

"We're looking for this woman in connection with a murder. Have you seen her?"

The man took the photo and examined it closely.

"Japanese, isn't she?"

"That's right, sir."

He shook his head.

"I'm sorry. I haven't."

"Well, never hurts to ask. We'd really like to get hold of her. She murdered her roommate in cold blood."

The man stood thinking.

"This is a real long shot, and if the woman in the picture wasn't an oriental, I'd not even mention it, but we don't get many oriental people out this way."

Fiore was suddenly very alert.

"Anything you can tell us might help."

"Fella comes in here from Goffs time to time. Brings me rocks he finds out in the Paiute Mountains. He was by the other day. He mentioned something to me that seemed odd. Some of the boys from the OX ranch was down at his store on the Fourth of July. Said he heard one of the cowboys telling someone else he'd seen an oriental woman out his way. Said it surprised him.

"Young or old?"

"Didn't say. Don't know whether the cowboy told the other person that. Just stuck in my head."

"Sounds like someone we might want to talk to. Can you tell us how to get to this place?"

"Sure."

He reached under the counter and got out pencil and paper. He drew them a map showing 66 and 95.

"Now, when you're on 95, you're gonna go through a place called Klinefelter. Old busted down motel there. When you get past it, you'll come to a place where the railroad tracks cross the highway."

"By that old service station?"

"That's the place. Don't go over the crossing. Just before you get to it, a road turns off to your left. That's old highway 66. Get on it and it'll take you right to Goffs. Can't miss it. Nothing else out there. Stop in at the store."

"Which store?"

"Only the one."

"Who should we talk to?"

"Chuck Sweeney. Tell him Don Clark sent you."

"Thanks for your help, Sir."

"Anytime, officers. Always glad to help the police."

When they got back in the car, Fiore said, "What do you think?"

"I think the old fart is right. It's a long shot.

Let's do town first. Don't turn nothin' up, we'll try this Goffs place."

They drove on into town and stopped at the first motel they came to, an ugly stucco building with the flat, rock-covered roof common on buildings where it rains but rarely. The motel itself was nothing more than an office connected to a string of single story rooms. The sign in the parking lot read "Have fun on the Colorado River. Colorado River Days 1959."

Salvatore went inside and came back with a chamber of commerce map of Smoke Tree. The two men drove to the Foster's Freeze. A little whitewashed building so bright in the sun it hurt their eyes. They parked in the shade of a huge aethel tree. They each got a root beer float and planned their search.

By the time they had completed most of the neighborhoods on the north side of town, they had not found anyone who had either seen or heard of Kiko Yoshida. They sat in the car after their last, unsuccessful attempt. Fiore picked up the map.

"Tommy Bones said try the library. When Tommy says to do somethin', best do it, so let's find the library. It's right in the middle of town. Probably gonna close soon."

The library was in an old complex cater-corner and across the street from the Santa Fe depot. They left the car next to a five and dime fronting the small park just beyond the station. They walked to the corner and waited to cross the street. Since the street was the part of Highway 66 that ran through town, they waited a long time, sweating in their blazers under the desert sun.

229

While they stood watching the passing cars, Fiore said, "I can't remember last time I was in a library."

Salvatore thought a minute.

"Hell, I can't either. High school, maybe."

By the time they climbed the concrete steps to the library, both of them were drenched.

They pushed through the double doors. It was cooler inside, but not much. At least the sun wasn't beating down on them.

The old, wooden floorboards creaked and groaned beneath their tasseled loafers as they walked to the librarian's desk. A thin, elderly woman looked up at them over her half-moon reading glasses, immediately curious about two men dressed so formally on such a hot day.

"May I help you?"

Fiore and Salvatore held up their Las Vegas Police Department badges.

"I certainly hope so, ma'am. I'm Detective Blake, and this is my partner Detective Kinston."

He got out the picture of Kiko and handed it to the woman.

"We're from the Las Vegas Police Department. We're looking for that woman. She murdered her roommate last spring. We have information that she may be in Smoke Tree."

The librarian seemed to consider carefully what he had said.

"I am surprised you're not accompanied by an agent of local law enforcement, detective."

"We just got this tip this morning. We wanted to follow up on it quickly."

"But you think she came this way last spring and is still here?"

"It's possible.

She's a college person, this woman. We thought she might get a library card."

"I see."

Salvatore and Fiore could tell she didn't believe them, but she was studying the picture as if she did when the day went south on them.

Lieutenant Caballo was in his office trying to catch up on paperwork from the previous week, but his phone would not stop ringing The calls didn't come directly into his office, but the dispatcher had instructions to ring them through if the caller asked to speak to Horse personally. Many callers did.

As he struggled to end the call with Lilly Menendez, he was wondering if he should make up a "do not forward" list.

"Mrs. Menendez, I sympathize with your frustration, but you can't file a complaint against the Smoke Tree Police Department with my office. Our departments cooperate with each other."

"Well, I guess that's good for you, but they don't cooperate with me. *No se supone para sevir todo el pueblo?*" she asked, so angry she was slipping in and out of Spanish.

"*Si, senora, ciertamente.*"

"Then why don't they come when I call? *Es que no les gusta venir a la parte mexicano de la ciudad? A caso el jefe sabe que hay gente mexicanos que viven aqui?*

"*Senora* Menendez, I'm sure the chief knows there are Mexican people in Smoke Tree."

"Well then, he needs to remind all those *policias blancos* who work for him. *Porque* Horse, I have called about my neighbor many, many times. He comes home *barracho* and drives over my yard. Sometimes over my garbage can. Last week he ran over my mail box. Next he's gonna run over my *nietos*.

Luego va en es casa. Sucia y convierte su musica tan fuerte como sea possible. That rock *y* roll trash. *Y sabes porque* he does this thing?"

"Yes, Mrs. Menendez, you've told me before."

"That's right, he beats up his wife, *y no quiero a nadie a escuschas sus aritos.* Poor woman."

"Mrs. Menendez …"

"*Por favor*, Horse, call me Lilly. I've know you since you were a boy."

"All right, Lilly, I'll pass this on to the chief personally."

"And one more thing..."

The dispatcher appeared in Horse's doorway.

"Urgent call, Lieutenant."

Horse put his hand over the phone. "Let me finish up here."

"You're gonna want to take this one right now, believe me sir."

"Okay."

231

He uncovered the mouthpiece.

"My apologies Mrs. Menendez, but I have an emergency."

"I understand, Horse. Thank you for your help."

Horse punched the other line.

"Horse, here."

"Lieutenant, glad I caught you. Jim Garret."

"What can I do for you, Mr. Garret?"

"Remember back in May when I called you about those guys from Las Vegas with the picture of the girl?"

"Yes sir, I do."

"They're back.

I never forget a car, and I even remember the license plate on that one 'cause I wrote it down to call you that day.

The car just showed up again."

"Where did you see it?"

"I saw them in my neighborhood, up here on Rio Vista. I was driving down the street when I saw them knocking on a door. I got curious, so I drove past them a ways and parked. They left the house and drove to the next block and knocked on the O'Brien's door.

After they left, I went to the house and asked Bob what it was they wanted. He said they told him they were Las Vegas Police Department Detectives. Showed him badges and a picture of an oriental woman. Told him she was wanted for murder in Las Vegas and they were following up a lead."

"Got 'em," said Horse.

"I'm sorry, what?"

"Where are they now?"

"After I talked to Bob, I found them on the next block over. When they drove out of the neighborhood, I followed them. They drove down Jordan Street hill into town and parked over across from the depot. Their car is in front of the five and dime by the park there. They got out and walked to the corner. They're standing there right now, waiting for a break in traffic so they can cross the street. Looks like they're going to the civic center. I ducked into the Jade to call you."

"Thanks, Mr. Garret. I'm on it."

He hung up his phone and keyed his intercom for the dispatcher.

"Who's close to town?"

"Dave Campbell's unit just came in from the north."

"Have him meet me at the civic center. Tell him to come code two and pull into the police department lot. Tell him if he gets there before I do, he's to wait for me in his unit."

Horse jammed on his hat. He took his gun belt off the back of his chair, looped it over his shoulder, and went out the door at a dead run.

When he pulled into the Smoke Tree Police Department parking lot, Dave Campbell's unit was already there. He got out when he saw Horse pull in beside him.

"Lieutenant."

"Dave. Got a situation here. Somewhere in this complex are two mobbed up guys from Las Vegas. They've been going around town impersonating Las Vegas police officers. Based on past experience and information about these two, I'm sure they're armed. Our goal is to arrest them without endangering citizens."

"Where do you think they are?"

"Well, we can be sure they're not at the police department. That leaves city hall, which is closed today, and the library, which is the only thing open besides the P.D."

Dave smiled.

"What in the world would gangsters be doing at the library?"

"We're about to find out."

"Want me to bring my shotgun?"

"No. If push comes to shove, we don't want buckshot flying all over the place. This is going to scare Helen bad enough as it is."

The two men walked out of the parking lot, onto the grass in front of city hall, and around the corner. They could see the library steps.

Horse pointed across Highway 66.

"That's their car over by the park. They're probably inside. It's best we go up the steps guns drawn. We might meet them coming out."

When they eased through the doors, guns pointing at the floor, they saw two men in blazers standing in front of the librarians' desk. They walked toward them, the old floor creaking under their boots.

One of the men turned around. His face did not register surprise or concern. He tapped his partner. The other man also turned toward them.

"Lace your hands behind your heads. Do it now!"

The two men complied.

Horse stepped slightly to the side. He could see the librarian sitting slack-jawed behind her desk. She was holding something but not looking at it.

"Sorry to scare you, Mrs. Sensabaugh. Please get up and go over and stand next to the card catalogue."

It took the librarian a moment to rise to her feet. She seemed a little shaky, but she managed to walk carefully out from behind the desk and over to where Horse had directed her.

"You men carrying?"

"Yeah. Shoulder rig."

"All right. My deputy here is going to take your guns. If you take your hands off your head while he's doing it, I will shoot you. Are we clear on that?"

Both men nodded.

"Don't just shake your head. Say 'yes'."

Both men said yes.

"Dave, hand me your gun"

Dave put his gun in Horse's left hand. Horse took it without looking away from the two men.

"Get their guns."

Dave reached inside the jacket of the man on the left and took the gun out of his shoulder rig. He stepped back, popped the clip out of the gun and put it in his pocket. Then he pulled back the slide to see if there was a round in the chamber. There wasn't. He pushed the unloaded gun down the front of his pants.

He repeated the operation with the man on the right. When he had both guns, he backed up next to Horse and took his own weapon from Horse's hand. The entire time, Horse never looked away from the two men.

"Got carry permits for the guns?"

"Sure," said Salvatore.

"For San Bernardino County?"

Salvatore didn't answer.

Horse spoke to the librarian without looking away from Fiore and Salvatore.

"What did these men tell you, Mrs. Sensabaugh?"

"They said they were police detectives from Las Vegas. They said they were looking for a girl wanted for murder. They asked me to look at this picture and tell them if I'd had ever seen her."

She held the photo up.

Horse did not look at it.

"Well, they lied to you. But they lie for a living. These men are gangsters. They're going to jail.

"Dave, please get the picture from Mrs. Sensabaugh and bring it to me"

When Dave retrieved the picture, he brought it to Horse and put it in his left hand. Horse slipped it into his front pocket without looking at it..

"Now Helen, we're going to take these two men out of here. I'm not anticipating trouble from them, but you never know. So, what I'd really like you to do now is go in your office and close the door.

Will you do that for me?"

"Certainly, Lieutenant Caballo."

"I'm going to send a deputy down to get a written statement from you. Once we're gone, you might want to write down exactly what happened from the time these men came in the door until right now."

She walked into her office. Horse heard her turn the lock.

"You two. Turn around. Now, take your hands off your head and put them far apart on the desk.

Farther apart than that.

Okay. Now, walk your feet back toward me while you keep your hands on the desk.

Now spread your feet.

Pat them down, Dave."

Deputy Campbell went to work.

"This one's got a switchblade."

"Check for ankle holsters."

He did.

"Neither one."

Horse walked forward and touched Fiore on the shoulder.

"You. Step forward. Now, take your hands off the desk and put them behind your back."

Fiore complied.

"Cuff him."

Horse repeated the instructions to Salvatore, then got his own cuffs off his belt and handed them to Dave.

When both men were cuffed, Horse said, "Turn around."

He took the picture out of his pocket and studied it. Then he held it up in front of the two men.

"Who is this woman?"

Neither man said anything.

"Okay, if that's how you want to play it.

Out the door and down the steps. And be careful. If you fall you could get a nasty bump going down those steps."

When the men were at the bottom of the steps, Dave and walked the men around the corner to the cruisers. They put Fiore in the back of Dave's car and Salvatore in Horse's.

Before Horse could close the door on Salvatore, he said, "Hey, how about it with these cuffs?"

He turned sideways on the seat.

Horse slammed the door.

"Dave, come with me."

He led Dave far enough away that the two men in the car couldn't hear them.

"When we get them to the station, book them both for impersonating law enforcement officers and carrying without a permit. Add the switchblade charge for the big one. Inventory everything they've got. Make sure the dispatcher witnesses you removing their LVPD badges.

When you're done, put them in separate cells. After they make their phone calls, get hold of the phone company and see who they called."

"Okay."

The two men stood silently.

"What are we waiting for Lieutenant?"

"Nothing special. Just letting our boys marinate for a while.

And Dave?"

"Yessir."

When you get them in their cells, turn off the air conditioning back there. And if we don't get any more customers this weekend, leave it off."

Dave smiled.

"Yessir. Welcome to Smoke Tree, huh?"

When he got back in his cruiser, Horse keyed his mic twice.

"Dispatch."

"Horse. Call in two more deputies. Have one help Dave book the men we're bringing in. Send the other one to the library to take a statement from Mrs. Sensabaugh.

"10-4"

Horse hung the mic back on the radio. He angled his mirror so he could see the man behind him.

"You boys are going to be with us a while. There's no court until Monday morning."

The man turned his dead eyes toward Horse but said nothing.

Chapter 17

Smoke Tree, California

And the Mountains

Of the Eastern Mojave Desert

July 8, 1961

I had to make a late delivery before I left work on Saturday. By the time I got home, got something to eat and loaded up my kitchen box with food for breakfast, the stifling summer twilight was settling over the desert. The final remnants of red were bleeding into the blackness above the horizon as I drove out of town and headed west on 66. The lights of Smoke Tree were beginning to wink on in my rearview mirror.

When my headlights swept across the traffic islands at Mr. Stanton's, it was after dark. I stopped next to one of the old pumps and got out. I went up the steps to the office and was just pushing open the screen door when he came out of his living quarters behind the counter.

"Well, I declare, it's Aeden Snow."

"Good evening, Mr. Stanton. Could I trouble you for ten gallons of gas?"

"Surely can."

We went outside. Mr. Stanton turned the crank and drew gasoline into the glass measure above the pump. When it was full, he unlatched the hose and hooked the nozzle into my tank. Gravity drained the gasoline into my car. Simple, elegant, no electricity required. When the measure was empty, he pumped it full again and drained five more gallons into my tank.

When he was finished, he put the hose back on the hook.

"That'll be six dollars, young sir."

Gasoline was fifty cents a gallon in Smoke Tree, more than twice what it cost in at the coast. At Mr. Stanton's, it was sixty cents, but in spite of the extra ten cents, I bought from him whenever I could. I knew he didn't get many customers at his station.

I handed him a ten.

"Step on up to the office while I get your change. There's somethin' I want to tell you might could be real important."

Inside, he rang up the sale on his ancient cash register.

"Last week when you was here and introduced me to your pretty lady friend …"

He paused.

"Yessir."

"Well, I'm not rightly sure because she had that ball cap on and all, but I think I mighta recognized her."

"From where?"

"That's what's got me worried. Back in the spring, May I believe it was, though I'm not completely sure 'cause at my age the days they seem to run on together. Nothin special to mark 'em, and I've already lived so many of 'em, if you get my drift."

"Yessir, I think I see what you mean."

"I know for sure it was before that day you found me layin' out yonder in the dirt.

Anyways, two men come in here. Bad men. Rough characters. Well sir, they claimed they was private detectives from Las Vegas come lookin' for some woman had gone missin' from her family. They showed me a picture. It coulda been that young lady was with you last week. When the one man handed me the picture, his jacket come open and I saw he was armed, which kindly took me by surprise.

When I asked about the guns, the other boy, not the one who had give me the picture, he said some real bad stuff about the woman. Called her a bad name. And I knowed then they wasn't workin' for that woman's family, or he wouldn't a spoke about her thataway.

So I told them to clear off. And the one who called the woman the bad name? He got real nasty with me.

Well sir, I was standin' right where I am now. I pulled my coach gun out from under the counter and run them off. And I remembered all that as soon as I saw your lady friend.

Then it kinda slipped my mind again during the week. More and more that happens these days. Ever since that day I fell down, seems like I remember stuff from when I was a young un better than stuff that happened yesterday. Darndest thing.

But this afternoon, when I was comin' round the building, I saw the back end of a big black car just a flyin' over the railroad crossing yonder, and I thought about it again. You see, it was the car called it to mind. It was the same kind of car them boys I run off that day was drivin'.

"Do you think it was the exact same car?"

"Couldn't tell you for sure, Ade. It was too far away by the time I seen it. But it reminded me about that other time. I wanted to be sure I didn't forget to tell you. So I come inside and wrote a note to myself. Generally, if I write somethin' down, it sticks in my head for a spell."

"Thank you, Mr. Stanton, for going to all that trouble. I'll pass that along to Kiko."

"Kiko! That was her name. I'll have to write that down, too.

Well, I've kept you long enough. You'd best be gettin' on."

As I drove up old 66, the smoke trees flickering past in the spill of my headlights, I turned Mr. Stanton's story over in my head. If it had indeed been Kiko in the picture, it was serious business. And it explained a lot. John Stonebridge found Kiko in Baker. The chances she came there from Las Vegas were pretty high.

It wasn't long before I was on Lanfair Road. I drove through the sandy bottom of Von Trigger wash and up to where the Joshua trees dominated the landscape. Usually when I drove through them at night, with my headlights picking up the yucca and cholla cactus and shrubs spaced between, I felt at home. But that night as I rolled though the familiar country, I was uneasy. As if something sinister might be coming. I tried to shake off the feeling, but it wouldn't go away. I kept looking in my rearview mirror, but there was nothing there but the blackness of a moonless desert night.

I made up my mind to get Kiko aside the next day and tell her what Mr. Stanton had told me. She could decide whether to pass it on to Mr. Stonebridge or not. It wasn't my call.

I was wiped out by the combination of heat, long workdays and evening workouts, but I didn't sleep well in spite of the cool air. After a restless night fitfully dozing off only to wake up to a vague feeling of dread, I gave up and got out of bed before first light. I started a fire in the stove and made breakfast. Strangely enough, three big cups of coffee calmed me down, and I was feeling better and finishing "To Kill a Mockingbird" when the world outside began to change from black to gray.

If I thought I would beat Joe to work by getting to the Box S before sunrise, I was mistaken. He was already working. I said good morning, got a nod in return, and went to work helping him add adobe bricks to a row he had already started. Like everything else I had ever seen Joe do, he had a knack for masonry work. We had the entire east wall finished by the time Kiko called us to lunch.

John was out doing some work on the stock tank at the south end of Watson's Wash, so when Joe got up from the table and went outside, Kiko and I were alone in the kitchen.

"You have something to tell me, don't you?"

"How can you tell?"

"Because you're usually Joe's shadow when you two are working. As soon as he went out and you didn't, I knew something was up."

I took a deep breath and crossed my fingers.

"This may be nothing. I hope it is."

I repeated what Mr. Stanton had told me. When I was finished, she didn't speak. Just sat absorbing the news.

"Is this important?"

"Let me think about it. Don't say anything to Joe or John just yet."

"All right. Whatever you want."

I went back to work with a sinking feeling in my stomach.

Kiko was the girl in the picture.

242

It was slower going in the afternoon. Fitting the bricks around the south side windows and the fireplace on the north wall was time consuming. The light was fading from the sky, and the evening hush was settling over the desert by the time we called it a day.

I walked toward the barn with Joe. We turned and looked at the room from a distance. Most of the adobe work was done.

"Looks good."

"Not bad."

High praise indeed from Joe Medrano.

"Finish this part tomorrow. Plaster next week. Whitewash the whole house."

We walked back to the mountainside behind the house. Joe showed me the roof tiles he had fired.

"Floor tiles tomorrow afternoon."

We were between the house and the barn when John pulled up in his truck. He got out and walked over.

"Jesus, Joe. That's beautiful! Hundred times better than the stucco box I would've tacked onto the side of the house.

Kilo's going to love that room."

If she stays here, I couldn't help thinking.

Kiko came outside.

"Dinner in ten minutes."

Kiko, John and Joe stood together talking. I turned to take in Table Top and Round Valley and the bulk of the Providence Mountains. Venus was just visible in the evening sky. The world seemed at peace. I wished it could be this way forever, but I knew it couldn't. Everything was going to come apart.

After dinner, we took our flan and coffee out to the veranda. When he was finished with his dessert, Joe got up.

"Don't leave, Joe. Please, stay and listen."

He sat back down.

Kiko told us everything that had happened to her, beginning when she was summoned to the executive offices at the Serengeti to meet with Eddie Mazzetti and ending with John rescuing her from the college boys in Baker. She was unsparing of herself in the telling. It took her a long time to tell it all.

When she was finished, we sat silently for a while.

Finally John said, "Good God, Kiko. You must have been terrified. You might have been killed that night."

"I was so scared. I thought they were going to catch me any minute."

"Did good," said Joe. "Good plan. Smart."

"And lucky."

"Don't believe in luck. Never had any."

I spoke up to add my part.

"When Kiko and I were driving back from the river, I stopped at Arrowhead Junction to check on Mr. Stanton, and he met Kiko.

When I was coming up last night, I stopped by again. Mr. Stanton told me about two men who came by his station. He thought it was in May. He said they had a picture. He said it might have been Kiko.

He said his memory's not what it used to be since his stroke, and he had forgotten about it until he saw her with me."

"Well, that was a while back," said John.

"That's what I thought, but then he told me he saw a car going fast over the railroad crossing yesterday. It was headed south. It was the same kind of car the two men were driving that day. It worried him so much he wrote himself a note to tell me about it the next time he saw me."

We were all quiet again. The night no longer seemed peaceful.

"So, what do we do now?"

"I go away. I'm putting the three of you in danger just by being here."

"You really think they can find you out here?"

"You heard Ade. They came looking for me in May. Now they're back out on the desert again. I've been thinking about this since he told me. I think when they didn't find me the places they thought they might, places like Salinas and Los Angeles and close to friends I had in college, they started over."

"We should go to the police."

Kiko laughed bitterly.

"The Las Vegas Police? These people own the police. There are probably people in the department who know about this and are helping them look for me."

"Kiko, we can protect you."

"No, John, you can't. I love it that you would offer, but they'll kill me and you and anyone else who helped me."

"Give them the money back. They'll leave you alone after they get it."

"They won't. I killed a man who was way up in their organization. It was an accident. They probably know it was an accident, but that doesn't matter. The only way to avenge his death is to kill me. These people are big on revenge. Getting the money would be extra."

"So, I run. And I keep running for the rest of my life. Because they will never, ever give up. I knew that when I was sitting on the chair in that fat man's room. My old life is over. It's never coming back.

That's why I took the money. I knew I'd need it if I was going to stay alive."

"And the money is in a locker at the Union Pacific Depot?"

"That's right. The key is in my purse."

"How much is it? Do you know?"

"I had no way to get it open, but the man who was trying to impress me said it was over half a million dollars."

"You're going to need every penny if you're going to disappear," said John.

"Yes. I have to go get it."

"You can't, Kiko. You can never go to Las Vegas again."

"I could wear a disguise."

"No. No. Too dangerous. I'll get it for you. I'll go tomorrow morning after breakfast. Joe will be here to protect you while I'm gone."

"And me too."

"No, Aeden," said John. "You have to leave."

"There's no way I'm leaving until this is over."

"Now listen,..."

"Trying to be a man," said Joe.

"That right. He's a boy trying to be a man. But he doesn't know what that means yet."

"Trying to be a man, already most way to a man."

"But..."

"Wants to stay. He stays."

John sat looking off into the night without speaking.

"Okay, but now you'll have two people to protect. Kiko and Aeden both."

"John, thank you for going to Las Vegas for me."

"Aren't you afraid I'll take the money?"

"I know you won't do that. I'd trust any one of you with that money and with my life. In fact, I already have, just by telling you what happened."

And with that, the discussion ended.

I didn't return to Lee's Camp that night.

Chapter 18

Smoke Tree, California

And the Mountains

Of the Eastern Mojave Desert

July 10, 1961

Two irritated, disheveled, unkempt, unshowered, sweat-soured and unshaven hard guys were ushered into Judge Sherman's court in Smoke Tree on Monday morning at nine o'clock. When their case was called, they were joined at the defense table by a world-weary man from the Los Angeles law firm of Kravitz, Karl and Klein. Jason Ablemann looked no happier about being in Judge Sherman's court than Salvatore Lupo and Fiore Abbatini. Ablemann and his driver had left L.A. in his Lincoln Continental in the middle of the night

He hadn't conferred with his clients. He didn't have to. They knew the drill. They had been down this road many, many times before. So had he.

Fiore was charged with impersonating a police officer and carrying a concealed firearm without a permit. Salvatore was charged with the same, plus one additional count for the switchblade. Both men pleaded not guilty.

The local prosecutor, who was out of his depth in dealing with an experienced criminal lawyer like Ablemann, asked that the men be held without bail. He cited their lengthy arrest records and the severity of the crimes with which they had been charged. Attorney Ablemann stood and pointed out that

247

while both men may have been mistakenly arrested for various crimes, neither man had ever been convicted of anything. Therefore the information was immaterial and irrelevant.

When the attorneys were done, the judge looked thoughtful and then set bail at fifty thousand for Salvatore and forty five for Fiore. He also set a date for the preliminary hearing.

Ablemann asked if cashier's checks for the entire amounts drawn on the Bank of America would be acceptable. The judge said if the checks were presented to the clerk of the court, the two men would be released, pending the hearing.

Fifteen minutes after the case was called, Jason Ablemann was on his way to the Bank of America with an attaché case full of cash. He was pleased he had guessed the bail amount within five thousand dollars.

Salvatore and Abbatini were returned to the custody of Lieutenant Caballo. Not long after they had been locked in their cells again, a deputy came into the hallway.

"You made bail."

He unlocked the cells. The two men followed him down the hall to the front counter. Their wallets, watches, change, and rolls of cash were returned to them, as was the picture of Kiko Yoshida. They knew better than to ask for their guns or Salvatore's knife. They did, however, ask for their shoulder rigs. Those were returned to them.

They were signing for their possessions when Horse walked out of his office.

"I'd like to say we enjoyed seeing you boys, but we didn't."

Neither man said anything. They turned to go.

"Hey, where's the car keys?"

"You owe us twenty five dollars before you get those."

"For what? The lousy food?"

"Towing fees. You don't pay, we keep the car."

Salvatore pulled the wad of bills out of his pocket. He peeled off two twenties and tossed them on the counter.

"Keep the change."

Horse turned to his deputy.

"Give him a receipt and his change. Don't give him the keys until he picks up both."

He turned and walked back to his office.

Their car had been left in the sun with the windows up the day before. The window on the passenger side had exploded in the heat. Most of the glass was outside the car, but there was some on the seat.

"Sonofabitch!"

Salvatore was so mad he grabbed the chrome door handle without thinking. It was blistering hot.

"Sonofabitch!" he said again, louder this time, shaking his hand.

They drove downtown and went into the first motel they came to.

"Need a room."

"Check in time is two' o'clock," said the young man at the desk.

"Come on. We won't be here long. Just need to shower and shave."

"I'd like to help you, but check in time is not until two."

Salvatore pulled out his roll of cash. He put a fifty on the counter.

"Gonna give you a choice, zit face. You can take the money and give us a room, some shavin' stuff, toothbrushes and toothpaste, or you can give me that 'two o'clock' line again."

The young man started to speak. Salvatore held up his huge hand.

"Not done yet.

Now, if you take the money and give us what I asked for, you can keep the change. If you give me that two o'clock shit again, I'm gonna come over this counter and rip your face off.

What's it gonna be, pal?"

The young man picked up the fifty dollar bill and walked out of the office.

"Sally! Hey, Sally!"

A woman emerged from one of the rooms.

"Yeah?"

"Which ones are made up?"

"Four, nine, eleven and fifteen."

249

He came back in and gave Sal the key to number nine.

The two men walked toward the room. They left the car parked in the shade of the overhang.

After showering and shaving, they stopped at a coffee shop for breakfast and discussed their situation.

"Should go see that guy in Golf."

"Goffs."

"Yeah. Member what Tommy Bones said about them busted shields or somethin'?"

"I remember. No way can we go back to Vegas without somethin' for him."

"Should we call him?"

"No way I wanna talk to that guy before we have somethin'."

"Okay. There must be a place in this town we can buy some guns. Shoguns would be okay. Make that shotguns and a hacksaw."

"I got the guns covered."

"Whadya mean?"

"Show you on the way."

They left Smoke Tree and started back the way they had come on Saturday. Hot air poured in through the gap where the window had been, making the air conditioner pointless.

When they got to Klinefelter, Fiore pulled off the highway and drove into the parking lot of the abandoned motor court. He parked in the shade of a salt cedar and got out and opened the trunk.

"Man, if you left back-up guns in there, they're long gone."

Fiore handed a big screwdriver and a pair of pliers to Salvatore, keeping a screwdriver and pliers for himself.

"Let me show you."

Salvatore followed as Fiore walked back and opened the driver's side door. Kneeling on one knee, he went to work.

"There's a .45, extra clips and another cop badge in the rocker panel on your side."

Salvatore smiled for the first time in two days.

"Hey, Abbatini? You ain't as dumb as you look."

"Eddie was worried about that deputy. Thought we might run into trouble."

A half hour after stopping, they pulled back on 95. A half hour after that, they were in the Goffs store.

They showed Chuck Sweeney their badges and the picture of Kiko. They told him Don Clark had sent them. They asked him what he had overheard a cowboy say to someone else about an oriental woman and where the cowboy might have seen her. Chuck got out a pencil and paper and began to draw them a map.

"You'll know you're almost to this intersection when you see the phone booth. Slow down and look to the left. You'll see a road going off to the west. It's the only way you can turn. That's Cedar Canyon Road. There are some ranches out there. The OX cowboy said the woman was with a kid in a pickup truck. Probably came from one of the places out that way."

They got back in the car, crossed the railroads tracks and turned right onto Lanfair Road. It wasn't long before the pavement ended.

"Guido and me was out this way somewhere back in May. We got on a road that turned to dirt like this one, but after a while it was paved again."

The drove on beneath the bright white glare of the sky. The road remained dirt. The heavy luxury sedan with its low clearance and soft suspension was strictly a highway cruiser. It was not made for these conditions. It shook, shimmied, lurched and plunged. When Fiore tried slowing down, the cloud of dust they were kicking up behind the car caught up with them and came in through the gap left by the missing window.

He tried speeding up almost to fifty. That worked better. There seemed to be a speed at which the wheels hit the tops of the washboarded surface and skipped along without making their teeth rattle. But when the long straight suddenly turned right and dipped down into Von Trigger Wash, the car slalomed and slid sloppily into the curve and the soft sand in the bottom. Alarmed, Fiore began to slow down again.

Put your foot in it," yelled Salvatore, coughing in the dust. "This thing gets stuck in the sand, we'll never get it out."

Fiore jammed down the accelerator, the wheels spraying sand and gravel. There was dust everywhere. Somehow, he kept it going forward and on the road until they climbed up the other side of the wash. He was relieved to be back on the hard road, bumps and all.

After a few more miles, they came to a phone booth.

"Look at that," said Fiore as they drove past. "What the hell's a phone booth doin' out here? There's no goddamned people."

"Beats me. Watch for the road he told us about. We should be comin' up on it."

They came to a "T" intersection, and Fiore turned left onto another dirt road.

"I didn't see no sign, but I don't see no other road neither. This must be the one."

They continued on through a forest of Joshua Trees. The road ran straight to the west, then turned north before turning west again. At the top of a steep hill, Fiore brought the car to a stop. They sat with the engine idling, looking down at the broad wash below, dust billowing around them.

"Man, when we hit the bottom, you'd better punch it. That's worse than the last place. Be sure you keep this bucket movin'. Get stuck, gonna make you carry me back to Vegas."

They dropped down into Watson's Wash. When they were almost at the bottom, Fiore shoved the accelerator to the floor and they went sliding, twisting and fishtailing through the sand and gravel, rocks pinging hard off the undercarriage. Somehow, they made it across. The road that rose up the other side was relatively smooth.

When they crested the hill, Salvatore pointed off to the right.

"Look at that big, white house up there. Start with that one."

A little farther down the road, they came to a sign that read 'Box S'. There was a square with an 'S' in the middle made out of wrought iron on the post above the sign.

A rutted road snaked off through the yucca, cactus, catclaw and sage.

"Shit."

"Hey, made it through that last place, can make it through here."

They did. And then they came to the west face of Pinto Mountain and the switchbacks that led to the top. Fiore eased the heavy car onto the first one.

Getting around the turns at the ends of the switchbacks was hard, but in spite of a lot of slipping and sliding and backing, they made it to the top and onto a long, straight driveway lined with whitewashed rocks that angled off to the northeast.

As they drove closer to the white adobe with the red tile roof, they saw a big corral off to the side. There were five horses in the corral. They were all staring at the car. Beyond the corral, there was a slender man at the end of the driveway. He was wearing Levi's and a blue, long-sleeved work shirt. His black hair hung down past his collar. A red bandana was tied around his forehead. There was a bucket at his feet, and he was bent over slightly, stirring something with a stick.

"Is that one a them Mexicans or a Indian?"

"Not sure. Sometimes can't tell 'em apart.

Indian, I think."

Fiore eased to a stop beside the man and hit the switch for his power window.

"Afternoon."

The man looked at him.

"You speak English?"

"Yes."

Chapter 19

The Mountains of the

Eastern Mojave Desert

July 10, 1961

Chemehuevi Joe

Joe and Aeden were making floor tiles from clay and red dirt. Joe heard the car before he saw it. He could tell by the sound the tires were making that it was coming fast. He walked over to the edge of the drop off and looked east down the road.

A moment later, a black sedan crested the hill above Watson's Wash. It was a big car, the west-tilting sun glinting off the broad windshield. It was coming faster now.

He stepped back from the drop off so he couldn't be seen from the road below and listened.

"What is it?" asked Aeden.

Joe held up his hand for silence.

The sound of the car changed as it passed from east to west, and for a moment Joe thought it would keep going.

Then it slowed.

Then it stopped.

Joe imagined the driver looking at the sign for the Box S.

The sound of the car changed again as it turned off Cedar Canyon onto the road to the house.

Joe turned to Aeden.

"Car. Trouble coming. Go in, get Kiko. Take her behind the house. Car gets here and stops, take her around the hillside into the draw leads to the ridge. Go way up in there.

I don't come, fifteen minutes, take her over the ridge, Bathtub Springs."

"Okay."

"Don't let her argue. Get her behind the house, fast."

Aeden turned and ran.

The car was on the switchbacks now. Joe could hear the tires fighting to gain purchase. He could hear it stop and back and start again as the driver worked to get it around the hairpin turns.

Joe walked over to where they had piled the cottonwood. He broke a stick off one of the limbs.

The car was moving slowly, but it kept coming.

Joe walked over by the house and picked up a bucket.

He walked to the end of the row of rocks lining the driveway and put down both the bucket and the stick.

He took the long-bladed, slender and very sharp skinning knife out of the sheath on his belt. He pulled up his left pant leg and slid the knife down inside his boot. He dropped the pant leg over it again.

He took a deep breath. He was ready.

He bent over and picked up the stick. He put it inside the bucket.

When he heard the car come off the last switchback, he leaned over slightly and began to make stirring motions with the stick.

The car was coming up the driveway now. When it pulled even with him, he straightened and pulled the stick out of the bucket. He looked over at the car.

There were two men in the car. They were very big. They were wearing blazers in spite of the heat.

256

The window lowered.

"Afternoon. You speak English?"

"Yes."

"I'm Detective Thorenson," said the driver, holding out a detective shield.

"That's my partner, Detective Wilkes."

The big man in the passenger seat nodded.

Joe thought the men certainly didn't look like a Thorenson and a Wilkes. But that didn't surprise him, since he knew they weren't policemen, either.

"Joe Medrano."

"Mr. Medrano, we're looking for a woman. She's wanted for murder in Las Vegas. Killed her roommate in cold blood. She's very dangerous. We think she might be out this way. Would you take a look at a picture for us?"

"Be glad to."

The man put the badge in the inside pocket of his blazer and pulled out a photograph. As he did, Joe saw the butt of a .45 automatic pointing outward from beneath his right armpit.

The guy was left handed. Joe thought that would help.

He stepped toward the car and took the photo the man was extending toward him.

It was Kiko.

He had known it would be.

He studied the picture.

"Murder, huh?"

"That's right."

"Be damned. Wondered about her."

"You mean you've seen her?"

"Oh, yeah."

He waved off toward the south.

"Seen her over at Gold Valley ranch."

He handed the picture back.

"Can you tell me how to find that place?"

"Come on, I'll draw you a map."

He stepped far enough away from the car that the driver would have room to swing the door open. He scraped at the dirt with his boot, smoothing out a spot. When he finished, he got down on his right knee, his left boot propped beside his left arm.

The man opened the door and got out.

Joe hoped he would close the door so his partner wouldn't see everything that was about to happen.

The man pushed the door closed.

"Kneel down here. I'll show you the roads."

The man hesitated. He probably didn't want to get his pants dirty, thought Joe. He looked like the kind of guy who would worry about that sort of thing.

Joe kept his face turned toward the cleared space. He was holding the stick with his right hand, the tip resting in the dirt. He thought it seemed less threatening that way. Not that either one of the men seemed to think he was going to be any kind of a problem.

Finally, the big man got down next to Joe with his left hand and left knee on the ground.

Joe reached to the top of the cleared space and drew a line toward the man.

"Cedar Canyon Road. Was just on it."

"Okay."

He intersected the line with one that ran perpendicular to it.

"Black Canyon Road. On down that way."

He gestured with his head and with the stick toward Cedar Canyon.

Just as Joe thought he would, the man turned his head the direction Joe was pointing with the stick. As if he could actually see through the car.

As soon as he turned his head, Joe did three things swiftly and smoothly.

He dropped the stick. With his palm facing the man's arm, he seized the man's left wrist just above his expensive watch and leaned to the right, pinning the hand to the ground. Simultaneously, he pulled the knife out of his boot.

Too late, the man realized he was in trouble. He tried to pull his hand free so he could reach his gun.

Mistake.

Had he swung on Joe with his free hand, with his superior size he may have had a chance. But he was too used to relying on his gun when things got tough.

Joe pivoted to his right, thrusting the long, thin blade up under the man's ribcage and into his heart.

His eyes opened in surprise.

He made a 'whuff' sound as the air left his lungs.

Joe kept the man's hand pinned to the ground.

His face was inches from Joe's, his expression bewildered, as if he could not yet believe what was happening. He struggled to speak, but all the air had escaped his lungs.

He was never going to get any more.

He sagged.

He slumped toward Joe.

Joe took his weight.

"Hey," Joe yelled, "Your partner's having a heart attack!"

The other man pushed his door open and came running.

As he cleared the back of the car, it looked to him like Joe was trying to support his partner.

"Help me!"

The man leaned down. As he put his left hand on his dying partner's shoulder, Joe pushed off the ground, straightening his right leg and driving hard with his left, shoving his burden against the other man.

As he did, he pulled his knife out of the first man's body.

"Hey, what the …," the man yelled as he stumbled back against the car.

Then Joe was on him. With the knife palm down in his left hand, he slashed backhand across the man's throat from right to left, severing the carotid artery. Bright red arterial blood sprayed across Joe and the man on the ground. With the car behind him and his partner's dead weight on his feet, he was trapped.

Salvatore "The Wolf" Lupo was already dead.

He just didn't know it yet.

He clawed for his gun with his right hand, but Joe turned his hand palm up and came back across Salvatore's throat from the opposite direction. His neck a gaping wound, Salvatore slumped partially across Joe and partially across Fiore Abbatini's lifeless body. His gun forgotten now, the mistakes that led to his death on a dusty, desert mountainside flashed through his mind as he pawed at his throat as if to stop the life from spilling.

Salvatore Lupo thought of sitting on the floor of his home in Sicily as a child. Thought of the smell of olive oil and rosemary bread baking in his mother's kitchen. Then he thought nothing at all, ever again.

When Joe was sure the man was no longer a threat, he stepped back. The man slid down Joe's body and finished collapsing on top of Fiore Abbatini.

Joe heard footsteps behind him. Three thoughts went through his head. There had been a third man who had been let out of the car below the top of the hill. The man was behind Joe. But he hadn't shot Joe because they needed to know where Kiko was, so Joe still had a chance.

As he thought, he was already turning and dropping into a crouch, the knife held palm down below his waist.

Aeden was walking toward him, holding a cottonwood limb.

Joe relaxed, straightened and shook his head.

"Sorry you had to see that."

"You all right?"

"Yes."

"Who are these guys?"

Joe shrugged.

"Came for missy."

Aeden walked over to the two dead men.

He stood looking down at them. Looking at all the blood. Then he giggled.

Joe knew what was happening. The boy had been primed to attack the two men. That's why he had the limb. Now there was nothing to do, but he was still primed, his heart pounding, his nerves keyed in anticipation.

Joe walked over and put his hand on Aeden's shoulder.

"Be okay. Were ready to fight.

That's good."

260

Aeden nodded.

"Put the limb down."

Aeden dropped the limb.

"Where's Kiko?"

"I left her up in the wash. Came back to see if you needed help."

"Go get her. Worried, scared up there alone."

Aeden headed off at a run.

Joe still had the knife in his hand. He leaned over and wiped it on the jacket of the man on top. Then he put it back in the sheath on his belt.

He walked to the stock tank behind the house and turned on the faucet. He took off the blood-soaked shirt and rinsed it and wrung it out several times. He walked over to the bunk house and hooked the shirt over a hook near the steps.

He walked back to the stock tank. He took off the bandana and soaked it in the water, turning it in his hands for a long time before wringing it out. Then he hung the bandana over the pipe while he laved water over his face, hair and arms again and again. The puddle spreading at his feet was pink.

Joe looked at his Levi's and boots. They were bloody, but not as bad as he had feared. He wet the bandana again and began to clean them. He didn't want Kiko to think he was some kind of savage.

Didn't want to frighten her.

When he was satisfied with his condition, he rinsed his bandana one more time and tied it around his forehead.

Chapter 20

The Mountains

Of the Eastern Mojave Desert

July 10, 1961

Aeden Snow

We were making floor tiles when Joe suddenly stopped and looked off to the east. I couldn't see or hear anything. He walked away from me toward the drop off.

He stopped again, still looking to the east.

"What is it?"

He held up his hand.

Then I heard it too. A car coming fast on Cedar Canyon road. The sound of the car changed as it passed us and moved to the west. Then the sound stopped, and I no longer heard anything.

"Car. Trouble coming. Go in, get Kiko. Take her behind the house. Car gets here and stops, take Kiko around the hillside and into the draw that leads to the ridge. Go way up in there.

I don't come, fifteen minutes, take her over the ridge. Bathtub Springs."

"Okay."

"Don't let her argue. Get her behind the house, fast."

There was no panic in Joe's voice. There was no hesitation either.

I turned and ran toward the house. I stopped before I went inside. I could hear the car now. It was making its way up the switchbacks

Kiko was standing in her new room. I took her by the arm.

"Come on. Joe says we have to get outside and get behind the house."

"Oh, God. They're here."

We went out the back door and stood waiting. With the house blocking the sound, I could no longer hear the car. Then it crested the hill and I heard it as it came forward up the long, straight driveway, gravel crunching under the tires.

It was hard to resist the temptation to peek around the corner, but I knew Joe wouldn't want me to.

"As soon as the car stops, we're going to start around the edge of the cut and head for the draw. Joe has a plan, and part of it is for us to get well up into that draw. That's what he wants us to do, and we're going to do it.

Once you're safe, I'm coming back."

The car stopped.

We set off at a run. We crouched down as we ran. I don't know why. It's not as if whoever was in the car could see through the house. As we ran, I could see the horses in the corral looking toward where the car had stopped.

We ran into the draw and headed uphill, deep into the brush and boulders. We kept running until the draw began to narrow. We came to a boulder big enough for Kiko to hide behind.

"If you hear someone coming and you don't hear Joe or me calling your name, something's gone wrong. Get out of here. Go quietly, but go fast until you come to the ridgeline. Try not to silhouette yourself as you go over the top.

When you're on the other side, go parallel to the ridgeline but stay below it. Keep going until you come to a side cut that leads downhill. It's deep enough that once you get in it, no one will be able to see you from up here. Follow it down to Bathtub Springs. There's lots of willows and catclaw there. You can hide and watch the hill. If you see someone coming, they'll probably come straight over the top from the draw we're in. Wait until they hit the bottom of the hill and are in Pinto Valley."

"How will I know they're in the bottom?"

"You won't be able to see them from where you are. And they won't be able to see you. When they disappear, climb the draw to the west and go over the hill. When you get on the other side, keep on going until it's dark."

"Aeden, I'm so afraid!. These are terrible people."

"I know. But they're not even sure you're here. Even if they come up here, they'll give up when it gets dark."

"I want to come with you."

"You can't. Joe's not risking his life for you to walk into a trap.

Please. Stay here. When it's safe, we'll come for you."

I turned and began scrambling back the way we had come.

When I came out of the draw and ran toward the house, I heard Joe yell something. I couldn't make out what it was.

I sprinted at full speed.

When I came around the house, Joe was on the ground on one knee. He seemed to be struggling with a man who was leaning against him. Another man was coming around the back of the car toward Joe.

He never saw me.

He leaned down and grabbed the shoulder of the man who was leaning on Joe.

I thought Joe was being outnumbered. Pausing, I picked up a cottonwood limb to swing, but Joe suddenly rose to his feet, pushing the man he had been holding against the standing man. At the same time, he pulled his left arm back. I thought he was breaking free.

The standing man staggered back against the car and yelled something. Then I saw that Joe had a knife. It was long and slender and wicked looking. It flashed in the sunlight as he slashed it backhand across the man's throat from left to right. Blood sprayed everywhere. The man tried to get his hand inside his jacket, but Joe turned his hand over and came across the man's throat in the other direction. The man gave up trying to get his gun and lifted his hand to his throat. Then he began to collapse.

Joe stepped back and the man fell down on top of the man on the ground.

I slowed but continued toward him, still holding the limb in both hands. Joe heard my footsteps. He whirled. I don't know what he was thinking, but he was dropping into a crouch, the bloody knife held palm down below his waist.

The deadly concentration in his eyes froze me in my tracks.

Then he relaxed, straightened and shook his head as if to clear it.

"Sorry you had to see that."

I don't know to this day whether he was talking about killing the man by the car or the look in his eyes when he turned on me with the knife.

"You all right?"

"Yes."

"Who are these guys?" I asked, feeling like an idiot as soon as the words left my mouth."

Joe shrugged.

"Came for missy."

I walked over to the two dead men.

The head of the man on the bottom was turned sideways, his vacant eyes staring at something he would never see. Blood had pooled on the ground below his open mouth. A big, black ant had already found it. The man on top was face down. His blood was everywhere.

"We're going to have more ants," I thought.

Then I giggled.

Joe walked over and put his hand on my shoulder.

"Be okay. You were ready to fight.

That's good."

I nodded.

"Put the limb down."

I hadn't even realized I was still holding it.

"Where's Kiko?"

"I left her up in the wash. Came back to see if you needed help."

"Go get her. Worried, scared up there."

I headed off at a run.

When I got to the draw, I started calling to her.

"Kiko! Kiko, it's Aeden. It's okay. Everything's okay. Come on down."

266

I kept hurrying up the narrow wash. It wasn't long before we met.

"It's over."

"Is Joe all right?"

"Yes."

"What about those people?"

"They won't bother you."

"Where did they go?"

"They're dead. Joe killed them."

She touched her hand to her forehead.

"Joe's not hurt? Not at all?"

"I don't think Joe can be hurt."

Kiko was shaken. She walked slowly beside me as we returned.

When we got back to the house, Joe was standing over by the car. His pants were wet and his boots were damp. He was still shirtless. His arms, shoulders and chest were corded with sinewy muscle

"Go in the house, missy."

"Are you all right? You sure you're not hurt?"

"Fine.

Go in the house."

"No. I want to see those men. See if I recognize them."

"Bad idea. Dream about them."

"I'll take my chances. I have to see them."

Kiko walked over to where the two men lay in a discordant, depressing, pile of death.

There was no hint of grace in their spoiled postures.

"I know that one. I saw him around the casino. I've never seen the other one."

She turned to Joe.

"You said I might dream about them. Won't you?"

"Add them, my list."

Kiko turned and walked to the house. Joe and I watched her until she went inside.

Joe turned to me.

"Clear a path for the car. Hide it."

Working together, we quickly moved floor tiles, tools and cottonwood limbs out of the way.

"You drive. Don't want blood on it. Going to need it."

The car was still running. I put it in drive and started forward. I could feel one of the bodies sliding across the left rear quarter panel.

I didn't stop.

I drove the car off the driveway, past the house and over behind the barn.

When I walked back, Joe turned to me.

"No need to be part of this."

"Yes, there is."

He looked at me for a long time, his eyes searching my face. I think he was looking to see if I was going to fall apart.

"Okay."

"What do we do now?"

"Get rid of them."

We went to the barn. We carried two tarps, a rope, a sack of quicklime, a big hammer and a can of gasoline out to the jeep. We drove over to the bodies.

The ants had already found them.

We spread one of the tarps in the back of the jeep. We got the two dead men into the jeep and onto the tarp. It was awkward and difficult. They were very big men. We folded the tarp over them.

We spread the other tarp on the ground. We got shovels and scraped up all the blood-soaked, ant-filled dirt and piled it on the tarp. When we had it all, we bundled it up and tied it shut. We put the tarp on top of the one already in the jeep and weighted them both down with the sack of quicklime.

"Talk to missy."

We walked into the house. Kiko was sitting cross-legged on the subfloor of her room.

"I'm going to miss you, Joe. You and Aeden and John. And I'm going to miss this room and this house and this mountain.

God, I hate to go!"

"I know.

Leaving. Be back. Say goodbyes. Be ready to go."

We walked out and got into the jeep, Joe at the wheel.

"Where are we going?"

"Know where Winkler is?"

"Sure."

"Back behind there. Old mine shaft. Hard to find.

No spirit road, these two."

We drove down Cedar Canyon to Black Canyon. We turned off onto the road to Wild Horse Canyon, then off that road over not much of a road to Winkler. From Winkler on there was no road at all.

Joe stopped the jeep on the side of the hill.

I thought I knew every mine shaft in the Providence, but I'd never seen this one.

We unloaded the jeep.

We stripped the two bodies of their shoes, clothes, wristwatches and rings. Joe left the guns in the shoulder rigs and put them back in the jeep. We dragged the nude bodies one at a time to the edge of a shaft that angled away into the hillside. We tumbled the first one in.

Joe said, "Stand back."

In a moment, some disoriented bats flew out into the light. The same thing happened when we dropped the next body down the shaft.

I carried the sack of quicklime to the opening. Joe cut it open.

"Stand back," he said again.

"Stuff blind you."

He untied his bandana and re-tied it over his face. He upended the sack.

A lot more bats came out.

We spent an hour throwing big rocks down the shaft on top of the bodies. When Joe was satisfied, we walked to the jeep.

We dragged the tarp with the bloody soil to the bottom of the hill and untied it. We brought down the men's shoes, clothing, wristwatches and rings.

Joe emptied the pockets of the pants and jackets and dumped wallets, badges, and rolls of cash onto the pile. He kept the picture of Kiko.

He stripped the contents from the wallets and added them to the pile, along with the emptied wallets themselves. He gathered up the wristwatches, rings and detective shields and carried them to a flat rock.

He went up to the jeep and got the big hammer. He pounded everything into very small pieces. He threw the pieces onto the pile.

I got the jerry can from the jeep, and we poured a quarter of the gasoline over everything. Joe picked up some dead grass and tossed it into the air.

"Good. Down slope wind. Blow the smoke out flat."

He popped a Lucifer match with his thumbnail and tossed it on the heap. It erupted into flames. The black smoke hugged the ground and fled down the narrow wash and out toward the open desert below.

We stood for a long time watching everything burn. When it was smoldering, Joe brought the Army entrenching tool from the jeep and scattered the chunks that were left. When they stopped smoking, we made a smaller pile and poured half the remaining gas on it. Joe tossed another match.

When that burned down, he used the tool to search for the scorched and blackened pieces of metal. He took off his bandana and twisted the pieces inside and carried them to the jeep.

We poured the remaining gasoline on what was left. The fire burned very quickly. When it was out, I scattered the ashes with the entrenching tool and watched as some of them blew away. I covered what was left with sand and rocks.

We got in the jeep and drove a mile from where we had put the bodies. We stopped and buried the remaining pieces of the watches, belt buckles and badges and rings in five separate holes. We smoothed over the dirt and put a rock on top of each place.

We drove back to Black Canyon Road and on to the Box S.

In the entire time, we had not seen another vehicle.

When we pulled into the driveway, John's truck was in front of the house.

Joe picked up the guns and shoulder rigs and looped them over his shoulders. We went to the soapstone sink in front of the bunk house, removed the guns from the holsters and washed the rigs clean of blood. Then Joe went to the car and locked the guns and holsters in the trunk.

When we went in the house, John and Kiko were in the kitchen. It was obvious Kiko had been crying. I think John had too.

There was a metal case on the table.

The mood in the room was somber. I don't think anyone knew what to say about everything that had happened.

Finally, John spoke.

"Joe, can you open this?"

Joe examined the latches and the combination locks.

"Can."

He picked up the case and walked out.

John and Kiko and I sat without saying much until he came back. He put the case on the table. There were holes where the combination locks had been. The latches were gone.

He opened the lid.

It was full of one hundred dollar bills, some banded, some loose.

"That's a lot of money," said Kiko.

Her voice sounded dull and lifeless.

John said, "I just hope it's enough. It's going to have to last for a long time."

Joe spoke

"Throw them off some."

"How?"

"Car, guns in the trunk, Albuquerque airport. Bad people think those two ran off. All that money."

"Maybe, but I can't count on that, can I?"

"No."

"Why Albuquerque? asked John. "Why not Los Angeles?"

"Too big. Maybe people watching. Can't watch everywhere."

Kiko looked at us.

"This is more money than I need. I didn't ask for this to happen. I didn't want it. Let me give some of this to each of you."

"Don't need it," said John.

"Me either."

"What about you, Aeden?"

"I'm with them."

"Best get moving. Long way to Albuquerque. Long way around. Can't go through Smoke Tree. Can't go through Vegas. Go Amboy, Twentynine Palms, Parker, Phoenix, then north.

Ready?"

Kiko nodded.

"Let me get you a bag for that money," said John. "Can't carry that ruined case."

Joe and I went outside. I brought the Chrysler out from behind the barn while Joe stood looking at the desert.

Kiko came out of the house with two bags. She walked over and dumped them on the ground beside me.

"I'd like a hug, Aeden Snow"

I hugged her.

"Thank you."

She hugged John, too.

"Thank you both. Thank you for making me safe. Thank you for saving my life."

"Thank Joe."

"I will, but I can never thank him enough."

"I'm never going to see you again, am I?" asked John.

"I'm afraid not. But I'll never forget you."

"Nor I you, Kiko Yoshida."

She picked up her bags. I opened the door for her, and she climbed inside.

Before he got in the car, Joe said, "Be back on the Greyhound. Maybe bring me up, Ade?"

"Sure."

"What for?" asked John.

"Finish the room."

"But Kiko's leaving."

"Remember her by. Make it perfect."

He got in the car and put it in gear.

Kiko turned and watched us through the rear window as they went down the driveway. She gave a final wave before they disappeared.

By the time John I walked to the end of the driveway, Joe was turning west on Cedar Canyon Road. He turned on his headlights in the deepening twilight. His taillights winked on.

We watched until the car drove out of sight.

Venus was up in the western sky. Coyotes were yipping over by Table Top Mountain.

Chapter 21

Smoke Tree, California

And the Mountains

Of the Eastern Mojave Desert

December 16, 1961

Aeden Snow

On the afternoon of December 16, 1961, the Grand Canyon shuddered to a halt at the Santa Fe depot. Billy Braithwaite and I were back in Smoke Tree for the first time since August. I got Billy's suitcase and then Billy off the train. His mother was waiting on the platform. She hugged Billy so hard I thought she was going to lift him out of the chair.

It turned out my dad was on a westbound freight. We had probably passed him somewhere between Barstow and Smoke Tree. Mom was waiting for me. She hugged me and held me at arm's length. Football season had added both muscle and weight to my frame.

"Aeden Snow, I think you're still growing."

She laughed and we hugged again.

"Let's go help Mrs. Braithwaite."

We walked to the parking lot. Mrs. Braithwaite already had the front door of her old Chevy open. Billy was still in his chair with his suitcase on his lap.

She turned and smiled.

I was pleased. A smiling Mrs. Braithwaite was almost as rare as a smiling Joe Medrano.

"Just like the old days in front of the school, Aeden."

"Just like."

I put Billy's suitcase on the ground and helped him into the front seat. I was about to put his suitcase and wheelchair in the back when I suddenly realized Mom and Mrs. Braithwaite had only talked on the phone.

Such was life in Smoke Tree.

"Mom, this is Mrs. Braithwaite."

"Mrs. Braithwaite, I've never thanked you in person for getting Aeden his scholarship. Perhaps when the boys are back in school, we can get together from time to time?"

"That would be fine. We could compare stories and make sure they're behaving themselves."

Mother laughed.

"I'll look forward to it."

Two days later, very early in the morning, I was on my way to the Box S. I stopped at Arrowhead Junction to visit Mr. Stanton. He was getting a little stooped. He had always been ramrod straight. As I talked with him, I realized he had forgotten all about Kiko and the two bad men from Las Vegas.

Not a good sign.

I said goodbye and headed on up the road.

I enjoyed my drive that day as much as any drive I have ever made. I often pulled off the road and walked into the desert to let the stillness settle around me. It was so good to be home.

When I cleared the last switchback and pulled onto the long driveway at the Box S, John Stonebridge's pickup was in front of the house.

He was out the door before I had come to a complete stop.

"Aeden. Great to see you."

The instant I stepped out of the car, I smelled smoke from a pinyon wood fire.

We shook hands.

"Good to see you, too."

"Just made a fresh pot of coffee. Come in, come in!"

We walked into the kitchen, and John poured us each a cup.

"Still take it black?"

"Yes."

I turned to look at the room Joe and I had built. Well, Joe mostly.

The tile floor Joe had returned and finished looked great. There were easy chairs on both sides of the fireplace. Logs burned on the andirons. The flames were reflected in the obsidian and the geode crystals embedded in the hearth.

"Come and sit with me."

We each took a chair.

"I often sit in here. It's become my favorite room."

"Joe did a great job."

"Joe and you both, you mean."

I laughed.

"I mostly carried stuff.

How's that fireplace work?"

"Just like Joe said it would. Burns hot, draws good, no drafts."

"Have you seen Joe since he finished the room?"

"Now and then. Sometimes he just appears when we're out working fence or water or feed somewhere. Don't know how he knows where we are. All of a sudden, he's just there."

"That's Joe."

We sat quietly for a while, sipping our coffee. These mountains encouraged long silences.

"John, have you ever heard from Kiko?"

"Not a word.

You?"

"Nothing."

"Hope she's all right."

"I hope so too. I like to believe she is."

We sat quietly a while longer, looking at the fire.

"You know, Aeden, we had her here for a while anyway. I wouldn't have missed that for anything."

"Me either.

But something bothers me, and I can't get it out of my head. I talked her into writing that letter to her mother. I think that's how they knew she was out this way and not in a big city or another country."

"The guys who could tell us whether that's true aren't talking. You know, Joe never told me where you put them."

"It's best you don't know."

"Maybe so."

"As much as I miss her, I'm glad she's not here. If she were, they would find her and kill her some day. They were going to kill her the day they showed up here. If it hadn't been for Joe, they would have."

"What a fierce man lives behind those quiet eyes."

We sat and talked a while longer. The fire burned lower. When John got up to get more logs, I got up with him.

"Thanks for the coffee. I should get back down the hill."

"Come by any time. And give my best to your folks."

"I will."

I was sadder driving back than I had been driving up.

Chapter 22

Cambria, California

April, 1962

Aeden Snow

I was in my room studying after dinner when someone knocked on my door. I yelled, "come in," and a kid from down the hall stuck his head into the room.

"There's someone downstairs asking for you."

When I walked into the lobby, Kiko rose from the couch.

I couldn't believe it was her. I felt like I had been holding my breath since July, wondering whether she was all right.

"Hello, Aeden Snow."

"Hello, Kiko Yoshida."

She came over and hugged me.

"Got a minute?"

"Of course I do! I have hours and hours if you want them."

I had to force myself to stop gushing.

We went out and got in her car and drove downtown to a coffee shop.

I got us each a coffee and carried it to the table. I still couldn't believe Kiko was in Cambria.

"How are you?"

279

"I'm fine, Aeden. And you?"

"Better, now that I know you're okay.

Where have you been?"

"Don't ask.

How's college?"

"All right, I guess. But it's too wet for me here. I thought it was bad in the winter, but the spring is even worse."

Kiko smiled.

"I know. It's just like Monterey."

Lord, I was being inane. There were a hundred things I wanted to ask her, and here I sat, talking about the climate!

"Why are..."

"What are...?"

We laughed about both starting to talk at once.

"Have you seen Joe?"

"You don't see Joe. Joe sees you. But no, I haven't."

"And John?"

"Yes. Over Christmas vacation. We sat in your room and drank coffee in front of a fire and talked about you. John misses you."

"And I miss him. And you. And Joe."

"Kiko, you can't imagine how glad I am you're here. I wasn't sure I'd ever see you again."

She looked down at the table. When she looked up she said, "I came to say goodbye."

"I was afraid you already had. That evening on Pinto Mountain."

"That was goodbye for a while. I knew I would see you again. Now I know I won't.

I'm afraid, Aeden. I'm afraid all the time. I can't keep living like this. Always moving, never feeling safe anywhere."

I lowered my voice.

"But Joe left their guns in the trunk of that car. It must have been found at the airport. They probably think those guys killed you and ran off with the money."

"No, they don't. They're looking harder. Because now, the score is 'little Japanese woman three, Mafia nothing.'

They won't ever stop looking. I had a close call last month. I might not survive next time."

"Where are you going?"

She leaned closer.

"Where would be the hardest place in the world to find a Japanese woman?"

I thought about it for a minute.

"Tokyo."

"That's right. Can you imagine them finding me there?"

"No, not really."

"I leave tomorrow from Santa Barbara. From there to El Paso, then on to Mexico City and Tokyo.

I didn't want to leave without saying goodbye."

"Since you're leaving, I'll tell you something that I'd be too embarrassed to tell you otherwise. I had this dream that someday, when I was older and had finished college and knew more about the world, you would still be at the Box S, and I would come back, and you would take me seriously."

Kiko smiled.

"I'm very flattered, Aeden. And since you've told me your dream, I'll tell you mine. It's not as different from yours as you might think. My dream was I'd live forever at Pinto Mountain with John Stonebridge. And you and Joe Medrano would always be around. And the four of us would always be safe and secure, far from the rest of the world. We'd have those marvelous, long evenings for the rest of our lives. Out on the veranda in the summer and in my room in front of the fire in the winter."

There were tears in her eyes.

"It's been a privilege to know all three of you."

She stopped.

I put my hand over hers.

"The next time you're out that way, give John and Joe my love. I owe my very life to the three of you."

We sat for a while without speaking.

The silence grew very long. There was so much I wanted to say before she left that I didn't know where to start. I pointed at her empty cup to give me time to put my thoughts in order.

"Let me get you a refill."

"Thank you."

I took both cups to the counter and got refills and a couple of cinnamon rolls.

When I turned around, she was gone.

I put everything down and ran outside.

Her car was pulling away from the curb. I saw her brake lights blink when she stopped at the intersection. Then she turned and was gone.

Chapter 23

Tokyo, Japan

1968

Aeden Snow

Six years later, I was on R&R during my tour in Vietnam. Most guys took R&R in Hawaii, but I went to Tokyo. I got a phone book and looked up all the Kiko Yoshidas. There were lots of them. I called them all, but none of them responded when I said, "This is Aeden Snow. I'm calling for Kiko."

Silly, I know. She would not be in the phone book. She probably wasn't even using the same name.

I spent the rest of my leave walking the streets of that huge city, looking for her. Of course, I never saw her.

But I took comfort that neither would anyone else seeking her there.

THE END

I hope you enjoyed this novel. If you did, I would be very grateful if you would write a review. Independent Authors don't have the resources of the publishing houses. We rely on our readers to promote our books by posting reviews. Please locate the book on Amazon. Near the bottom of the page, just above the "More About the Author" Section, you will see a gray button that reads "Write a customer review." Please click on it and leave your thoughts about the book

*This book is a companion to three other books in the **Smoke Tree Mystery Series**. The first is "The House of Three Murders," the second is "Horse Hunts," and the fourth book in the series is "Death on a Desert Hillside." They are available on Amazon. Lieutenant Caballo and Aeden Snow are important characters in the first book. The second book introduces the enigmatic Chemehuevi Joe. The fourth book features Lieutenant Caballo and Chemehuevi Joe.*

Cover photo by Ginny George

Made in the USA
Monee, IL
14 September 2020